SCARS OF STONE

BOOK 2 OF PACTS ARCANE AND OTHERWISE

JOANNA MACIEJEWSKA

Scars of Stone

Pacts Arcane and Otherwise: Book 2

Copyright © 2021 by Joanna Maciejewska

http://authorjm.com

Editing by Arran McNicol

Cover art and design by Joanna Maciejewska and Inq So

ISBN (paperback) 978-1-7346067-4-4

ISBN (hardcover) 978-1-960158-06-2

ISBN (ebook) 978-1-7346067-3-7

Published by Joanna Maciejewska
PO Box 243
Bushland
Texas 79012, United States
info@authorjm.com

Printed and bound by IngramSpark.
Australia: Ingram Content Group AU Pty Ltd, Melbourne, Victoria. US: Lightning Source LLC, La Vergne, Tennessee / Allentown, Pennsylvania / Jackson, Tennessee, United States. UK: Lightning Source UK Ltd, Milton Keynes, United Kingdom. Europe: Lightning Source UK Ltd, with facilities in Germany, France, and Spain.

The authorized representative in the European Economic Area is Lightning Source France, 1 Av. Johannes Gutenberg, 78310 Maurepas, France. compliance@lightningsource.fr

ALSO BY THE AUTHOR:

Pacts Arcane and Otherwise

By the Pact

Scars of Stone

Shadows over Kaighal

Demon Siege

Shadows of Eireland

Humanborn

Myth-Touched

Snakebitten

Other books

Memories of Sorcery and Sand

Collections

Scourges, Spells, and Serenades

To Piotr Schmidtke
who over 20 years ago saw a spark in my writing
and kept it burning since then

1

Lefna's full lips trembled, and even though she forced them into a smile, her watery eyes told all. Ryell could swear he heard a sniffle before she approached his table. With the late afternoon slowly shifting into an evening, the Jagged Swordsman was still quiet. Only a few patrons sat around the tables, and it seemed that the stillness of the inn seeped into Lefna's thoughts, bringing fears instead of calm.

"They'll be fine, don't worry," he offered, but his own mind haunted him with unwanted images, and he fought to conceal his worries.

He should have insisted on going with Kamira, no matter how many times she had objected. Or maybe he should have never asked for permission and simply joined the two of them as they departed. He clenched his fists in frustration. In hindsight, it was easy to come up with solutions, but the memory of Kamira's unyielding expression when she turned down his offer left no doubt he wouldn't have succeeded no matter what he chose. And Veelk, of course, would have sided with her, guarding her like a jealous dog.

Thankfully, wrapped in her own emotions, Lefna missed his reaction. The last thing he wanted was to upset her more.

"They were supposed to be gone for no more than four weeks!" She rubbed her eyes, smudging her tears. "They didn't take enough supplies for a longer trip!"

Ryell eyed her with interest. The mention of supplies was hardly a reason to panic, but the way she reacted told him of some other, unspoken worries. "I'm sure Veelk will hunt if they run out of food," he replied, the first thought that came to mind. "Maybe that's what slowed them down."

Lefna took a deep breath and gave him an appreciative nod. With a weak smile, she set a jug of ale in front of him and rushed away to tend to other patrons.

With a sigh, he filled his mug. It was the Light's blessing that she didn't know where Kamira and Veelk had set out to. Ryell had seen the desert only from a distance, when his ship reached Tyorane and made its way north along the coastline. The memory of the endless, sunburned dunes stayed with him for a long time and made him believe the continent they'd reached was a harsh, unwelcoming place. At least he could seek a little comfort in the thought that Kamira had traveled through that land before, and she had Veelk to protect her, but that last realization made him close his fingers around the mug tighter than a reassured person would. The mage killer had too much influence on Kamira, keeping her away from the right path and from anyone who was willing to help her. Ryell hadn't earned enough of her trust to pull her away from Veelk. He couldn't help wondering what kind of a dark secret bound the two together, because a Tivarashan noblewoman wouldn't have been keeping company with someone like Veelk willingly. She couldn't have. At the same time, she never, even when they were alone, asked for Ryell's aid. And then she left him in Kaighal, heading out into the desert alone with that cursed...

His frustration grew, so he diverted his thoughts to Atissa. The mere memory of her gentle yet passionate touch and of the magic she was so eager to share with him eased Ryell's mind. Several years younger than Kamira, at least from what he could tell, Atissa still had that air of innocence about her, even if it meant her actions at times were like those of a child. He couldn't help smiling. Sheltered all her life, Atissa had never experienced the harsh side of it and hadn't learned how to deal with challenges, but her actions were not malicious. But were they truly?

The unpleasant memory of when she refused to help his people returned to him in an instant, and Ryell found himself thinking about Kamira again. She helped him without delay, without asking for any payment or even gratitude... He shook his head, trying to chase the image of the callous arcanist out of his head. She'd chosen to wander the desert with a mage killer, so he shouldn't waste his time. Neither of the women who'd absorbed his attention in Kaighal was worthy of what he was offering, yet he couldn't find the strength to walk away from either, bouncing from one to the other like a helpless trapped animal testing the limits of its cage.

A muffled scream drew his attention, and once he recognized Lefna standing between the tables with her hand to her mouth and eyes wide, he followed her gaze.

Two travelers walked into the inn. Veelk entered first, hunched and moving slowly, nearly staggering, and while he held the door open, Kamira stepped inside. Every detail of her state burned into Ryell's mind as the inn's imbued lamps lit up her face and revealed the dirt on her skin and parched lips. A limp distorted her smooth moves, and her arm rested in a makeshift sling.

Ryell kept staring, but Lefna broke free of her stupor. Several steps and she was already back at the counter, filling a tray with a jug of wine, cups, and bowls of fresh food. Before Ryell blinked, she headed for the stairs, the tray and a key in her hands.

"Bath?" She looked over her shoulder.

Veelk shook his head. Once he let go of the door, he took time to help Kamira walk. "Maybe later."

Lefna climbed the steps balancing her burden, and Ryell looked after her in awe. The innkeeper must have been proud of his daughter, whose first thought was of serving her guests instead of asking questions or giving in to emotions. At the same time, she made Ryell feel useless. The way Veelk glared at him when they passed his table made it clear he would not welcome any help, and Ryell's blood boiled. Tiredness aside, the mage killer was unscathed, not a single injury on his body, while the woman he was supposed to protect had suffered from more than one. *Some protector he is!* Ryell clenched his fists.

Veelk paid no attention to him. He lifted Kamira and carried her up the stairs then muttered a few words to Lefna, who was already heading back. Then he disappeared around the corner on the upper floor. The patrons, who had so far silently watched their passage, returned to their drinks and conversation, and the Jagged Swordsman once more looked quiet and calm.

Ryell hesitated. The need for news fought with the courtesy of allowing them to rest first.

Lefna approached his table, her hand on his shoulder in a failed attempt to comfort him. "Better leave them alone.

It's been a long time since I saw Veelk in such a mood. Something serious must have happened on their journey."

"They've been attacked." Ryell hadn't expected to state the obvious.

"No, it's not that. They get in trouble all the time, and all you can hear is Veelk teasing Kamira about being too weak or too stubborn." She shook her head, a glimpse of amusement brightening her face, likely at some memories, but then concern took over again. "Last time I saw him like this was when—" She covered her mouth with sudden realization. "When something really bad happened to them," she said after Ryell's insistent glare.

"How bad?" If he could learn more about it, maybe he would understand what kind of power Veelk had over Kamira, and he'd figure out how to free her of the mage killer's influence.

A patron called out, and Lefna sent him a smile over the shoulder. "I have to go. Besides, it's a nasty story. Father would kill me if I repeated it to patrons."

Before she rushed away, Ryell held her forearm. "I have to know." As two men at the next table eyed him with barely concealed hostility, he let go. "Please."

The corners of her lips curved downward, but her nod was all Ryell cared about. "I'll be with you as soon as I can."

With uneasiness, she hurried off to other tables, and he finished his ale with a pang of guilt. Forcing the innkeeper's daughter to gossip about her patrons was below a royal guard's honor, but at the same time, with the fall of Devanshari, he could hardly call himself such. If Lefna knew the story, it couldn't have been a secret anyway, and when he learned the details, he would know how to speak with Kamira. A little discomfort for Lefna wasn't a high price to pay. Reassured, Ryell relaxed in his seat, waiting for her return.

~

RYELL WOKE up to a gentle knock on the door. His eyes, sticky from lingering slumber, refused to open after an entire night of restless, shallow sleep. He was ready to pull a pillow over his face and ignore the visitor, but when the knocking became more persistent, the memory hit him. Lefna! She promised she'd wake him up.

He was at the door in a leap and three steps, and she gently smiled at him, holding an empty tray.

She pointed at the door at the end of the corridor. "They're up. I brought them breakfast, and they seem... in a brighter mood today. But if I were you"—she gave him a critical look—"I'd get a bath and food first."

He followed her gaze to the crumpled clothes he'd slept in. "That might be a good idea." Not that he wanted to waste time, but if he was to win Kamira's trust, he had to look like a royal guard, and not like a poor refugee wasting his life away in a foreign city.

With most of the guests either sleeping or gone, the room downstairs had an eerie feel of emptiness and silence to it, weighing heavy on Ryell's mood as he recalled Lefna's story from the previous night. No wonder Kamira had been so distrustful, and Veelk had such a firm grip on her if they were betrayed by their companion. Ryell wouldn't be even surprised if she saw another treacherous Garivan in him, and she feared that their blossoming friendship would turn sour with the betrayal she must be expecting.

The inn's bath chamber was empty as well, and he hastily saw to his cleanliness while his thoughts still circled

Kamira. Possibly, she perceived high mages as threats or traitors as well, so Ryell's relationship with archmage Yoreus wouldn't help, but to deny it meant deception that could aggravate her wariness should she discover it. Honesty was a better option even if it meant he had to work harder for her trust.

A sudden thought brought a cringe to her face. He might have had obligations binding him to Yoreus, but Kamira had her own secrets too, and played games with the archmage like the one back in the tavern when Ryell met her first. Yet she refused to offer even a small amount of trust, putting the burden on building it entirely on him. He shook his head, chasing the bitter feeling away. The mage killer must have been poisoning her with his own hostile attitude. Without him, she'd surely be more open, and if Ryell found a way to convince her to go back to the High Towers, she'd be out of Veelk's reach.

With a sigh, he dried himself, and a surprisingly soft towel brushing across his skin reminded him of Atissa. Once more he pondered why he'd even wasted time on Kamira, why he endlessly searched for the way to bring her back to the Light's grace, running in circles, while the archmage's daughter was all he could dream of: beautiful, willing, and still somewhat innocent.

Lefna walked in and put a pile of fresh clothes on the chair. "Thought you'd need these." Her eyes slipped along his naked body, but she neither blushed nor stared. "Breakfast is ready too."

Ryell gave a quick nod, more uncomfortable with his own nudity than Lefna was, and welcomed her departure. When he got dressed, the polished brass plate that served as mirror showed him a less appealing image than he'd hoped for. Unconscious and taken from the Devanshari pier right before the demonlings swarmed it, he'd had no time to pack, so all of his clothes were of Kaighal's make, following local fashion, and the bloodstained and dented armor was hardly a suitable alternative. His face bore the marks of the essence deprivation—though, thanks to Atissa's generosity, he didn't look as starved as some of his compatriots—and lacking the daily guard's routine, his body was losing its nimbleness.

He ran his fingers through his hair, resisting the urge for more grooming. There was only so much he could do, and in the end, Kamira had seen him before, bloodied, bruised, and balancing on the edge of death. If he tried too hard, she'd likely suspect deception.

Out in the main room, he downed his breakfast, paying no attention to the few travelers eating theirs and seeking no conversation. He hardly felt the taste of porridge and diluted cafra juice locals drank with their morning meal, but still complimented the food when Lefna approached.

"Don't worry, they seem back to normal now." Lefna's words and pat on his shoulder made it clear his expression wasn't as collected as he'd hoped for. "I think Veelk was cleaning the wound on her leg, and she's complaining a lot, but it's more like their usual bickering."

Ryell grunted in response, staring at the rest of his food, but she didn't leave him alone, so he looked up at her.

"Something else is wrong, isn't it?" Her voice carried that sincere concern she only had for regular patrons. "Is it because of what I told you last night?"

With a shake of his head, he forced a smile. "I think I just worry too much." He grasped the first thought that would get him out of sharing the truth. "Seeing Kamira like this and knowing that something might have happened to her..." He let his voice trail off in hopes Lefna would leave it at that. Explaining his motives and tangled feelings to an inn's maid would be both embarrassing and frustrating.

"It's normal when you care about someone." She offered a smile. "But I better let you finish your food. Kamira's probably already wondering where you are."

Ryell's heart skipped a beat. This might have been nothing but an empty phrase meant to comfort him, but maybe indeed Kamira was waiting for him. He finished the last few spoonfuls and washed them down with the remainder of the juice. Lefna winked at him as he rushed toward the stairs, so he made an effort to slow down.

He'd been so wrapped up in his concerns that he never considered what he'd say to Kamira, and as he approached the door, he desperately looked for the words that would earn her trust.

Before he knocked, Kamira's voice reached him from behind the closed door. "I don't need to be fed. I can eat with one hand just fine. But I need my hair done."

"I'm not putting all that debris back on your head," Veelk replied. "You can live with it being not done."

"But I can't eat. The hair's getting in the food."

Ryell caught a tease in her complaint, and he hoped Veelk would once more refuse, so he could offer to help.

"And that's why I'm feeding you."

The mage killer's tone suggested he considered the topic finished, and Ryell smiled. They indeed seemed in better mood, and he knocked on the door, lured by the playfulness in their voices while the images of the battered Kamira from the previous evening faded from his mind.

Silence followed, and Ryell waited to hear the steps or hushed conversation, but no sound came before the door opened. Ryell, caught unprepared, stared at Veelk, and the mage killer took a step to the side, revealing the visitor's face to Kamira and making it clear that an invitation—if any—would come from her.

Kamira was sitting on the bed with a bowl on her lap, staring at Ryell in silence. Her arm rested in a fresh sling, and her face was clean of marks and dust. With her hair loose, she'd lost a lot of the malicious demonologist look, and Ryell's instincts responded with compassion for the fragile woman she seemed, but the intensity of her gaze reassured him that her personality remained as it was.

"Come in." Her permission carried only tiredness.

Veelk offered no greeting as he moved to the side, and Ryell's muscles tensed as he stepped through the door at the sight of Veelk's keshal resting against the wall and within reach. They clearly hadn't been expecting a guest, but an assassin. Whatever transpired in the desert, it must have been more than a skirmish with some riffraff.

Kamira looked at Veelk, and a smile warmed her face. "Go, see her. I'll be fine." She rubbed her skin on her forearm where she used to wear her nightfly bracelet.

Ryell glanced at her other arm, but it bore no jewelry either, leaving him to wonder whether she'd removed the set because of the injury or if she'd lost the unique crystal pieces. Veelk stared back at Kamira. Their body language suggested they communicated with more than words, and then he nodded and left.

"How are you feeling?" he asked, the first question that came to mind. "Lefna mentioned something about a wound."

To his surprise, she smiled. "I've been better. Usually it's Veelk who gets all beaten up." She made an inviting gesture toward one of the chairs.

He'd much rather sit at the edge of the bed, close enough to catch the scent of her magic, but he followed her unvoiced wish, ignoring the whispers of how much it spoke of her trust. Given time, if he didn't slip, he'd remedy that. Yet he pulled the chair toward the bed with a teasing smirk, far enough away to keep the distance she wanted, but at the same time cutting it a bit.

"I should have gone with you." He had to say it even if he was risking an argument.

Her expression softened. "It's good you didn't. Otherwise I'd have your death on my hands."

"You didn't die, and neither did Veelk," Ryell pointed out. "And maybe if I was there, you wouldn't have your arm broken, and the Light knows what other injuries." At her grimace, he reined in his frustration. "So, what happened?" he asked softly.

She looked to the side as if trying to conceal her grimace. "There was an explosion of magic deeper in the desert, and its wave reached us. We barely had time to do anything, and raising a barrier... My pact is limited. When the destruction passed, I was defenseless, and the desert nomads attacked."

"Why?" Ryell couldn't help himself. The excitement that she'd shared the story with him instead of denying him an answer pushed him to take chances. There had to be more to the story if she was convinced he would have died there.

A shrug was her first response. "They didn't tell, and we didn't bother to ask. It might have been a simple robbery, or they thought I had something to do with that eruption of magic." Kamira's eyes dimmed. "If chronicles are to be believed, this looked a lot like the Cataclysm, just... less powerful."

"People have seen it even from Kaighal. Got a lot of them worried. You saw it close, didn't you? What was it?"

The look she gave him was sharp and inquisitive, and

her voice was cold when she asked, "Is it you or the archmage asking?"

Taken by surprise, Ryell struggled to keep his face straight, his memories of conversations with Yoreus too clear all of a sudden. "From what I could see, the archmages were concerned about it, but Archmage Yoreus doesn't share his thoughts with me." To thread between truth and lies was beyond a royal guard, but openly admitting he did Yoreus's bidding would ruin any remaining trust between them.

"Not his thoughts, just his daughter."

His face burned, because there was no denying it when she made such a direct remark, and he stuttered, searching for words. Kamira burst out laughing, but he found no malice in it, only amusement.

"It's so like Yoreus... Using his own daughter to play you." She giggled as she spoke.

"He asked me to protect his daughter, and Atissa... she wanted something more," he admitted. At the same time, he had to fight to resist the ire at her biting remark of Atissa being but a pawn in her father's hands. She was too innocent to play games like that. "And I... My body is addicted to magic. You went with me to Prince Allyv's asylum, and you saw the ones who hunger for it, the ones desperate enough to swallow imbued stones to ease their suffering. I'm no different, just lucky enough that someone is willing to share their magic with me." He didn't want it to sound like an accusation, but there he was, implying that Kamira didn't offer him what Atissa did.

"I can understand that," she said with a touch of softness, as if she could relate to his hunger, but then her features hardened again. "What I can't understand is what you're doing here."

With all their differences and all his obligations to

Yoreus, Ryell weighed his options, and only truth could salvage what little trust she might have had. "I worried about you, and I missed you." He shrank under Kamira's inquisitive gaze, but he couldn't blame her for remaining suspicious and sighed with surrender. "I made my promises to Yoreus before I knew... Before I realized..." He shook his head, as the right words weren't coming. "The world was much simpler when I hated all the arcanists the same." It didn't come out as lighthearted as he'd hoped for, and he turned his head away with an awkward smile that might as well have been a grimace.

"So, what are you going to do now?" she asked with enough amusement to put him at ease. "Hate all the arcanists again?"

"No," he replied. "But I do wish you weren't one. Demons destroyed my home and slaughtered our people. I can't simply forget it." Ryell shifted uneasily. He needed to change the direction of their conversation. "Can I ask you something? Why did you get expelled?" He'd heard enough gossip, because even if Kamira's name didn't come up often in the conversations he overheard around the Towers, the mentions of "that student who got expelled" were frequent enough. The story sounded like a cautionary tale for children, so Ryell had had a hard time learning the details, even from Archmage Yoreus himself. On one hand, Kamira's deed was supposed to be beyond any acceptable boundaries, but on the other, Yoreus always referred to it as "a triviality" when he spoke of her possible return.

Her face dimmed at his words, making him realize how unpleasant the memory must have been. At the same time, her reaction allowed a sliver of hope that she cared, and, given an opportunity, she would consider going back to the High Towers.

"I refused to sleep with my teacher." A grimace twisted her mouth.

His eyes widened. All that gossip, all those reminders, and... "Just for that?!"

"I might have added a few insulting words to the 'no' part." Her playful tone told Ryell she was back to her usual self, as if she chose not to dwell on the past, and his hopes faded. "It's in the past. I don't think of it much. And I don't regret it."

She smiled, but more to her own thoughts than to him, and then shook her head. Whatever thought she might have had, she was discarding it, so if Ryell wanted to make her reconsider, he needed to make her doubt her own choice first.

"I don't know if I understand," he said with caution. Kamira wasn't quick to anger, but if she suspected he had ulterior motives, he'd suffer the consequences, likely cold responses and scathing remarks. "Ever since I was a child, I wanted to be a royal guard, but my family was from a minor noble house, and we lived at the borders of Devanshari." To speak about it brought sudden pain as the memories of the war surfaced. Most of his relatives had perished when the demons first attacked, before the barrier could be raised, and he knew nothing of what happened to those who survived. They might have made it out of his family lands only to die months later in the slaughter of the capital. Too busy with Yoreus's requests and Atissa's charms, too obsessed with finding a way to bring Cahala to justice, he'd never even asked after them, and guilt overwhelmed him. Forcing back his focus, Ryell discarded those thoughts and continued. "I did everything I could to join the border patrol first, and then our capital's garrison. It took me years, but finally I was offered a place among the royal guards. I can't imagine giving it up, no matter the humiliations I had to suffer..." He bit his tongue, realizing too late that there was a difference to being a pushover for guards from the wealthier families and having to sleep with someone to secure as little as a student's position. "I apologize."

"No need," she replied, her voice hushed, as if contrary to her reassurance he'd struck a painful chord. "When I first went to the High Towers, I had every bit the intention of becoming an archmage one day, and I worked hard for it." She stared off, reminiscing. "But in the end, it was all pointless when not jumping into Kerl's bed was more important than my skills or knowledge. Even if I found another way, I'd become part of the corruption that rots the Towers from within."

"But if you had another chance," he said, unable to resist. "Maybe with another archmage—"

In a sharp move, Kamira turned her head toward him, and Ryell found himself trapped by her gaze, composed and unyielding. "Do you really think Yoreus wants anything other than to humiliate me and have power over me? You heard yourself how he speaks to me."

Ryell swallowed and gave a reluctant nod, because no matter what argument he could conjure against it, his own or the archmage's, the pieces of Yoreus's conversation with Kamira remained fresh. He still wanted to believe that it was Kamira who'd pushed the archmage into such behavior with her taunts, but he couldn't deny that Yoreus had acted more hostile than benevolent.

"So, how's being an arcanist different?" he asked, the first question that came to mind. He risked hearing about demons, but even that seemed better than dwelling on what real motives Yoreus could have to want Kamira's return to the High Towers. All of a sudden, Ryell felt like a pawn in a game he didn't understand.

The question brought a smile to her face, and that alone was worth suffering through whatever her answer could be.

"Students of the arcane arts are expected to learn and to grow, to bring pride to the teachers. They are challenged and pushed to work harder, even to question the teaching and find new solutions, or draw conclusions from their own mistakes. I learned more in a month as an apprentice arcanist than in a year at the High Towers." As she spoke of the past, her voice softened and carried a longing undertone.

Ryell hid his relief at the lack of demons, but the words themselves sounded like an arcanist's attempt to prove her school's superiority. "It sounds quite... blissful."

Kamira burst out laughing. "It was everything but that. You see, in the High Towers, well-placed flattery helped you get away with things, while studying with Master Tijhran meant I got to taste the consequences of every single mistake I made, and no compliment or excuse would allow it to slide. On the day I made my pact, he took out a bottle of his best wine, and we drank late into the night, but in the morning he still kicked me out with nothing but a few of my belongings and told me I had to prove my worth by supporting myself for six months with my art before he'd offer any more teaching."

"And did you?"

Her laughter filled the room again. "Of course I did! I was determined to prove he had never had a better student. But the first weeks were harsh. Then I found a small village that had no medic or herbalist. I mostly helped with broken limbs and infected wounds, not really using much magic, but..." She chuckled. "I was still bold enough to send Master

Tijhran a letter asking if he'd like me to come back, because if not, I was set for life."

It was Ryell's turn to burst into laughter, and he savored it. "Taking care of farmers and their livestock?"

"I didn't mention *that* part. And when he politely replied that it was up to me, and he'd already chosen a replacement should I decide not to come back..." She grinned. "I was back at his door in a week."

Her face radiated joy as she spoke about her teacher, and Ryell couldn't help thinking that this arcanist had to be very similar to Kamira: stubborn and ambitious, with a bit of a rebellious nature. The docile and obedient students never strayed from the high mage path.

Atissa's face resurfaced in Ryell's mind. She might have had that rebellious spark about her, but it seemed more of a childish whim than anything else, and her behavior around Yoreus was always obedient and servile. In a way, Atissa reminded him of the spoiled daughters of Devanshari noblemen he'd gotten to know all too well once he received his post in the capital. Kamira, on the other hand, was older and more mature, so her rebellion stemmed from disagreeing with the way the High Towers were. Even if Ryell considered her perspective flawed, he could relate to that refusal to submit. After all, he wouldn't have become a royal guard if he yielded to the rules of his kingdom.

"You're staring at me," she said, part reprimand, part curiosity.

Lost in his thoughts, he'd missed the silence that fell between them. "I... It's because you look so different with your hair down. Why do you put it up?" He grasped for the first excuse that came to mind, though he actually liked the way she looked.

"It's practical." The shrug accompanying her words

suggested that she hadn't thought about it much. "It doesn't get in the way when I travel or fight."

"And all the bones and feathers you put in it?" Ryell glanced at the table, where an array of her accessories lay scattered.

"At first, I did it only to annoy my family." She smirked. "The look on my aunts' faces when they saw me... It was worth it. Then it became a habit, and now it's a way to ensure no one mistakes me for a high mage."

The challenge in her words became clear when she looked straight at him, and all Ryell could do was to nod, cursing his own curiosity. His questions were bound to drive a wedge between them even deeper, at least until Kamira learned to trust him more. As much as he wanted to spend more time with her, he risked ruining the friendly mood of sharing amusing stories. It was time to take his wins and leave the rest for the next time... if there even was to be one.

With a heavy heart, he looked her in the eye. "I know you don't trust me, and I don't deny my... obligations to the archmage and his daughter," he said, "but I enjoy your company, and I was hoping that... I could visit again. Ask you about your health, and maybe share more laughter. It's the least I can do in return for all you did for me and my people."

"I'd... like that." Her face revealed that he'd surprised her, and Ryell took that little victory.

"Thank you." He stood up. At least it felt like he'd made a step forward in building trust, no matter how small it was. "I took enough of your time today, and you need to rest." He hesitated, but it seemed she wouldn't accept a kiss, not after he had admitted how close he was with Atissa, so instead he bowed.

"It was nice seeing you," she said.

He stepped out into the corridor, comforted by the warmth of her response and the hope of being welcomed back in the future, but when he closed the door, his hands were shaking. He cared more than he was ready to admit, more than the pawn he was supposed to be should care. After what Kamira had told him, he couldn't deny the possibility that the archmage had used Ryell to play his own game. Taking a deep breath, he turned to leave, but then he heard someone else speaking in the room.

"He wasn't being fully honest with you."

The deep tone echoed with wisdom and little else, no emotions, nothing, and Ryell froze. From what little he knew, summoning demons to speak with them took time and effort, but it couldn't have been anyone else. He debated whether to reenter, but Kamira's reply held him fast.

"Neither was I with him."

2

"At least he didn't try to kill me," Kamira added when Veranesh ignored her remark about honesty.

The nightflies circled in the air above the bed. During Ryell's visit, Veranesh had kept them hidden but close by, and she appreciated his vigil. Anyone could expect her to use magic to defend herself or to attack, and they would prepare for such an instance, but no one except for Veelk knew of the crystal creatures.

"You're avoiding the question of his truthfulness." Veranesh's dry voice continued to contrast with the creatures' playful flight.

"It's not a question," she fired back. "I'd much rather know why Yoreus is using him, and what the old fox really wants from me. Information, that's certain. But what else?"

The game with Ryell had tired her, and if she didn't need all the possible insights in the archmage's schemes, she'd have told Ryell to go back to the Towers, to the woman he was so eager to embrace while she was away. Kamira almost huffed in frustration at the memory of their previous meeting, when Ryell made his interest clear, quite bluntly so, and now he had the nerve to attempt acting the same while all that high magic emanated from his body. Had she allowed it, he'd have undoubtedly sat beside her, throwing friendly remarks or even trying to charm her.

She glanced at the nightflies, but couldn't tell whether her ire showed and if Veranesh noticed anything.

The aura of high magic was gone with the one who carried it, but she still boiled at Ryell's admittance of being under Atissa's thumb. He didn't seem a player himself, and Kamira could assume that he indeed desired her, especially with the aura of arcane magic surrounding her, but she doubted the feelings for her he believed to have were real, and he definitely was not a friend.

A knock on the door sent the nightflies darting to cover.

"It's me." Veelk entered without being invited. "I saw Ryell in the corridor. By the look of his face, I'd wager it wasn't a pleasant time."

Kamira narrowed her eyes. When he was leaving, Ryell seemed content enough, but if he caught Veranesh's remark and her response, it could have changed his mood. Next time, if there was any, she would have to be more careful, or Ryell was bound to discover secrets she didn't want to share with him.

"She was quite gentle, considering he sleeps with another," Veranesh said as the nightflies emerged.

Veelk arched his eyebrow then glanced back at the closed door and again at Kamira. "That's a pity. He seemed to have taken to you."

Kamira discarded that remark with a shrug. No matter how honest Ryell might have seemed, she couldn't discard the possibility that he was as seasoned a player as Yoreus or any Tivarashan noblewoman with whom she'd dealt in the past. A royal guard could have had enough opportunities to try his hand at intrigue and deception. But discussing Ryell and his intentions would make them go in circles.

"We need a plan." She looked straight at Veranesh. "Because the ambush showed how unprepared we are." Even in the privacy of their room, she chose words with caution, avoiding the mention of Uganel's name.

Silence fell, but she waited patiently. The demon would arrive at the conclusion she had in mind.

"You consider yourself incapable of the deed," Veranesh said.

"We almost died because I couldn't hold the barrier long enough." The memory of the event made her crumble inside, but she kept her composure. At least she'd gotten to experience firsthand what an attempt at freeing Veranesh could be like.

Veelk walked over to the table. "Wounded and in pain against a storm of magic. A lousy arcanist indeed," he said as he took the chair Ryell had left.

As much as she'd enjoy falling back into their casual bickering to pick up her mood, she kept her eyes on Veranesh. "This was the limit of the energy I could channel," she said. "Regardless of how much I'd be willing to practice or sacrifice, the human body has its limits."

The nightflies circled in the air, and the chaotic moves of two creatures must have reflected Veranesh pondering her words. "You have something in mind, don't you?"

Kamira hesitated, looking between Veelk and the nightflies, and gave a cautious nod. She had weeks of strenuous journey back through the desert to recall every single detail from their confrontation with Uganel, and all her thoughts led to one conclusion. Veranesh could have offered her all his power, but without the ability to survive channeling it, she'd be as useless as defending from

Uganel's destruction. She might have found a way, but both Veelk and Veranesh had to agree, and she couldn't decide who would be more likely to say yes. On the other hand, it hardly mattered, because neither of them would be able to convince the other.

After a deep breath, she pointed at Veelk's arm. "Your scars... They channel magic both in and out, right?" she asked.

His expression changed, as always when she asked about things related to his tribe. No matter how many secrets they shared, how many times they saved each other's lives, and how deep their trust was, when it came to his kinsmen, he still retreated to old habits. She didn't blame him, because in the end, he always gave her as much of an answer as he could, and this time was no different. "They draw it from the demon world whenever it's necessary for healing or reflexes, and into it when they take care of spells thrown at us." He looked her over. "But the stones need to be bound with the flesh to work. You can't simply wear one or hold them."

If it was that simple, she wouldn't need that conversation. "Would your people make an exception for me?" She glanced at the nightflies. "If you agree." Veranesh could well be opposed to the idea, because higher demons guarded magic they granted, and with the stones as a part of her, he'd lose that power over her.

"Suzhaul won't agree even if I was the one to ask." Veranesh crushed her hopes, but at least he wasn't disagreeing with the idea itself. "He's too engrossed in his... endeavors to risk that aiding me would make other kanyalari confront him and pull him away from his pursuits."

With the way Veranesh spoke of Suzhaul's plans, Kamira

couldn't help wondering what secrets they shared, and what the goals of Veelk's demonic patron were.

"Sounds like him." Veelk showed neither surprise nor respect for his tribe's demon. "But there's someone else we could ask. A man who knows the secrets of the blending and isn't bound by my tribe's rules."

Her jaw dropped. "Your people taught an outsider?!" The last thing she'd expected of the tribe that was more protective of its secrets than of its members was to give it away to someone they couldn't fully trust.

"It's a long story... and a long shot," he said, ignoring her outburst. "I don't even know if he's still alive, and if he is, finding him will take some favors for Gildya."

"Gildya..." When the understanding dawned on her, Kamira stared at Veelk. "Your people taught an adept?!" A way to keep secret, teach it to a member of an organization that shared them freely among its people and used them to gain wealth and influence.

"No need to yell." Veelk shot her a warning glare. "My tribe had a huge debt to pay, and Suzhaul approved. Koshmarnyk was taught our techniques, but he's not allowed to pass this knowledge to anyone else."

She knew better than to question the trust Veelk had in this man, even if she considered sharing such knowledge akin to playing with fire. "So, we just need to reach out to that... Kosh-mar-nyk? The name sounds tribal."

"That's the name we gave him." The tic at his lips' corner indicated amusement. "After all, he had to be of the tribe, one way or another. But he disappeared some years ago, and if anyone knows where he went, it's Gildya."

Kamira leaned back on the bed. "Master Tijhran used to sell imbued stones to some adept. I could ask him to introduce us." She turned to Veranesh. "Such information might be costly. I'll need quite a few powerful stones." Likely, no ordinary stones from minor demons would do, even if she wanted to try to bargain with them first.

The nightflies shifted in their flight, and one of them hovered close to Kamira. "Not the most pleasant thing, but nothing compared to the pain I go through by the high mages' doings. Although you should rest and heal before you set out again. With... the immediate threat gone, you have time."

She gave him a nod. As much as she loathed the prospect of idleness, possibly spoiled by Ryell's further visits, traveling with a broken arm was too much of a hassle. It was enough that she'd made it back through the desert. Now her limb needed to heal. When she got the stones blended, the magic within them would hasten the process, but until then, she only had natural mending. "I'll write a letter to Master Tijhran. Perhaps he'll be willing to visit Kaighal."

"Then it's settled," Veranesh said.

One nightfly wrapped around the wrist of Kamira's healthy arm, while the other coiled around her neck, forming a necklace.

"Are you sure about it?" Veelk asked when the nightflies froze into jewelry. "Once bound, the stones are not easily taken out. And even if you manage to remove them, the scars will stay forever."

"I know. But I don't need them all over, like you. Only on my arms, since arcanists use them to draw and channel. Wearing long sleeves till the end of my days seem a small price for saving my own life, and maybe the world too." During their journey back, she'd had enough time to think about it.

"Just maybe? I thought you finally trusted the demon."

She couldn't help glancing at the nightfly on her wrist before replying. The creature was still, and she did not sense Veranesh's presence. "I do. At least in matters of his freedom and keeping his word. He might not be as evil as the high mages try to paint him, but... beings like him have a different perspective. Once he's free, there's no telling what he'll do." She shivered, as it wasn't hard to guess. He'd go after the high mages, and their hold on Kaighal would put the whole city at risk.

"We'll worry about it when the time comes." Veelk must have caught the shift in her mood. "Right now, we need to find Koshmarnyk."

She snickered at Veelk's approach to problems, on a one-by-one basis. He never seemed overwhelmed by anything, and it put her at ease. With her concerns lightened, she glanced at him playfully with a new thought on her mind. Of course, it would never work, but the prospect of his dry response pushed her to try nevertheless.

"I still need my hair done."

KAMIRA GROANED TRYING to tie her hair with one hand. All the muttering and cursing couldn't help her, and Veelk had left to see about restocking their supplies with a remark that she didn't need her hairdo staying in the room. She regretted not having asked Ryell for help, but that, of course, would have brought problems she wasn't ready to face. It was one thing to keep secrets from a man not worthy of her trust, and another to consciously mislead him into believing she desired intimacy with him.

A knock distracted her, and the hair she was about to pin escaped her fingers.

"By the pact, come in!" Still frustrated with Veelk's unwillingness to help, she let anger slip into her words. "It's not like I'd undress myself while you were gone." Not that Veelk would have been bothered with her lack of clothes. They'd tended to each other's wounds so often that there wasn't much left to hide.

The door opened, and when a small figure stood in the entrance, Kamira realized that Veelk wouldn't bother knocking, as the room was also his. Unable to see the face beneath the cloak, she froze, certain it wasn't Ryell either. She brandished the wooden hairpin, though only as a distraction. If it came to fight, she'd use magic and awaken the nightflies.

"I think you expected someone else." First Archmage Irtan lowered the hood. "But I hope I still can come in."

Kamira swallowed words of refusal and nodded. Avoiding Irtan would only raise his suspicion.

The archmage entered, and while he closed the door, his back was turned to Kamira, giving her an opening to strike if she wanted to take it. Instead, she breathed out with relief. He wouldn't have been so casual if he had come to kill her.

Irtan walked to the table and took a seat without waiting for invitation. His moves, still full of confidence, betrayed him every once in a while, revealing that the archmage's body was advancing in years faster than his mind. It'd been —how many?—at least seven years since she'd seen him last.

They stared at each other, and the silence deepened.

"I care little for games," she said. "So don't expect pleasantries and empty talk."

The wrinkles on Irtan's face shifted when he laughed. "You haven't changed much since the last time we spoke. At least when it comes to conversational habits." He looked her over, his sharp eyes lingering on the sling. "I see your new life doesn't treat you too well."

She fought off a grimace creeping onto her face as she glanced down at her broken arm. It was the worst time to look feeble or miserable. "It seems you haven't changed much either, or did you just not hear the 'I care little for games' part?"

"It's not a game. I'm actually curious how you've been." Irtan's smile, gentle and friendly on his aging face, reassured her that, contrary to his words, he *was* playing a game. "I was sad to see you leave."

Of course, she could have reminded the archmage he had done nothing to prevent her from being expelled, but after years of bitter thoughts and words, she wasn't about to repeat them aloud and drag herself into a pointless discussion. Especially given that, with the recent revelations, she had even less to regret than she did right after she left the Towers.

Irtan sighed but kept smiling. "I guess I shouldn't have expected any sentiment from you, though I did hope you missed the Towers at least a bit."

It was her turn to laugh. Then she looked the archmage in the eye. "Enough games. Let's get done with it. Why have you come?"

In an instant, he became serious. "I'd like to ask you about some events. You're an honest person, so I hope to learn from you that which I'll never know from other archmages. I grow old and tired of their games myself."

Kamira offered a short nod as acknowledgment. She'd always considered Irtan wiser than the other archmages, and he was the one to mention Master Tijhran's name before she left the Towers, but deception ran through high mages' blood even denser than magic, and she wasn't about to trust him blindly. One did not become the first archmage if one didn't know all the steps in the Towers' political games.

"I've been told that you approached Archmage Yoreus with an offer," Irtan continued. "You planned to explore the old Towers in the desert, is that correct?" He glanced at her. "No, I can see it's not. So what would be your story?"

Irtan must have pressed Yoreus if the snide archmage had shared information about his dealings with Kamira, even if, undoubtedly, he presented it in a way that would divert any suspicions from him. With that, she had no choice but to admit her involvement, and she could only hope that the same story she'd told Yoreus would be enough for Irtan. "Are you aware of what I do?" A few questions could help her determine how much Irtan really knew.

"Not quite, I admit. I only know that you've successfully finished your arcanist training with Master Tijhran, and you travel a lot."

At a high mage referring to her teacher as "master," Kamira moved from her spot on the bed. Such rare courtesy, especially from an archmage, was worth recognition and reciprocation, so she poured them both thin wine. Whether he'd consider it safe to drink was another matter.

"I explore old places, bringing artifacts from the past to those who can pay." She only dipped her lips into the wine, and she saw Irtan doing likewise—enough to be courteous, but far too little for it to dim their wits. "Mostly collectors and Gildya adepts. Sometimes a high mage who is interested in such research buys a trinket or two, but they rarely want to deal with an arcanist."

"And Yoreus is an exception?"

Kamira allowed herself a bitter smile. "I'm sure he despises me as much as everyone else, but he desires old artifacts, and we traded several times when I had something of interest to him." She looked the archmage in the eye. "But this time, it was him who approached me. He said he knew of an entrance to the old Towers and was willing to give me that information if I would bring something back for him."

"And that was?"

"A book, leather-bound, handwritten." Kamira faked indifference with a shrug. "He didn't tell me what it was about, only where to find it."

Irtan nodded slowly as his eyes narrowed, and she couldn't help thinking he knew exactly which book Yoreus had in mind. "And did you find it?"

Faking a huff of frustration, she replied, "I couldn't even find the entrance he described, let alone some book that had probably already fallen apart. Instead, I wasted a lot of time and resources." If she could lead him to believe that the coin was all that mattered to her, maybe he wouldn't dig any further. "Yoreus wasn't impressed, but I don't think he ever is."

"It seems the same applies to his truthfulness," Irtan said dryly.

"Why would you believe my words over his?" She had to ask, but at least she managed to cover her surprise with the suspicion an expelled student would have if an archmage favored her all of a sudden.

Irtan's blue eyes gripped her. "You're my friend's best student, and in every letter he sends, he makes sure I regret allowing that expulsion to go through."

As his words sank in, Kamira stared at him. An arcanist and the first archmage being friends... Irtan was too cunning to lie about something she could check, so she couldn't assume he was trying to deceive her. Maybe he intended to shake her composure with the news, or drive a wedge between her and Master Tijhran. A cold shiver went down her spine, and she hated to admit that Irtan might have succeeded with the latter, because with such friendship revealed, her secrets might not have been as safe with Master Tijhran as she thought.

"Is there anything else?" Better to cut the visit short than to give Irtan more opportunities to manipulate her. "I have more important things to do." Like getting that cursed hair tied up, but the archmage didn't need to know that.

Sadness flashed on his face. "I'd like to ask you about the two power surges in the desert, one quite recent and violent, but somehow I'm sure you'll be as unwilling to share any information as Tijhran was. I appreciate you taking time to talk to me, even if you weren't as forthright as I wished." He sighed. "But I can't blame you for that, especially not after what happened to your master."

Kamira's blood froze, and her heart skipped a beat as she stared at the archmage.

"You didn't know he was attacked." It wasn't a question, but a realization, and when Irtan placed his hand on her arm, she didn't move away. "He's been wounded, but he's alive," he added with compassion that sounded genuine.

"How did it happen?" she said through a clenched throat, even though no matter how the events unfolded, they must have been her fault. After all, Veelk had caught someone spying around back when they visited. And Hafnis... A man like him, with no loyalty to his teacher and an ax to grind, could have flapped his tongue as well, before he'd met his end at Veelk's hand.

"He was attacked at home, by a demon brought into this world in flesh." As he spoke, his eyes locked on her face.

As shaken as she was, she still managed a neutral

expression and a suspicious tone. "No demonling could be a threat to Master Tijhran."

"I have reasons to suspect that a higher demon was involved."

She allowed herself widened eyes. "One of those who were said to have attacked the overseas kingdom?" With the Devanshari all around Kaighal, she couldn't pretend to be oblivious to the events on the other continent.

"Possibly. I also have a reason to believe that it's connected to your journey into the desert, to the Towers' ruins." He raised his hands before she could reply. "Hush. I do not want to hear you evading the truth again."

Kamira let her displeasure show. "You're back to playing games. I don't suppose you could simply tell me what you know of that higher demon?" Asking how he knew of it to begin with would be stretching her luck, and with the knowledge of the high mages' involvement in Veranesh's imprisonment, she had her guesses anyway.

Irtan hesitated, and when his face hardened for a glimpse, Kamira was certain he'd tell her nothing. Yet the first archmage smiled. "His name is Uganel, and from what I've discovered, he might be interested in what happened in the desert."

"I appreciate your courtesy," she said, using words to conceal her relief. There wasn't another demon about, so her teacher was safe for the time being. "Not all high mages would be kind enough to share the name."

"You didn't ask how I know it." Irtan regarded her with curiosity.

She couldn't help sneering. "You're the first archmage; it's your... obligation to know things. As to how..." She allowed herself a playful expression. "I wouldn't think an expelled student would be privileged to the Towers' secrets, so I didn't ask."

"You're right, but perhaps... You could return to the Towers, and we could trade secrets." Irtan waved his hand before she could put together her refusal. "I know, I know. Arcanist pride and all." The tone of his voice suggested he never expected her to agree, and he held no grudge, but when he looked her in the eye, he became serious. "We live in dangerous times, and I can sense a change coming. Don't get caught in its wave." He stood up. "Once again, thank you for your time and answers."

As he walked toward the door, Kamira bowed, both out of habit and genuine gratitude. Allowing Irtan to play his game might have been dangerous, but it turned out to be worth it. "Likewise, archmage. I hope you got the answers you came for."

A glimpse of sudden movement caught Kamira's eye when she was raising her head, and her training took over. She brought up a barrier before she even recognized what the projectile was, and the mug of wine splashed against it. Kamira gritted her teeth, because in the end, Irtan had succeeded at playing her. If he had used magic, she'd have countered with all the power she had, and one of them would have died. But a mug couldn't have been considered a real assault, and at the same time exposed her power.

"Now I have." Irtan stood motionless, a gentle smile softening his features, as if reassuring her she shouldn't expect another attack. "Master Tijhran was right to praise you. Your skills are indeed impressive. And that smooth energy flow... You must have made a pact with quite a demon. A higher one, perhaps?"

Ignoring the tease in his voice, Kamira weighed her decision. Even if she could stand her ground against the archmage, such a duel would draw too much attention. Her barrier dispersed, magic obedient to her will. "I think it's time for you to go, first archmage. We've learned enough from each other."

Irtan walked to the door. His casual stride tempted Kamira, and she bit her lip, fighting the urge, but the memory of the mug he'd tossed, forcing her to act and reveal her true power, cooled her blood lust. He might be old, but he was the first archmage for a reason. If he turned his back to her, it meant he was confident he would defeat her if needed.

He looked over his shoulder with a smile, and it was obvious he knew exactly what Kamira was considering.

"Give Master Tijhran my regards," he said as he put the hood over his head again, "should you happen to see him before I do."

She waited until the door closed before she allowed herself a show of emotion: a grimace and clenched fists. Clearly, the archmage's mention of her teacher was meant to shatter her trust, and she had to admit, Irtan had succeeded in sowing that seed of doubt. If she wanted the truth, she needed something more than a letter. She needed to speak to Tijhran face to face.

With that thought, she packed up her necessities, cursing the injury every time she needed both hands, but when Veelk came back with the supplies, she was almost ready.

"I need my hair done, and I'm going downstairs to ask Lefna to help me," she announced as soon as the mage killer walked in. "And when I'm back, we're setting out for Gaunash, so you better be ready."

Veelk inspected the mug in the puddle of wine of the

floor, then looked at her. "It's unlike you to act so abruptly... and spill your wine."

"Master Tijhran's been attacked, and the first archmage threw his mug at me."

His eyes widened and his body tensed. "He came here?!"

She waved her hand. "To fish for the information Yoreus skimped on." She collected all the hair accessories and opened the door. "I'll tell you everything on the way."

3

Alluvendran looked at the sheets of parchment covered in ancient tongue with several rough sketches nowhere near the detail of a blueprint, and then at the small device that emanated magic even he sensed. An empty laughter grew in his lungs, but tight lips kept the mockery at bay. The cellar given to him as a workshop reminded him much of his previous prison, with its dark corners and bare stone walls. He might have been released, but he was far from free. At least his new lodgings provided a lot of space, and he could think of many uses for the equipment collected within its walls. Wasting time chasing a madwoman's dream was not one of them.

"Well?" One word was enough to convey Cahala's impatience.

He couldn't resist half a smile but otherwise kept the sarcasm to himself. "This task might not be impossible, my lady, but for me alone it would take years, if not my whole life. Time, as I understand, you do not wish to wait."

The grimace on the queen's face was just as much answer as her next words. "So what do you suggest instead?"

The tone of her voice made it clear she expected more than mere pondering, and with no offer of bringing assistants in to speed up his work, Alluvendran could weave his web.

"Why rely on something that might be destroyed or stolen? On something that would need recharging every so often"—he poked Gildya's device—"or would be too big to move, limiting your ability to travel freely?"

"Get to the point," Cahala said blandly.

Her deception didn't work, and Alluvendran caught the interest on her face. She'd listen however long he'd make her. But to delay meant also waiting longer for his real freedom, so he pulled a sleeve up, revealing imbued stones melted into his skin. "They can look much more beautiful than this, and they can be smaller, too. But most importantly, they can feed your body with the magic it craves, and no one will ever take them away." He didn't bother telling her the solution he offered was considered a crime by Gildya Magna. A woman who had people slaughtered to achieve her goals would either not care or find a way around.

Cahala leaned closer, and a cloud of her perfume's flowery scent veiled Alluvendran like a promise. He exhaled, watching his own breath tease her elaborate hairdo, and waited. She reached out, and her finger danced around one of the stones, brushing against the adept's skin as well. It woke up his long-forgotten instincts, but the hunger in the queen's eyes was of another nature. Besides, no matter how his body reacted to her, her personality spoiled any possible carnal pleasures. Not to mention the queen's dog, Phuran, always skulked nearby. Alluvendran knew better than to check what this zealous man would consider an insult or a threat to his mistress.

"Will they work forever?" She finally looked up, but stayed close to him.

"As long as you live, my lady."

With a nod, she took a step back, not a woman giving in to her curiosity and desires anymore, but a queen again. "Very well. You'll teach our brightest scholars how to do it, and once we confirm it works, you'll receive your freedom."

He should have expected that. "I'll perform the task myself, as many times and for as many people as necessary. But I won't teach, nor will I have anyone watch me while I work."

Cahala's face tensed. "We can have you killed. One word is enough."

Alluvendran let out a short laugh. From the corner of his eye, he caught Phuran approaching, but he cared not for the threatening glare of the Devanshari man. "Will this be your decision, then, my lady? My death is likewise the death of your desire." Challenging her like that wasn't even playing with fire. Yes, she could have him killed, but only *after* he performed the blending. The hunger in her eyes told him enough, rendering the threat useless.

A grimace curled her perfect red lips, but her gesture stopped Phuran from drawing his blade. "Fine. You will be allowed to keep your secrets, but if we ever sense any deception, we will not hesitate to have you killed and find someone else to serve us."

"Fair enough."

The queen's displeased face made him wonder whether he'd be granted his freedom—and his life, for that matter— upon the completion of the task, but even if she made him pay for his refusal to teach, Alluvendran's resolve wouldn't change. Some promises were not to be broken, and he gained the knowledge of blending the stones along with the trust of people he didn't want to—and never would—betray. The images of their copper-skinned silhouettes resurfaced, surprising even Alluvendran, who thought the memories long since faded.

"I'll need some time to regain my skills and a few volunteers to practice before I'm ready," he said. "When I learned the art, I cared not how the stones looked, but now it's of the utmost importance to preserve and enhance your beauty, my lady."

The compliment pleased Cahala, and her expression softened. "We'll have some women and imbued stones delivered to you. Ask Phuran for anything else you might need, and he'll see to it." She looked him over. "We'll personally be checking on your progress."

"I'd be honored, my lady." He bowed and didn't lift his head until Cahala walked away.

A servant picked up Gildya's device and carried it out, but Phuran stood unmoving. He watched Alluvendran intensely, and his palm, resting on the saber's hilt, moved slightly as if he was about to draw his weapon, but then he turned without a word and followed Cahala.

Alluvendran smiled. He recognized the threat, but thought little of it. Like the queen, her dog sensed trickery everywhere. Their vileness outmatched that of many adepts and high mages Alluvendran had met back before his imprisonment, and his smile ebbed at that thought. Keeping his part of the bargain was a given, but he'd be a fool to trust they would keep theirs. At least now it became nothing but a side task in the studies he wanted to perform anyway. Cahala had agreed willingly to receive the stones, and as long as she didn't realize she could enhance her body with the stones even more, he could give her what little she wanted.

If she knew, she'd make more demands, but before that, he would not only complete his part of their agreement—he'd also add several imbued stones to his own body and maybe solve the problem of the collar too, regaining his full strength. That would even out the odds should they refuse him his freedom after their dealings concluded.

Seeing to the blending of the stones could take as much as weeks or months, if she wanted them for all of her servants, but it was nothing compared to years in Gildya's prison. His smile returned as he pushed the tables around, setting up the workshop for his needs and making plans for the future.

PELINA GRIMACED when the fourth archmage, Kerl, reached for the bottle again. Its glass rang against the crystal cup while he tried to pour the wine, spilling some over his hand. She'd never get those stains out. Another evening spent cleaning his attire meant wasting both time and magic on mundane chores again, which brought her to question her life choices once more. He was an archmage, demons curse his ass, and he was supposed to teach her, not use her as a servant. When Kerl chose her to be his personal apprentice from several dozens of the Towers' students, Pelina thought her life had finally taken a turn for the better. Little did she know, that foolish young girl! Memories flowed, and while Kerl guzzled the wine, she remembered his shaking hands touching her skin. A shiver went down her spine, and she put away a book, never turning her eyes away from the archmage. *I better get out before he remembers I'm here.*

Maybe she should bring him another bottle... Her hesitation lasted only for a heartbeat, and then she walked through the chamber, resisting the urge to rush. Kerl was already drunk enough to have his senses dulled, and he was used to her walking about, but any abrupt movement could snap him out of his stupor. When the door closed behind her, a sigh of relief left her mouth as Kerl called her name. *Just in time.*

She sent a smile to a passing-by mage. His face revealed a mixture of curiosity and amusement, so he must have been aware of the fourth archmage's habits, but he looked away when their eyes met and rushed off. She grinned at his back, watching the retreat, but didn't linger by the door, unwilling to try her luck. Should Kerl stumble outside, no flattery nor magic would save her.

With the evening's approach, the Towers became quiet. The high mages and apprentices retired, and Pelina wandered the corridors considering her options. The library tempted her with the knowledge Kerl refused her, but it was also the first place anyone would look for her, and she knew the fourth archmage well enough to expect him to send servants after her. The dining chamber would be filled with students having their evening meal, and Pelina avoided their company. Her ears and cheeks burned at the memories of whispers behind her back and overheard words. They laughed at her for having a drunkard for a teacher, and even though some of the mockery was accompanied by looks of jealousy that she'd been chosen by an archmage, it didn't soothe their stabs.

I better go for a walk, maybe stop by a tavern. Of course, if she kept spending her evenings drinking in the city, she'd soon join her teacher in his habit, but getting out of the Towers was still the best choice. Kerl would drink himself to sleep as usual, and she'd be back in her own bed before midnight. And contrary to her teacher, she knew that one mug of ale was enough.

The guards didn't bother her as she exited, and Pelina paused at the gate to take in the sight of Kaighal. The Towers, built on the hill overlooking the city, provided a perfect view, and she liked to look at the sea over the rooftops before descending the winding path. After that, walking down felt like venturing into the guts of a living creature. Kaighal never slept, and under the darkening sky, its lights flickered like the numerous eyes of a strange beast. Only at the foot of the hill did the shapes of the buildings emerge sharper from the dark, revealing not a monstrous creature, but a welcoming city.

She walked the streets while merchants packed away their wares and citizens gathered around taverns. A fire-spitting performer caught her attention, and she stopped to watch the tongues of flame burst into the air, awing the spectators. She pictured herself in the man's place, juggling fire and water, and making snowflakes dance in the wind. She smiled at the idea, but when her eyes focused on the performer's tattered clothes and a hat on the ground with only few coins inside, the memories of Kerl's fat hands touching her or his wine-soaked breath on her face became less unappealing. If she persevered, she had a chance of becoming a teacher in the Towers, maybe even an archmage one day.

The spectators clapped and cheered, but only a few reached for their purses, and Pelina threw several coins into the hat before walking away. Copper was hardly enough to help him improve his life, but at least he would be able to pay for food and a place to sleep for the night.

Music called for her in the distance, and Pelina picked up her pace at the prospect of spending an evening among the cheerful crowd. Forgetting about her problems might have been running away from them, but until she finished her schooling under Kerl, there was little she could do anyway. Once she secured a teacher's position in the Towers or perhaps found a wealthy patron in need of her skills, she'd be free of that old lecher forever.

She took a turn onto one of the smaller streets, and the lights of the Plenty Fish tavern flickered in the distance.

"Excuse me, pretty lady, do you have any spare coins?"

A beggar's voice made Pelina twitch. She hadn't noticed him standing in the shadow by the wall.

She gave him an apologetic smile. "Just gave them away around the corner." Archmages' apprentices received a small allowance, but if she wanted some ale tonight, she couldn't afford more generosity.

The beggar took a step closer. His clothes, though rough and dirty, were not rags, and his eyes held a smug stare. Pelina backed away at the sight of an ugly smile stretching his lips, and her back hit against something... someone. An arm locked her body in place, and before she could call out for help, a piece of cloth filled her mouth, its taste nauseous.

The false beggar approached, grinning as he pulled out a rope. Pelina struggled to break free, but the man holding her from behind didn't give her a chance.

"Now, now. Don't fight, and we won't hurt you!" a repugnant voice said by her ear.

If only they didn't gag her! Had she her voice, she'd have shown them what a mage, even an apprentice mage, was capable of. The stench from the cloth in her mouth dimmed her senses, and as the poison in it took over her body, she drifted off into nothingness. In her last conscious thought, she couldn't help pondering the cruel fate. Fleeing from her problems, she'd run into bigger ones.

4

Ryell's fists clenched whenever he thought of Veelk. The mage killer's unexpected return had ruined the plan to learn more of Kamira's conversation with the stranger, but the one sentence Ryell heard made his blood boil. His nails dug deep into his palms, marking his skin, and Ryell gritted his teeth. He should forget about her. But his heart objected to the reason, reminding him of Kamira's face and the scent of her hair. No matter how hard he tried to replace that picture with the memory of Atissa, his own mind betrayed him. And even when he persuaded himself how foolish it was to waste time on a deceitful demonologist, his feelings demanded he wouldn't give up on returning Kamira to the path of the good and the righteous. The evil didn't claim her, not yet, but she refused to listen to reason. It had to be that mage killer's influence... It had to be. To succeed, he needed to find a way to separate them and spend more time alone with Kamira.

He walked through the streets deep in thought, paying little attention to his surroundings. The crowd thickened as he approached the merchant quarter, but one glimpse at his expression and clenched fists made the common folk step aside. Then, as he ascended the winding path to the High Towers, only occasional passersby would give him a startled glance.

He needed to talk to Yoreus, but Kamira's words tainted the trust he had in the archmage. They reminded him that she had a reason to keep her secrets to herself around him, and he couldn't help questioning both Yoreus's intentions and Atissa's feelings. After all, he was neither powerful nor influential, yet the second archmage treated him like an honored guest.

The doubts set in when Ryell walked through the High Towers entrance, exchanging a brief nod with the guards. He chose the stairs, instead of using one of the magic-imbued platforms to travel between levels. Climbing helped keep his body in shape and gave time for his mind to clear before he spoke to Yoreus.

But when he finally stood before the archmage's quarters, his thoughts still haunted him with doubts.

Overcoming hesitation, he put his knuckles to the door and listened to their dull sound against the wood.

Yoreus called from inside and arched his eyebrows when Ryell entered. "You look troubled." He put a book away.

Ryell walked over to the table and sat down at the archmage's gesture. The subtle wealth of the archmage's quarters weighed heavy on his uneasiness. Before, he saw them as comforting, but Kamira's words cut deep into his calmness. A powerful man like Yoreus couldn't see Ryell as more than just a pitiful refugee. Even if Ryell held a noble's title and a position of a royal guard, these things mattered little in Kaighal, and had to matter even less for someone who ruled over it.

"Kamira came back to the inn." Ryell spoke in a cold,

detached tone. "She's wounded and she mentioned an attack."

The archmage's eyes lit up. "Did she say anything? Who attacked her? Where was it?"

Ryell weighed his information, but nothing that Kamira had told him seemed a secret. After all, he concluded, she wouldn't have shared any with him in any case. "Some desert bandits. From what I understand, they got caught by a magic storm before it happened."

Yoreus leaned forward. "So she saw it? How close was she? Did she say anything about its source?"

Ryell shook his head. "She wouldn't say anything more."

"Hopefully, when she rests and feels safe here, in the city, she'll be more talkative." Yoreus didn't hide his disappointment.

"I don't think she'll tell me anything." Ryell's voice remained cold. If he wanted a chance to win Kamira's trust, he needed to keep the archmage at a distance. "Somehow, she knew of you and Atissa." The memory of Kamira's words brought a bitter taste to his mouth, and he grimaced. "She said I stank of high magic."

To his surprise, Yoreus didn't laugh. "In comparison to us, the arcanists seem to have a heightened sensitivity to magic. Maybe it comes from their connection to demons." He rubbed his chin. "But I doubt she was truly able to recognize the origin of that magic. You could tell her you're seeing someone here to help you with... your condition."

Ryell grimaced. "I'm a guard, not a spy. I can't lie as readily as some people." He bit his tongue at the last moment, before accidentally accusing the archmage of deception. "Kamira got enough from my reaction to figure out everything she needed. And from what I understood, there isn't a way for anyone to convince her to come back to the Towers, though her reasons are unclear." Regardless of what he told the archmage, Ryell could hope to find a way to make Kamira abandon her demonologist ways, but if there was one, he was certain it didn't include Yoreus's participation.

"She's as stubborn as I remember." Yoreus sighed.

"I don't think I can help you with that matter further," Ryell said before the archmage could come up with another plan. "I don't think I'm of any service to you anymore." He stood up.

Yoreus shook his head. "I wouldn't dare to look at you as another servant or a tool to be used and thrown away." He gestured for Ryell to retake his seat. "If you wish to leave, I have no right to insist, but I'd be honored if you stay."

Ryell didn't sit down, his body stiff as he looked at the archmage. "I have nothing more to offer, and the thought of not being able to reciprocate your hospitality—"

A burst of laughter interrupted him.

"That's not true," Yoreus said as soon as he stifled his amusement. "It is I who is indebted to you. You've achieved something I could only dream of doing, and for that I'll be forever grateful." The archmage's expression softened as his inscrutable mask fell. "You've changed Atissa, Ryell."

"What do you mean?" Ryell could only hope his question came across as confusion, not suspicion.

"We high mages boast that our magic doesn't come from easy pacts with demons. Instead, we strive for perfection and put effort into reaching for the energy that is not tainted by a demon's presence," Yoreus said. "We were the ones to save the world in the past and defeat a powerful demon brought here by the arcanists, but ultimately, because of that, high mages fall prey to the very flaw that became the downfall of the arcanists: pride."

"And Atissa...?"

"Being an archmage's daughter doesn't help one stay humble, and as I mentioned the other day, it's my fault as well." Yoreus looked away. "But let's not dwell on it. I'd rather show you what you've achieved. Atissa was supposed to come back a while ago, so she might be here any moment." He stood up and indicated her room. "Why don't you wait there and see for yourself?"

Ryell hesitated. The archmage's words piqued his interest, but common sense moved him to wonder if he had become part of another of his games. A knock on the door made the men exchange glances, and Ryell, acting upon curiosity, hid.

Yoreus opened the door himself. "You're late."

"I'm sorry, Father, I lost track of time," Atissa replied. "I didn't realize there was so much to do. These people have been suffering for months now, and I couldn't just walk away."

Ryell heard the steps from the main room but dared not peek through the cracked door. He leaned against the wall, listening intently. Atissa seemed genuine. At the same time, it was so different from what he knew of her. With Kamira's remarks having sowed suspicion in his mind, he expected deception... He scolded himself for giving in to such thoughts. Atissa didn't know he was eavesdropping. She'd have no reason to pretend in front of Yoreus.

"So, has your curiosity been sated? Are you ready to go back to your duties and studies?" Yoreus asked.

Silence followed, but then Ryell heard Atissa's voice again. "If you approve, I wish to visit the asylum again when my duties allow it. Maybe I can convince several other students to help out as well. These people need us, Father. They might be foreigners, but it's Kaighal they sought refuge in, and I feel like we should show them what high mages stand for."

"Very well," Yoreus replied, and Ryell could swear there was pride in his voice. "As long as it doesn't affect your studies, you have my permission. I'll also discuss the matter with other archmages, so that more students may join you."

"Thank you!"

Atissa's feet pattered on the floor, and Ryell pictured her hugging Yoreus. He smiled at how passionate she was, be it in happiness or in anger, but the thought didn't linger, replaced by the memory of Kamira's laughter. The demonologist reserved her emotions, and her smile seemed more valuable, especially when she gave it to Ryell, not Veelk or anyone else. Yet those word he'd overheard, that swift admittance that she was deceiving him, still stung. It didn't matter whether she had reasons to keep truth from him. His fingers curled and his shoulders slumped at the memory of the distrust she'd openly expressed.

"I'm sure Ryell will be delighted to hear about it," Yoreus said.

At the sound of his name, Ryell snapped back to reality, focusing once more on the conversation in the other room.

"No! You mustn't tell him!" Atissa said. "Father, please... I don't want him to think I'm doing it to impress him or make up for the argument we had. For that... For that I'll have to apologize myself."

When her voice broke, raw emotion ringing in it, Ryell's heart almost shattered. Drowned in his own guilt, he couldn't scold himself enough for allowing Kamira to sow doubts. Swayed by her crafty manipulation, he'd suspected an honorable man and distrusted his daughter, who might have been spoiled a bit but were otherwise good-natured.

"Well then, my dear child, you better run to the baths to

refresh yourself," Yoreus said, amused, "because I expect Ryell's visit today. He has some information for me."

"You should have told me earlier! He better not see me like this!"

The sound of shuffling and quick steps distracted Ryell and left him unprepared for the door to Atissa's room to swing open. At first, he hoped she wouldn't see him. She dashed toward the clothes folded on her bed, but as he shifted and she spun around, their eyes met. He didn't even know how to apologize for the transgression. Though it was Yoreus's plot, blaming it on the archmage seemed petty, but any explanation would have to involve him. Yet, as the rush of blood through his heart slowed down, he realized that Atissa wasn't angry. She was looking at him, her expression revealing hope and fear.

No matter how spoiled she was, in that one moment her posture expressed nothing but innocence, and Ryell's heart panged in response. Despite what Kamira said about high mages, Atissa could become someone to prove her accusations false. Yet, at the very thought of the demonologist, a memory followed. The gaunt face framed with black hair made his hands shake and his throat clench. But Kamira had been pushing him away, while Atissa's feelings seemed strong and honest. Even if Yoreus might have been hoping to glean Kamira's secrets through Ryell, his daughter was not part of it.

Discarding all his doubts, he opened his arms.

That movement broke the spell that held Atissa still. In a few steps, she was in his embrace. Her body emanated warmth and magic, and Ryell's nostrils filled with the scent of her perfume and sweat. They stood like that for a while, but soon she moved away. "You heard," she said. "I—"

He put a finger on her lips. "No need. You deserve a bath. We can talk later."

In return, he received the brightest smile he had ever seen, one that could dim the vivid image of the gray-skinned woman still staring at him from his memories, her black eyes cold and uncaring.

Atissa nodded, and Ryell followed her out of the room. Yoreus still sat in his chair, but remained silent.

"Do you see now what I mean?" the archmage said after the door closed behind his daughter. "This is an Atissa I've never seen before, the high mage I always wished her to become. Selfless, concerned, and ready to help. For that, I can't express my gratitude enough... And I hope that one day, instead of calling you my dear guest, I'll have the privilege to call you a family member."

Ryell couldn't help but look for traces of deception or jest on the archmage's face, but his expression showed only gratitude.

"That's..." Ryell stumbled for words. That might not be something he wanted, so he offered a deep bow. When in doubt, retreating into etiquette offered a way out without commitments. "Such words flatter me." Yet, as his head lowered, under his half-closed eyes, Kamira's image still haunted him.

"But you're not convinced." Yoreus surely had a gift to notice things Ryell would prefer to remain hidden.

With the question so straightforward, he couldn't avoid it, and once more he cursed his obligations to the archmage. But when their eyes met, a sudden thought came to his rescue. Something he could offer as an explanation and maybe even an excuse to keep his distance. "I came to Tyorane dreaming of revenge, and I'm yet to fulfill that desire," he said with confidence. "The things I'd do to reach my goal might make me a traitor in the eyes of my own people, or a wanted murderer in Kaighal." His own words made him ponder the possibility of killing Cahala, but he discarded those thoughts. It wasn't time to explore futures that could never come true, though he had to admit, they made a sound argument against anyone acquainting with him. "It's not the kind of man I'd wish Atissa to have as... anyone special."

To his surprise—and disappointment—Yoreus didn't falter. "I'm sure an honorable man like you has just reasons to seek revenge. Be assured that I would do whatever is within my power to support such endeavors, should you ever decide to trust me with details."

Ryell shifted uneasily. At the back of his mind, the image of Kamira laughed at him, because he couldn't help the feeling he was being manipulated again. He'd come to Yoreus in hopes of severing ties. Instead, the archmage had tightened their relationship and almost wriggled his way into Ryell's secrets. "Thank you, I—"

"Don't mention it." The archmage waved his hand. "Come, sit down. One would think you're a supplicant, not a guest, the way you insist on remaining unseated. Have you eaten yet?"

With no choice, Ryell sat down, but his newly found trust was fleeting. Atissa might be innocent and genuine, but he couldn't help thinking that Yoreus was playing him. The interruption had steered them away from the topic that would see Ryell retreat. As if the archmage knew exactly when to stop pushing. "I'll gladly keep you and Atissa company during your meal."

Yoreus rang the bell for the servants. He offered small talk as they waited, but Ryell paid hardly any attention to the conversation about Kaighal's gossip and some trivial matters concerning the High Towers. His thoughts circled Kamira, both her warnings and her admittance of dishonesty. He could only hope that after they'd eaten, he'd find some solace and oblivion in Atissa's embrace.

As SHE CLOSED the door behind her, Atissa resisted the urge to eavesdrop. When Ryell arrived, she'd already spent enough time with her ear to the door, following the conversation inside and waiting for the right moment. Thankfully, not many students frequented the highest towers where the archmages had their quarters, or there would be no end to the gossip on how the archmage's daughter eavesdropped on her own father. Not that he would care, since he was the one who'd told her to listen, but she could do without vicious remarks other students would generously offer. At first, their jealousy of her position amused her and tickled her pride, but as years passed, it became nothing but a source of annoyance.

She rushed down the spiral stairs. Built four hundred years ago—and in quite a rush, from what she knew—the High Towers lacked the space for all the necessary conveniences that places like Gildya Magna boasted. Of course, the archmages' pride prevented them from moving the school somewhere else, or at least adding more buildings to the original structure, leaving her and all the others to use common bath chambers. She'd much rather wait and benefit from the privilege the archmages enjoyed that allowed them to bathe in privacy within certain times, which some extended to their private students, but she needed to wash off the filth and stench of the Devanshari asylum. She'd expected the place run by a prince to be cleaner and better kept... Had she known, she would have never set her foot in there.

At first, she couldn't even understand why her father had insisted on it. Lies were to be carefully woven; she wouldn't argue that. Yet it seemed pointless to waste such effort on a lowly Devanshari she had under her thumb anyway.

Of course, after she'd waited for him to enter her father's chambers, hidden behind the bend of the stairs, and witnessed their conversation, all those efforts seemed more than necessary.

Ryell was slipping away from her, and, blinded by her confidence, she'd never noticed. Atissa clenched her fists and must have grimaced, because the servant approaching from the other direction rushed to the side, getting out of her way. It couldn't have been that silly argument they had, for which her father punished her so harshly, because she'd seen Ryell since then, and he seemed to hold no grudge. Unless she misread him, and he was waiting for some kind of an apology.

The bath chambers weren't as full as she'd feared they would be. Few of the bath tubes, separated by dividers for privacy, were occupied, and three students soaked in the small pool heated with imbued stones, their chatter echoing within the walls. They threw Atissa curious glares, and a hushed comment sparked a bout of laughter, so she rushed to the side and pulled the divider across.

A spell was enough to fill the metal tub with hot water, and Atissa lowered herself inside. Most of her work in the asylum required magic, as Prince Allyv asked her to help relieving the symptoms of the addiction, but walking up and down the stairs on top of making it to the poor district and back was straining enough. Soothed by the heat, her muscles relaxed, and her mind was free to wander.

Sentence by sentence, she went through the conversation her father had with Ryell. Even though it was obvious Ryell came to cut ties, at first, she couldn't quite conjure any reason for such a decision. Then she remembered the bitterness when he spoke about that arcanist, Kamira, and how she exposed Ryell's affiliation with high mages. Somehow, her accusations affected him... As a former student, she likely knew her way around manipulation and deception, and was trying to drive a wedge between Ryell and Atissa's father. But to what end? If she needed a spy in the Towers, she would try to ensure Ryell remained close with Atissa.

She huffed, amused. Clearly, she'd been attributing too much to that demonologist. No matter what her father claimed and suspected, Kamira was no one. Perhaps her motive was simply getting revenge for being expelled. Then it would make sense to pull Ryell away, to jab at Atissa's pride, and to deprive her father of a useful tool.

Satisfied with the conclusion, Atissa reached for the bar of soap she'd brought with her. Its exotic scent mixed with the steam still rising from the tub, and she hoped it carried throughout the bath chambers, reminding all those jealous women that no matter what vicious remarks they could come up with, they wouldn't change that Atissa was an archmage's daughter and his private student, while they still scrambled for attention of any worthwhile teacher.

Another time, such payback would hardly be enough, and Atissa would find an opportunity to return their jabs, but she had more important matters to see to. As the soap traveled along her skin, adding the scent that Ryell seemed to like, her thoughts circled him again.

He was nothing but a tool, and one that might have outlived its usefulness. Her father insisted on keeping him around as if he could still gain any insights to the supposed plot that Kamira was weaving. Such behavior was so unlike an archmage that it gave her pause. He might have been keeping Ryell around, because he wasn't done with the demonologist, but there could be another motive too.

Atissa smiled involuntarily when she thought of Ryell. Yes, he was only a tool, but she liked him, too. He was foolish and naïve, that was certain, and at the same time he had something noble about him, something pure she yearned to be hers. Maybe her father had noticed that and decided to keep close relations with Ryell because of her. Maybe Ryell was meant to be her reward... She narrowed her eyes. He could also be her test. If she didn't manage to keep strings on a man so simple and trusting, her father could deem her unsuitable for the more complicated games the archmages were playing.

With that thought, she rushed her cleaning. There would be time later to soak in a bath and enjoy hot water, after she ensured that Ryell was still addicted to her... or to the magic she shared with him. If she wanted to become an archmage one day, she couldn't fail at such a simple task, beaten by a wandering demonologist. She'd show her father she was worth all the schooling and earn his trust, so that he would share the secrets she knew he'd been keeping. An archmage or not, she'd join their game and carve her way to the future position among them.

And after that, Ryell would truly be her reward. At least —Atissa smiled again—for as long as she enjoyed his company.

ALLUVENDRAN SIGHED and stared at the pieces of imbued stones, chipped and polished. Their shapes and colors danced in front of his eyes as he moved them around his worktable in a pointless attempt to rearrange them. *This is ridiculous.* By no means was he a jeweler or artist, and this shouldn't be his task.

Behind him, in the corner of the cellar workshop, three women sat chained to the wall and watched his every move with a mixture of fear and hope in their eyes, but they didn't try to beg or disturb him anymore. As much as Alluvendran pitied their plight, he couldn't set them free, so he'd drugged them instead. It brought him an illusion of peace, and spared them most of the pain that came with the blending of stones. Yet his blood still boiled at the memory of when he first learned who his "volunteers" would be, and the pointless argument with Phuran. With his crude threats, the Devanshari man made all the women agree to the treatment, and then wanted to hear nothing more of Alluvendran's objections.

Two of them already bore the marks of his experiments, their skin adorned with shards, and he cringed at Cahala's constant dissatisfaction. She expected immediate beauty when cutting skin was involved... He shook his head. Wounds would heal eventually, just like his own had, and the stunning results she expected boiled down to picking the hue of the stones and a pattern. One study subject would be enough for all his needs, but the queen kept insisting on testing it on multiple women.

He gritted his teeth. If she didn't trust him to do a good job, why not pick a servant or a maid to be treated first? They'd testify that the stones inhibited the withdrawal symptoms, and Alluvendran could fulfill his part of the agreement instead of playing around with stone shards and doing what bordered on torturing women.

The chains behind him rattled, and he turned at a muffled gasp.

Phuran stood above the women, having approached as silently as usual, and Alluvendran's fury rose at the captives' widened eyes.

"What do you want?" He allowed his tone to leave no doubt what he thought of courteous greetings toward such a cruel thug like Phuran. "I made it clear I want to be left alone."

Phuran's lips curled, and the grimace on his face was the ugliest smile Alluvendran had ever seen. "Don't worry. I'll just take my toy and leave you to your work."

A toy. That was what this woman was to the Devanshari... Alluvendran tensed, but the shackles around his wrist reminded him that he was as powerless as the captives. "I'd rather you leave without my test subjects," he replied in a cold tone. "How am I supposed to finish preparations to the queen's satisfaction if you and your men constantly have your way with these women? They're bruised and they heal slower, and the magic within the stones becomes corrupted with all the grief they experience." Thankfully, Phuran couldn't have known how the blending worked, so Alluvendran could allow himself to embellish the truth.

"Don't get so worked up. I'll get you a new one," Phuran said. "And I might even tell my men to leave her untouched." He laughed and forced one of the women to stand up. "But since these are already spoiled, there's no harm in having a bit more fun, is there?" Phuran removed the lock, freeing the chain from its clasp, and pulled his victim closer.

Alluvendran stiffened when the Devanshari's hands closed around the woman's breast while his tongue traced her chin. A clear challenge glared from his eyes, locked on the adept.

Despite his urge for confrontation, Alluvendran did nothing. Getting himself killed wouldn't help the women, so until he found a way to get rid of his collar, he had to keep his rage at bay. As Phuran dragged away his victim, the adept's fists opened and closed in response to the storm within him. He might have made an agreement with Cahala, but that man, that *animal*, was not part of it, and his thoughts wandered toward the possibilities of getting rid of Phuran one way or another.

The eyes of the two remaining women pleaded in silence, and he took the flask off the nearby table. "I'll give you something to sleep peacefully," he said in a soft voice, kneeling down.

They drank the mixture he offered, but he couldn't give himself similar comfort. Drugging the women was anything but a solution to the problem, and he couldn't even be certain they would live after he was done with his task. He turned away from their faces, their expressions softening as sleep took them. After ten years of captivity, he didn't expect the feeling of powerlessness to bother him, but in Gildya's prison he hadn't had to witness the suffering of innocents, nor had he engaged in questionable practices. He resumed his work.

The more he thought about it, the more he questioned whether agreeing to help Cahala was indeed a better choice than death.

5

When Kamira entered, Master Tijhran was sitting in his library as if nothing had happened. Yet his leg was stretched before him, and in the aroma of salves and herbs in the air, she smelled a more pungent odor in the mix. The bandages looked fresh and clean, but the small patch of red told her the wound still bled. Her teacher's gray hair was in disarray, and he wore an outfit more suitable for staying in bed than arcanist work. Never in her years of studies had she seen him so disheveled. It must have cost him a great effort to even make it to his library.

"What a pleasant surprise," he said, even though he must have heard her voice as she spoke with the servant downstairs, a man that Tijhran had to employ recently— she'd guessed only because of the injury. Her teacher never bothered with help before that, and if needed, he had students to perform menial tasks. She almost smirked at the memory of scrubbing the floor using wind and water, or preserving food while channeling magic into ice. In Tijhran's house, even chores were a lesson in magic.

"Courtesy of the first archmage," she replied. "How

come your supposedly favorite student learns of your injury from him and not from you?" she added in a half-accusatory manner.

Tijhran offered her a disarming smile. "I should have guessed the archmage would flap his tongue too much. Fishing for information, I presume?" As expected, he didn't address the actual accusation.

"He had the audacity to complain that your letters have been scarce and brief."

His laughter filled the library. "I'd wager he forgot to mention that his own letters lacked volume lately." He became serious. "From what I read between the lines of the last one, though, the archmages are very concerned about a certain event in the desert. Were you involved?"

She hesitated only for a moment. "Yes." Already on her way to Gaunash, she decided to trust her teacher to be on her side. If he had been sharing any information with Irtan, the archmage wouldn't come to ask her questions. And hiding the truth of what happened from Tijhran wouldn't keep him safe, since he had already been attacked. He deserved to know. "The same demon who attacked you ambushed us, and we had to fight."

With eyes widened, her teacher leaned forward. "That power…"

"It wasn't mine," she said quickly. "It was the demon's. We barely survived, but we defeated him." As much as she trusted Master Tijhran with everything else, the secret of a demon-destroying spell wasn't meant for humans. Veranesh had been careless enough to share it with her, and she would use it when she saw fit, but other than that… she would do anything in her power to ensure no one else learned of it. Other yalari were likely too suspicious or cautious to ever reveal it to any other human. At least, she hoped they were. No matter how appealing the destruction of *some* demons might be, the consequences to the world would be too dire to risk fanatics running around and destroying them.

Tijhran shook his head with a mixture of disbelief and pride. "Just like in the old times. But tales of battles aside, no matter how much I'd want to hear all the heroic details, have you learned anything useful in your travels? Did that demoness offer any insights?"

He didn't ask about the price she would have to have paid for such information, and she appreciated the courtesy, although for an entirely different reason. If he did, once more the conversation would get close to the spell too dangerous to mention, and she would hate lying to Tijhran... if that was even possible.

With that in mind, she skipped the details of meeting with Pardayi and went straight to the point: "It was the demons who gave the high mages means to imprison Veranesh. He's the source of high magic." She couldn't help her grim tone.

The intensity of Tijhran's stare left no doubt he'd rather hear she was jesting, so she allowed him the time needed for such a revelation to sink in.

"Four hundred years..." he muttered. It must have been the first time ever that his hands trembled, or at least the first time she had witnessed it. Then he pulled himself together and shook his head as if chasing thoughts away. If he felt any anger toward the mages, he didn't reveal it. "That's in the past. What of the present?"

To that, she didn't have a good answer. "I'm no closer than I was. I know what they did, but not how they did it. They couldn't have been in the Towers when the Cataclysm happened."

Tijhran leaned forward, a glint in his eyes and a mischievous smile dancing in a corner of his lips, and for a moment she saw only an excited scholar, not a demanding teacher. "They couldn't have and they wouldn't have, but they prepared nonetheless, didn't they?"

She waited patiently, his excitement contagious. It seemed that she'd accidentally handed him a piece of a puzzle, and in return, he would share one with her as well.

"Tell me, my dear former student, have you noticed anything unusual during your time in the High Towers?" His smile grew wider. "Something that surely didn't belong to the school of high magic, yet the archmages made no effort to dispose of it. Quite the contrary, they seemed to make a good use of it."

"Of course!" Kamira almost smacked herself on the forehead for not having figured it out earlier. After all those years she'd spent there, one would think that an oddity would stand out, but truth to be told, the joy and excitement of learning arcane arts washed most of her memories of the High Towers away. "The circle for the initiation rite." If she strained to remember, it had all the qualities of the arcane circle, similar markings and layout, though details escaped her. After all, when first she walked through it, and then passed it by on occasion, she knew nothing of the other school of magic.

Tijhran gave her a nod—the same way he always praised her for a question answered or a task performed well. "I never understood why the initiation rite, the very ritual that was supposed to enhance the students' sensitivity to high magic, was performed with the use of something as purely arcane as a circle. If what you have learned is true, this circle is the means to force a pact onto... the demon."

She appreciated that he didn't mention Veranesh's name.

Perhaps his servant wasn't likely to eavesdrop even if Veelk wasn't keeping him busy, but with so many powerful people and demons involved, caution could be the difference between death and survival. "I wish I could study it, but getting into the Towers won't be easy."

"Perhaps you won't have to." Tijhran pointed at his desk. "If you would be so kind, second drawer from the bottom. There should be a journal there."

The leather-bound book she found in the drawer was thick with additional sheets of paper, and upon her teacher's inviting gesture, Kamira leafed through it. All the notes were in Tijhran's handwriting, and most of them speculated on the meaning of various arcane symbols. She flipped back to the beginning, and there it was, on the bigger sheet of paper, carefully folded and inserted into the journal... the initiation rite circle, drawn in such detail that it couldn't have been a sketch made from memory. "How?" she muttered. To her knowledge, Tijhran was never a student in the High Towers.

"A decade or so ago, in one of my letters to Archmage Irtan, I expressed my curiosity about the circle," Tijhran replied jovially. "Of course, my interest was purely of a scholarly nature, and I hoped—how did I put it in the letter to Irtan?—oh, I hoped that finding a link between high and arcane magics would bring the two schools closer and encourage arcanists to seek tutelage in the High Towers."

She couldn't help laughing. "And he actually believed you?" Out of all the men and women leading the high mages, Irtan was probably the most cunning and insightful one.

Tijhran shrugged. "Maybe he did, maybe he didn't, yet nonetheless, he obliged my request and sent me the drawing of the circle." He pointed at the journal. "Feel free to read through it and copy what you might need. I didn't get anywhere with my research, but I didn't know what you've discovered. I'm sure your demon might offer insights as well."

"Or Irtan played you and this is not the real circle," she said. "I have no proof, but I think at least some of the archmages know the truth. If he was protecting their secrets, he wouldn't let you have it so easily."

"It looks genuine enough, but, of course, I can't be certain. As much as I value my friendship with Irtan, neither of us has any illusions about sharing." He looked her in the eye. "But even if he omitted or altered parts of it, it still might provide you with enough insights to move on with your plans. Unless, of course, you prefer to convince the archmages to let you have a peek at the actual circle."

The corner of her lip twitched at the thought of making such request. Irtan, perhaps, would oblige, if only because of his hopes to glean any knowledge from her, but Yoreus was another matter, and she couldn't count on, even after all those years, that no teacher would recognize her. The word of the expelled student back in the High Towers would spread. The second archmage would quickly learn of it, and confronting him on his own ground and terms didn't appeal to her. If she died in that fight, all of Kaighal would suffer.

"Thank you. I'll take whatever help I can get," she replied.

"Now that this is settled," he said in a lighthearted tone, "maybe you would like to entertain an old, injured man with tales of your exploits? I'd be keen to hear about your battle —as much or as little as you're willing to tell."

She shifted uneasily. To tell such a story while omitting certain happenings would require more time and thought to prepare. "It's not a tale of glory." She looked him in the eye. "And some things... I won't be able to share."

Her heart ached at the thought he would think she considered him unworthy of trust, but Tijhran nodded. "Demons don't like when arcanists share their secrets, and I'm sure you've gathered quite a few," he said and looked at the library's door. "Is your friend joining us? I thought I heard him downstairs, but I can't sense his magic close."

"He took it upon himself to check your house's protections," she replied. "Seeing as you were attacked here, I thought I could not win the argument about an arcanist being safe in his home."

The wrinkles on his face shifted as Tijhran let out a hearty laugh. "I might have had my reservations about him, but it seems you couldn't have hoped for a better friend. Now then, assume for one evening the duties of my student, tell the servant to go home, and return with wine and a good tale. I consider it the payment for sharing my journal."

An evening spent on telling stories and avoiding revealing secrets seemed like a waste of time in comparison to studying the initiation rite circle, but at the same time, after the rushed journey to Gaunash before she'd even had time to recover, such an evening would offer her some rest she desperately needed. In the morning, with a clearer head and better focus, she would tackle research. Therefore, she responded to his smile with her own. "Of course, my dear teacher."

As much as they hated the artifact, the place where it once stood had become—much to Myrkan's amusement—their gathering spot. He couldn't decide whether his brethren were drawn to the magic lingering around the garden patch, seeking a trace of home in that magic-less world, or if their instincts drove them to ensure no human got near... as if those pitiful creatures were capable of fixing an object shattered to pieces.

No matter the reason, whenever they were to gather, his companions picked the same spot, and the three yalari looked at Myrkan as he walked up to them with dark blood staining his claws. Trupyad's disappearance would cause more questions and likely do more harm than admitting to have killed the sly yalari, which could serve Myrkan's purposes if he played it right. When he stood before the others, he looked straight at Derazin.

"That was a lousy plot." He spat. "Did you really think Trupyad could kill me?"

A mixture of disbelief and fear struck Derazin's face. The plump yalari must have realized that even a mere accusation undermined his position among the others. "That's ridiculous!" His high-pitched voice conveyed anything but confidence.

"I agree." Myrkan savored the moment. "Sending him to kill me was ridiculous. You should have come yourself if you wanted to get rid of me so badly."

"You're insane!" Derazin regained some of the lost confidence, but his widened eyes betrayed the fear he was trying to hide. "I won't give in to the game you're playing. Why would I bother killing you?"

"Because you want to go back, and I'm in your way." This wasn't entirely true with the votes they had cast, but Myrkan didn't need the accusation to stick. All his words had to do was divert Derazin's attention from the real reasons behind Trupyad's death. As soon as the fat yalari got cornered, he would take any way out offered without asking too many questions. He might be powerful, and his domain spread across a vast area, but deep under the layers of flabby skin and soft flesh, Derazin remained as cowardly as a clawless asayalari.

Derazin's fists clenched while the other yalari watched him with a mixture of suspicion and curiosity. "And I will, as soon as we're done," he said. "We voted. I wouldn't have risked this alliance turning against me only to bring forth what will come anyway. And I definitely wouldn't have sent Trupyad."

"If not you, then who?" Arujhan's voice remained calm, but his eyes challenged Derazin.

"That's a question Trupyad should answer." Derazin's plump lips stretched into a smile. "But Myrkan conveniently disposed of him instead of bringing him for questioning. Until he revives in our realm, we can't even have a pactee to summon him."

Arujhan smiled, but no warmth accompanied it. "Isn't it what we all would do?" he asked. "Leaving a traitor to live would be foolish."

Myrkan stared at him. "So what do you propose?" He didn't hide the challenging tone. He'd already had an agreement with Arujhan, so the other kanyalari would see through the game and, perhaps, use it as an opening to deal with Derazin. "Everyone knows what he thinks of me."

Fyertash remained silent, but his focused expression suggested he was watching the dispute closely. Unfortunately, Myrkan had no way of letting him know of the arrangements made, but Fyertash had enough wits to wait and observe instead of rushing to conclusions... or actions.

"I wouldn't risk a valuable alliance to get rid of a minor pain like you." Derazin's posture, though non-aggressive, expressed contempt when he leaned forward. "Whatever reason Trupyad had to attack you, I know nothing about it. And if you don't—"

Arujhan lifted his claw. "We won't speak about it anymore. Trupyad's gone for now, and I doubt any of us will miss him." It took as little as a change in his voice to impose his authority. "Perhaps Trupyad worked for someone else, someone who would like to see us fight." He scrutinized each of them with squinted eyes. "This covenant stands, no matter what hatred or grudges you might all harbor."

Myrkan grimaced, staring at Arujhan. "Very well. I'll let this one go. We have an invasion to prepare for, and several new humans ready to serve in exchange for a pact."

"I'll handle them." Derazin walked away, not giving Myrkan as much as a glance, and his departure looked much like a retreat.

Myrkan licked the blood off his claws. The red stains had served their purpose, and he wanted them gone before they completely dried. The metallic flavor tasted like victory. As his eyes met with Arujhan's, the powerful kanyalari gave a short, quick nod. Myrkan cared little about approval, but he appreciated the recognition of his well-played game. Not only had Myrkan ensured that Derazin couldn't question his motives for killing Trupyad, but by openly opposing Arujhan, Myrkan kept their agreement a secret. The only thing left was to let Fyertash know before he perceived a threat where there was none.

"Since it's settled, there's no need for my presence here." Without bothering for any parting words or courtesy gestures, Arujhan took off.

Myrkan turned to the last remaining yalari.

"That was a risky move," Fyertash said as soon as

Arujhan's wings disappeared from sight. "What if he took Derazin's side?"

"I knew he wouldn't." Myrkan allowed a smile of satisfaction to creep up his face. "I'm certain he saw Trupyad when he was departing, and left dealing with the little eavesdropping hoyve to me."

Fyertash tensed, and his eyes narrowed as his gaze traveled from Myrkan to the spot where Arujhan had been sitting. "You talked to him?"

"We talked some, yes." Myrkan savored the feeling of power that came with the words and Fyertash's uncertainty, letting the silence set in before speaking again. "About things that might interest you as well, should you be wise in your choice of allies."

The corner of Fyertash's lip tipped upward. His posture relaxed as if he perceived danger no more, but Myrkan couldn't tell whether that ease was genuine. "You've made a deal with him."

"And I want you to be part of it," Myrkan replied. "My domain can be yours, if you support Arujhan in what's to come."

"And you'll be taking Derazin's?" Mockery rang clear in the yalari's voice. "I'd be surprised if Arujhan didn't take it from you once we're done."

Myrkan shook his head. "I'll be given something else, something of equal value to me. That's why I agreed. I'd recommend you do the same."

Fyertash's face brightened as he nodded. A foolish, hasty reaction, if Myrkan had his say, but maybe that was the reason the otherwise quite cunning yalari never got anywhere in a power play.

"A covenant within covenant. Secret meetings, whispered agreements, and"—Fyertash glanced in the direction of Derazin's departure—"some healthy backstabbing." He stretched, relaxed and smirking. "Took us long enough to get there."

Myrkan nodded. Betrayal was part of their nature, and only a fool would expect covenants such as this one to last. Fyertash must have been aware that Arujhan could just as well turn back on his former allies, but his unconcerned expression suggested he cared little of such an outcome. "So, you agree, I take it?" Myrkan asked.

"I never liked Derazin," Fyertash replied. "That hoyve doesn't deserve half of the domain he has. And Arujhan is powerful enough to ensure I get to keep the domain you abandon for as long as I do his bidding."

As much as he despised such a servile approach, Myrkan recognized the wisdom behind Fyertash's words. The cunning, if a bit spineless, yalari might survive in Arujhan's shadow longer than Myrkan expected. "Very well. Then it's settled," he said and headed back toward the port.

In the end, he cared little about Fyertash's future or survival, and with his own domain soon claimed in the human world, all the yalari's plots and betrayals wouldn't be Myrkan's problem anymore.

6

Veelk grimaced and stared at the thin beer the tavern maid served him. The girl's tired eyes only glanced at him in passing, and he didn't want to flirt. The room of the run-down tavern was full, and the stench of sailors' and port workers' sweat mixed in the air with the nauseating scent of cheap perfumes local gaharras wore. The beer tasted worse than a demonling's blood—having tried both, though not voluntarily, Veelk could aver that. Any other time he'd rather be in the Jagged Swordsman or Hircifa's Peony Garden, enjoying finer drinks and finer women, but this kind of place attracted people he was hoping to find.

As he reluctantly took another swig from the mug, he looked around. It seemed that his luck was in short supply, because so far he'd spotted no one worth approaching. Sailors at another table eyed him, maybe drawn by his grimace. Veelk returned the glare, ensuring they knew better than to pick a fight. It might not have been his lucky day, but luck wasn't needed when it came to tavern brawls.

With nothing else to do, he gnawed on the information he'd gotten from the adept that Master Tijhran recommended. Several imbued stones sufficed to make the man talk, but Veelk didn't like what the Gildya member had to say.

Koshmarnyk confined for the past ten years. An unexplained attack on his prison. Cahala qi'Devanshari also making inquiries about him. It seemed safe enough to assume she was the one to break him out, as the adept insisted Gildya was happy with having Koshmarnyk locked up. They also didn't have to make a bloodbath of their own people to get rid of him. Yet that didn't explain what the foreign queen wanted with his friend. Adepts didn't announce what kind of studies Koshmarnyk engaged in, and Veelk wasn't surprised about it. If they hated the idea of blending imbued stones with flesh so much, they would make sure others didn't get... *inspired* to follow such a path. At the same time, money could buy anything, so Cahala had likely learned of Koshmarnyk's knowledge and skill. With her kingdom overridden with demons, she might have been dreaming of creating an army of enhanced soldiers who could drive them out.

A bitter smile crept onto his lips when he thought about how foolish such an endeavor would be. Stones helped with strength and speed and protected from magical attacks, but they couldn't replace training, courage, and skill. And even then, no man was a match for a higher demon. Veelk huffed as the images of his fight with Uganel returned. Many times during their way back to Kaighal he'd thought of it, and always arrived at the same conclusion. No matter what he could have done differently, the outcome would have been the same. If Cahala wanted her kingdom back, she would need something more than a handful of humans with stones in their flesh.

At the same time, with both of them having disappeared,

Veelk had only guesses and speculation instead of answers or leads. That was why, instead of indulging in the pleasures of life, he was sitting in this mockery of a tavern. Even if Cahala was nowhere to be found, money changed hands and gossip traveled along with it, so someone, somewhere in Kaighal, was bound to know at least a bit about what had happened in Gildya's prison or after that.

He waved at the maid to bring another beer. Kamira had offered to ask Prince Allyv about his mother, but Veelk preferred if she kept away from the place full of people who hated arcanists, even if they had good reasons for such feelings. Besides, he doubted the princeling would know anything. If he was involved, he would have disappeared too.

"I'm tellin' you, it's easy money," a patron said to his companions as they took a table nearby. "That man pays good coin for youn' lasses."

The hushed conversation almost died in a sudden din at the other side of the tavern, and Veelk was straining to hear when he caught a glimpse of gold in the scoundrel's hand. The man's rat-like features stood out against the tanned and muscular sailors frequenting the tavern. With the looks like this, he might yet prove that Veelk's luck wasn't entirely gone.

"It's a foreign coin. What good will it be?" asked another man.

"Gold is always gold." The ratface played with the coin, keeping his companions' attention on its luster. "And those pale wimps are willin' to part with it."

Veelk kept his face straight and his eyes on the beer but fished for every word. The only people in Kaighal with lighter skin were the Devanshari. It might have nothing to do with Koshmarnyk and Cahala, but learning more never hurt. Any information about underhanded dealings among the refugees could turn out to be payment enough for the knowledge Veelk needed.

"But capturing girls? Don't know. Seems too risky."

"Me and Jally done a few and nuthin' happened. Whatever they need them for, no bodies ever turn up, so the girls just disappear—right, Jally?"

The third man at the table nodded. His eyes were sunk into his round face, but they looked around with cunning. "We've been careful. They want more, so maybe they need them as slaves. I heard their king kept a lot of slaves overseas."

Ratface laughed. "And looks like their royal gaharra still wants them."

Veelk looked around with a grimace as if looking for a fight. It gave him time to inspect the three men before they turned away, avoiding confrontation. He took in the details of their faces and postures, and then he returned to scanning the tavern, hoping no man would be stupid enough to respond to his challenge. A fistfight with drunken sailors could prove entertaining but would draw too much attention.

"So? Are you in?" the Ratface asked.

"I'll pass. It's not exactly my kind of work." The third man stood up.

"Your loss." The one named Jally shrugged. "But don't complain you can't afford to pay for your gaharras."

The jab missed, and the man threw him a disgusted glare as he walked away. "Don't complain when the guards catch you, or when that foreign scum decides to double-cross you."

Jally and Ratface kept drinking after the third man left, so Veelk had time to consider his options. His hands itched to reach for the two's throats, to squeeze the information out of them first and then their lives, but pawns like them knew little. Their deaths could alarm Cahala or that "man" the Ratface mentioned. Setting a trap seemed a better solution. Wait till they took another woman and follow them, or rather their overseer, to the Devanshari lair.

Veelk sighed both at the thought of risking a stranger's life and at the solution to that: he had a perfect victim at his disposal. In the dark, with her hair loose or braided in the local girls' fashion, Kamira could pass as young enough to interest the men. She'd be taken straight where they needed to get, and Veranesh's nightflies could lead Veelk there. With magic at her disposal, she wouldn't be defenseless, and she was smart enough to stay alive... Unless they learned she was an arcanist. As much as the people in the asylum seemed restrained enough in their hate, he couldn't count on similar behavior from those who didn't shy away from kidnapping women.

He stared at the beer, then left it unfinished at the table. The plan was good, and if whoever captured Kamira expressed their hate toward arcanists... Veelk smiled at the thought. He was certain that, if needed, she would unleash enough magic to outmatch the Cataclysm itself. And her demon—Veelk had no doubt—would only encourage her to do so.

~

FEEBLE BARGES BOUNCED on the waves in the ruined Devanshari port, and their sides sank deeper in the water as rows of asayalari marched aboard, obedient to the kanyalari's will. The pactees wove the energy into protective cocoons around the vessels, but Fyertash still doubted all the ships would make it across the sea.

"You seem tense." Arujhan approached, and his wings caught the morning breeze like the sails of the last Devanshari ships that left the port months ago.

Fyertash allowed himself a grimace. "I don't like the thought of going over there blind and with almost no army." They'd only taken enough asayalari to keep their pactees safe. More could be summoned once they arrived at the other continent... provided they had time for that. Although Fyertash didn't oppose that solution when Myrkan suggested it, he did see its weak points. Yet such weakness could serve him well if the tides turned, so he kept silent about it. At least silent enough to maintain his image of a servile yalari. Now that Arujhan asked openly about it, he had to give him something. And, in the end, this could also serve Fyertash's plans. "There's no doubt Uganel failed, but without knowing exactly what happened, we might be headed straight into a trap." He stared at the sea, confident his face expressed nothing, save the uncertainty a yalari like him would feel. After hundreds of years, acting weak and submissive had become second nature to him.

"It's a valid concern." It came as no surprise that Arujhan used that patronizing voice of his, but Fyertash didn't even flinch. "But four of us can stand against anything. And Veranesh remains trapped."

"Or so we are led to believe." Fyertash arched his eyebrow, adding a mocking smile. Any kanyalari, no matter how inferior to the others present, would still attempt at least some confidence. No, Fyertash took that back—the likes of Trupyad never did. But he wasn't like him, so concealing his true insights too often would wake others' suspicions instead of putting them to rest. They knew he was cunning, so he had to show it. The game was to convince them he wasn't cunning *enough*.

Arujhan looked down at him. "We'd sense if it was otherwise."

Of course they would, but the concerned and fearful yalari Fyertash played wouldn't be able to resist similar speculation. "We've already sensed a disturbance. And someone did destroy Uganel by means only yalari know. Whether it was Veranesh somehow, Suzhaul, the Four, or another player to join our game, we don't know." That lack of knowledge worried Fyertash, because without it, his own game became even more dangerous.

The other yalari remained silent, and Fyertash waited. Revealing any emotion could prove deadly, and he could only hope Arujhan would come to the desired conclusion: they needed eyes overseas.

"Get ready," Arujhan said eventually. "I'll tell others you set out to scout. Return when you learn what happened. And... assume the high mages might not be our allies as much as we'd like to think."

A flash of satisfaction passed through Fyertash's mind. So many centuries, and he still hadn't lost the touch, playing those more powerful as easily as a pack of confused asayalari. Yet instead of taking the order, he gave Arujhan a glare. "Myrkan's wings are stronger. They'd carry him faster over the sea."

"I'll need Myrkan by my side should things go sour with Derazin."

"And I'm expendable?" He allowed himself a hint of sarcasm, curious how the other yalari would react. Such momentary rebellion hardly mattered for the outcome, because either he would agree to do Arujhan's bidding or he'd be forced to do it. Yes, being seen as weak had its advantages, no matter how humiliating it was at times.

Arujhan considered him in silence. "You're sensible. Unlike Uganel, you'd rather bring the information we need to deal with the threat than pick a fight you can't win."

Fyertash didn't bother pointing out that Arujhan had called him a coward, since it offered no gain. It was one thing to sate his minor curiosity, and another to push the powerful kanyalari so far that he would give in to his rage. "So be it. I'll set out soon, then."

"Prove yourself useful, and I won't forget it. You'll have your own domain and protection."

A short nod was all that Fyertash gave in response, and Arujhan walked away, his dark wings standing against the white marble of the ruined city. Only when he disappeared among the debris did Fyertash allow himself a smile.

Playing with fire was less deadly than trying to play a yalari such as Arujhan, but he got what he wanted. He'd be the first to reach Tyorane, learn of Uganel's failure, and discover plots that could interfere with his plans. He almost burst out laughing at the memory of the other yalari's promise. Arujhan's protection and his own domain meant nothing when a memory of one kanyalari lingered clearly in his mind. Renalea's gaze had faded centuries earlier, but Fyertash still remembered the months of her torment and her final moments. And now, after an eternity of his own suffering, he had the opening he'd been waiting for, a fleeting opportunity that could bring him the revenge he desired... or become his undoing.

He headed for the crumbled building and retrieved the travel sack he'd hidden there. As soon as it was secure at his waist, he spread his wings. If he hurried, he might have a few weeks to plan and act before the barges arrived. With his last gaze upon the asayalari army embarking, Fyertash pushed himself into the air. With so many things unknown, the thought of how narrow his chosen path was would stay with him through the whole journey to Tyorane.

7

Kamira woke up to damp air and dimmed light. Her body rested in an uncomfortable position, and there was metal against her neck. Heavy chains bound her hands, and a closer look revealed small gems that blocked the flow of magic. It seemed that Veelk's plan had worked, and the men who'd assaulted her in the dark alley, two mindless thugs she could otherwise have taken on her own, were indeed henchmen for Cahala. She'd gotten where she needed to be, but other than that, nothing went according to plan. She hadn't expected to be unconscious where they took her to... wherever she was. Instead, she had hoped that once she learned Cahala's whereabouts, she could dispose of her thuggish escort and wait for Veelk outside rather than inside. Not to mention the chains that limited her use of magic.

A gentle movement around her ankle reassured Kamira that the nightfly was still there, so the thugs settled for her moderately stuffed coin purse and the flashy but cheap jewelry she wore like many common girls in Kaighal would, and didn't bother to search her too thoroughly. Maintaining contact with the creature proved burdensome, but it wasn't impossible. Whatever they made those binds for, it wasn't to restrain an arcanist. At the short impulse of magic she sent, the nightfly uncoiled. Before Kamira blinked, Veranesh made it dart away, hiding in the darkness, and the faint flutter of its wings faded.

With it gone, she could only hope that Veelk would find her fast. The shackles prevented her from using magic, save maybe a few tavern-worthy tricks, and it reminded her of how she felt when Veranesh broke her old pact. If anybody attacked her, she'd have nothing to defend herself, and for that one moment, Kamira regretted ignoring Veelk's remarks about her lack of physical prowess. She glared at the metal around her wrists... Not that being a master fighter would change much in her situation.

It seemed that when it came to survival, she would have to rely on the skill set she'd considered useless ever since she left her homeland. A traveling arcanist had no need for the art of manipulation and deception... Until she did, which, strangely, coincided with Veranesh entering her life.

Someone moved several tables away, and Kamira inspected an underground workshop: tables filled with contraptions, tools, and gems, and a man working on a device she didn't recognize. His brown skin looked pale in the light of the lamps, much like the complexion of Devanshari women who avoided Tyorane's sun whenever possible. At a second look, she didn't miss his wiry muscles tightly wrapped around bones that revealed longstanding malnutrition. Such features would match a prisoner's life, so it seemed she was in luck.

The man caught her gaze and walked over. "Are you... hurt?" The intense stare of his brown eyes followed the question, and there was some curiosity on his face.

He must have expected her to act confused, ask questions or plea for her life, but Kamira saw no reason for deception. She shook her head as he squatted down and offered her a flask of water. The hem of his shirt pulled from his wrist, revealing gems in his skin just above the heavy shackles.

"They look uncomfortable," she said when their eyes met.

"No more than yours."

Next to her, two more women sat chained to the wall. Their closed eyes made them look like puppets. The man offered water to them as well, but neither reacted.

"I could help you with yours if you help me with mine," she offered.

He glanced at her. "They'd require more than a key."

"I can see that. But if the imbued stones in the shackles stopped working, the metal brace itself wouldn't be a hassle for you, would it?" And if the ones in his skin were indeed like Veelk's scars, they wouldn't be affected by her magic.

He didn't reply at first, giving her an inquisitive look. "Are you with Gildya?" No fear in his voice, only distrust.

"No."

"But you aren't here by a chance."

"No. I was looking for you."

He let out a short laugh. "It's amusing how people despise me, yet they still want things from me. Because that's why you're here, aren't you? To promise me my freedom in exchange for something you want: a device, a service, some piece of knowledge."

She couldn't blame him for such a perspective. After all, he'd been freed from one prison only to end up in another. She shook her head, wondering whether he'd even believe her. "Your freedom comes first and won't be part of the trade," she replied. "There's a man coming for us, and once we're both free, we'll talk. You'll decide whether you want to help me and on what terms." She put all her confidence into those words, but the doubt had already settled. The man in front of her seemed cautious, and she couldn't discard the possibility he'd refuse. At the same time, there was no other way. If she couldn't have his trust, she wouldn't give him hers.

"A man? Just one man?" His expression shifted, amusement softening the hard edges of his face. "That might not be enough."

"It should suffice." She'd spent enough time with Veelk to know that unless Cahala had a whole army with her, he wouldn't consider it an uneven fight. "But we'd better be out of our chains by then."

He smiled. "Such an unlikely tale, but skillfully spun. Were I in your place, I couldn't have told a better one myself. I can't help but wonder, though, what will you do now, when you're out of cards?"

She should have expected he'd need more than vague promises. "Am I? I can prove I come from a friend... Koshmarnyk."

He laughed. The sound, dry and short-lived, had no warmth to it. "Now that's a name I haven't heard for some time. I'm quite curious how you came across it." He held her chin in his hand, but the grip brought no pain as he moved her head around, inspecting the skin on her neck and shoulders. "No scars, and you're not of the tribes. So tell me..."

"Kamira."

"Tell me, Kamira, how come a Tivarashan woman knows something that only people of the mountain tribes know?"

That one suspicion she could put to rest. "I'm Veelk's friend."

Koshmarnyk responded with a half smirk. "Now you've mentioned two names I haven't heard in a long time. Is he the one coming?"

She should have expected that her friend's name would warm the adept to her, at least a bit. He'd likely reserve his doubts until Veelk actually arrived, but at least she could be certain that would prove her truthfulness. "Yes." The chains rattled as she lifted her hands. "We're both defenseless if the guards get here first."

He hesitated. "I gave Cahala my word. Even if she never intended to keep hers, I won't break mine."

As much as she could relate to such sentiment, she said, "Cahala will die tonight, regardless of whether you agree to help me or not. When we leave, there will be no trace of you here."

His eyes lit up. "Are you planning to kill someone in Gildya? Or to assassinate the Tivarashan queen?" His question was only half in jest, as if he couldn't help his curiosity, having pieced everything together: that she needed him for something secretive and dangerous.

Kamira hesitated only for a heartbeat. Parting with secrets wasn't easy, but if she wanted his help, she needed his trust. Trust that could be earned by giving the same. "I'm going to bring the high mages down."

He regarded her as if making sure she was serious, and then produced a key from his pocket. "I see how you're friends with Veelk." He unlocked her chains.

The restraint on her magic lifted when the irons fell, and Kamira again had Veranesh's power at her disposal. Without delay, she brushed her fingers over several stones melted into Koshmarnyk's shackle and poured energy into them until they cracked. A crude solution, but it worked well.

"An arcanist!" he said amused as he watched her work. "No wonder you're so hardheaded about the high mages."

There was more to that, but stories could wait, and she still wasn't sure how much she should share. With a nod, Kamira freed his other arm and moved on to the collar. It didn't escape her that more gems marked his clavicle, and she couldn't help her curiosity about his motives. Mage killers powdered their gems and inserted them into scars, making them almost invisible, but Koshmarnyk didn't seem to care about concealing the changes he'd made to himself. She caught the glimpse of a few, but he could have many more, all over his body. The picture her mind conjured made her cheeks burn, because in the end, it was of no concern to her. She leaned closer, hoping Koshmarnyk wouldn't notice her fluster as she worked her way around the metal, cracking the stones one by one.

"It's going to take a moment," she muttered, her breath rustling his shoulder-length hair. "These are bigger."

When she moved away, relief softened Koshmarnyk's face, and he reached for the collar. Nothing could have been clearer proof of the power his stones lent him than the shriek of bending metal as he pulled it apart with his bare hands.

"Thank you." He offered a meager smile as the collar clanked, hitting the floor. "I wonder... why did you free me? Why not wait till I gave you what you wanted?"

"What if what I want is your trust?"

"That's right. The trade comes later."

She took that as a good sign. Koshmarnyk didn't come across as a man who trusted easily, and she wouldn't have expected him to, but she must have given him enough to at least consider her words. Kamira could relate to his approach. Without Veelk's reassurance, she'd have hesitated before taking Koshmarnyk's restraints off. When she thought of the stones she'd caught a glimpse of, she doubted even Veelk knew the extent of this man's changes.

Koshmarnyk stepped away, taking his binds and packing them alongside several tools.

"Let me help you," a female said all of a sudden.

Kamira inspected the woman beside her. With her dark hair and deep brown skin, she must be local to Kaighal, but her young face didn't look familiar.

The woman took the scrutiny calmly. "I hear what you said about the high mages. I want to help."

Koshmarnyk glanced over his shoulder. "I thought you were awake." He said nothing more, and Kamira understood he was leaving the conversation—and the decision—to her.

The woman must have caught it too, because she focused her eyes on Kamira. "You're that student that got herself expelled, aren't you? They still make you a cautionary tale for newcomers."

Kamira narrowed her eyes. "And why would a high mage help someone like me?" Her distrust toward the high mages fought with curiosity. If this woman was playing a game, she wouldn't have so readily revealed who she was.

"Because I'm the fourth archmage's apprentice. Don't tell me you have no idea how he is. Besides"—she swallowed and looked at Kamira's hands—"I've been chained to the wall, no more capable of freeing myself than a commoner." She rattled her chains. "I don't even know a spell that could be useful in such a situation, because Archmage Kerl was too busy with his other... interests to give me the knowledge I'd need."

As much as she could relate, both to the young mage's

experiences with Kerl and the desire to get revenge, Kamira's own endeavors were too much at risk already. "You're of no use to me," she said in a detached voice, one her father used frequently when dealing with people of lower status.

"Am I not?" The woman raised her chin. "No matter what your plans are, you'll need someone in the Towers to be your eyes and ears, and studying under Kerl means I have a lot of time."

Kamira couldn't resist a smile. So, after all, the woman had enough wits about her, and despite her young age, she knew her way around the mages' games. "What's your name?"

"Pelina."

"Kerl still as much of a pig as he was when I left?"

"I think he drinks more now, but nothing else has changed. Most avoid him at all costs." Pelina's voice turned bitter, but she pulled herself together. "I'm just an apprentice, but I hear things. The first three archmages are onto something. Kerl was quite frustrated when he talked about their secret meetings in the middle of the night. I think Archmage Yoreus has his own game, too. He visited Kerl several times, and they made sure to send me away. Once I saw him arguing with Loktra. Something about the arcanist being his concern. He never mentioned any names, but... he might know that you're planning something."

Kamira nodded, reserving a smirk for herself. Of course Yoreus had suspicions. After all, he'd sent her to the old Towers. And despite the fact that Pelina hadn't told her much new, save the suggestion that the secrets of high magic might not have been shared with all the archmages, it at least proved she could be useful. At the same time, trusting her could turn out deadly.

With some time left before Veelk found them, Kamira could ask more questions. "Why haven't you left? Or done something?"

Pelina looked away, her skin darkening with a blush. "I'm not as brave as you are. I'd never be able to do anything on my own, and until now I believed it was better to just make it through the schooling. But you seem to have a plan. I can get back at Kerl by helping you, even if it makes the Towers collapse."

The way she spoke, with frustration and bitterness, made her sound genuine, so either she was honest or better at deception than many Tivarashan noblewomen. Either way, she could definitely be of use if Kamira was careful enough. With Ryell too much under Yoreus's influence, he couldn't be trusted, and Pelina could at least become a second source of information—a more reliable one, if there was any truth to her words.

A nightfly darted from the darkness and wrapped around Kamira's wrist. No words accompanied it, but the sudden appearance of the creature startled Pelina and put Koshmarnyk on guard.

"Veelk's near," she told him, appreciating Veranesh's silence. A flying piece of jewelry required enough explanation, and there was no need to add a higher demon to it.

Before he replied, two guards entered with their blades unsheathed. "Master Phuran! The adept!" called one of them.

Koshmarnyk glanced at Kamira as he stepped forward, enough to the side to not obscure her line of sight. "I trust you can fight?"

The guards charged from both sides of the table, and as one swung his blade for Koshmarnyk's neck, the other swung for his legs. Koshmarnyk avoided the lower swing by lunging at the other guard. There was no finesse in his move, but Kamira had to admit he was efficient. With quick strikes, Koshmarnyk disarmed the soldier, positioned himself behind him, and wrapped his arm around his opponent's neck. His posture made it clear he would use his human shield as necessary, and the other soldier hesitated.

That gave Kamira the opening she needed. The guard never saw the ice shards coming. As large as Kamira's arm, they disappeared into the man's body, throwing him into the table. Within heartbeats, he slumped to the floor, dead.

The muffled crack of the other guard's neck announced the end of the fight, and Koshmarnyk let the dead man fall beside his companion. The adept glanced at her with a half-smile. "I'll take that as a yes."

That note of relief in his voice suggested he'd worried she'd panic or scream, and she couldn't blame him. Arcanists rarely looked like warriors, and having Veelk to do the heavy work helped her keep the image of a weakling. Despite Veelk's complaint about her martial prowess, such deception had proven useful more than once.

A third man entered. As were the others, he was of Devanshari origin, but his moves revealed a seasoned warrior, and his two blades spoke to an aggressive fighting style.

"I should have expected as much," the man spat.

"I'm a man of my word, Phuran." Koshmarnyk took several steps back, drawing the man deeper into the chamber and away from Kamira. "But I didn't promise I wouldn't defend myself when your men tried to kill me."

Phuran growled as he leapt over the table and scissored the sabers at Koshmarnyk before Kamira could draw energy again. His focus remained solely on the man in front of him, and Kamira wasn't surprised. Beside her, Pelina watched the fight with wide eyes, and her startled expression made it clear she wouldn't be of help. She was a child of a sheltered life in the Towers, a cruel one at times, but safe and mostly free of direct violence. And with her disguise of a townswoman, Kamira herself didn't look like anyone Phuran had to concern himself with.

Kamira drew energy forth, but held it. With the two men so close and constantly moving, she couldn't risk it. Koshmarnyk wasn't Veelk, and she couldn't be certain he'd survive her spell if she missed.

Phuran's blades flashed in the lamps' light, slashing relentlessly at Koshmarnyk, and the adept moved with equal quickness to avoid their bite. Over and around the tables and equipment, the flurried attack continued.

Kamira flexed her fingers, ready to throw magic, but the men kept moving and no moment felt right enough. Yet she was running out of time, with Koshmarnyk weaponless and likely weaker after his long imprisonment. Frustrated, she released the nightfly. Even if her control over it was far from perfect, it still allowed more precision than spells. Twice she went for Phuran's hand, and twice she missed. Phuran swatted at the nuisance on her third attempt, and if not for Veranesh's taking control, the crystal would have been shattered. Veranesh's evasion was precise and instant, and Kamira envied his skill.

The attacks missed, but they were enough to interrupt Phuran, who paused his onslaught and took a step back. "Demon's gaharra!"

Each of the sabers now pointed toward a different opponent, and Kamira readied to raise her barrier.

"Shouldn't you be protecting your queen instead?" Koshmarnyk asked. "I'm not the one who's going to kill her, and neither is the arcanist." He positioned himself between Phuran and Kamira, providing the Devanshari a clear exit, but once more avoided standing directly in front of her. If their opponent attacked, she'd be able to use her magic to protect them both.

Phuran cursed under his breath, and while keeping his eyes at Koshmarnyk, he made his retreat.

The adept watched the door, and Kamira glanced at Pelina. The sight of the shivering woman reminded her that she could have been like her. Pelina had no muscle tone whatsoever, and no other signs of physical exercise. Kamira might have neglected her own strength and agility in favor of magic, but traveling, climbing, and crawling into places forced her muscles to work regularly. Pelina, on the other hand, looked every bit a soft-bodied high mage, devoted to studying magic, who never walked further than the local tavern or market. And without her magic, she was just a scared, naïve girl.

Kamira sighed. Such thoughts were dangerous.

"What's going on?" Another voice slurring from sleep broke the silence.

They all looked at the woman who had just woken up as she scanned the corpses. Her eyes widened, and so did her mouth. The scream accumulated in her lungs, and the nightfly shot through the woman's heart before anyone had a chance to react. Then it flew over to Pelina.

"No!" Kamira shouted. Her eyes blurred as she fought for the control she couldn't take, but to her surprise, Veranesh gave in and let her call the nightfly back to her wrist.

Koshmarnyk glanced at her and the crystal creature, and she hid her grimace. An arcanist did not shout at things she supposedly controlled, and her reaction had likely brought questions and suspicions. Perhaps the adept would wait for a more opportune moment to ask questions, but that still left Pelina. If Kamira had any choice, a high mage would be the last person to ever learn about it.

"Thank you," Pelina whispered.

Kamira gave her a little nod in response. *I hope I'm not going to regret it.* But the thought of explaining to Veelk and Veranesh why she kept a high mage alive, and their imminent disapproval of such a risk, no matter the gains, reassured her that there would be plenty of regret to come.

PHURAN STORMED out of the cellar against the instinct that urged him to kill Alluvendran and deal with the demonologist, but the adept's words had struck the right chord. If he was still down in the workshop, he couldn't have taken out the outside guards. At the same time, with his collar gone, he and the demon-worshiping woman had something to do with the attack, no doubts about that. Yet the queen's safety was the most important task, even if Alluvendran had played that card to ensure his own survival, and Phuran ran through the empty corridors of the mansion's ground floor. Shadows danced on the floor and walls, with the few lamps bringing them to life and revealing the struggle that took place. Without stopping to search for the assassins, he rushed up the steps.

He'd left the queen with the finest of Devanshari guards, but that thought didn't bring much comfort when he jumped over several servants' and mercenaries' bodies. His surroundings were eerily quiet, suggesting that whoever had attacked them made an effort to leave only dead behind. With that thought crawling down his spine like a demon's claw, he barged into the queen's room through a shattered door, disregarding his own safety.

Blood lust colored Phuran vision red at the sight of a tall, broad-shouldered man who was piercing the last of the royal guards with a long spear. His copper skin and clothing told of tribal origin, and the weapon reminded Phuran of old tales that brought him to a halt. What was a mage killer doing there? The only logical explanation was that Gildya had found out who attacked their prison and sent the mage killer to dispose of the adept.

A movement by the bed caught Phuran's eye. The queen, wearing nothing but her nightgown, sat curled in the corner, and every bit of her posture and expression screamed of fear, but she made no sound. He had no doubt that she was reliving the last days of her kingdom's fall, and in her eyes, the tribal assailant must have been demonic.

He readied his sabers. "You'll pay for what you've done here." When they were fleeing Devanshari, he'd promised himself to ensure that such horror would never find its way onto the queen's face again... But all it took was a single tribal man to destroy his efforts.

Slowly, as if with no concern, the mage killer withdrew the spear's thin blade from the last body. His white teeth flashed a momentary grin. "I hope you'll prove more of a challenge than your comrades."

Phuran sprang toward his opponent with a flurry of short, quick slashes. The mage killer met him with his spinning spear. The keshal had longer reach but was a slower and more cumbersome weapon, so Phuran hoped to overwhelm his adversary with relentless offense. But the tower of muscles before him proved much more skillful than he'd imagined. What spear didn't block, the mage killer evaded.

Their skills truly are everything the tales say. Phuran sidestepped with an aggressive swing, forcing his opponent to pivot, but the mage killer ducked. His spear swept a wide, low arc for Phuran's hip. Blocking would end Phuran's assault, even if only for a moment, so instead he retreated just outside the blade's reach, and back forward once the blade passed. His weapons never ceased their constant motion.

The mage killer's eyes showed the battle fever invigorating him, but to Phuran's regret, he didn't give in the fighting rage. When Cahala began to move, the mage killer didn't even glance behind him as he said, "I'd stay where you are, if I were you." His breathing showed no strain from the battle. "The spear has a longer reach than your dog's knives, and you might get stuck."

Phuran gritted his teeth. He needed to get between them. If he pushed the mage killer away, the queen would be able to flee. He lunged with two quick swipes, but had to abandon the second swing for dodging a quick thrust of the mage killer's spear. Yet his recovery and return to offense was instant. One blade hammered his opponent's spear down, and the other whipped at his throat. He meant it to be a deathblow, a much-needed, quick end to the duel.

Something caught the light of the lamps, and Phuran realized too late his opponent had used only one hand to execute his trust. A crystal dagger tore into Phuran's shoulder, and he cursed. In many fights where strength and skill were matched, it was often a single wound that decided the victor. No matter how long he could continue, with the blood flowing and muscles torn, he'd tire quicker than his opponent. *I've lost.*

He snatched the dagger from his flesh and threw it at the wall. The crystal resembled the nightfly the demonologist used, and he expected the weapon to come to life as well, but it stayed buried in the wood, motionless.

The mage killer adjusted his spear, narrowed and focused eyes following Phuran's every move, but he didn't attack, as if he preferred to stay on defense. Phuran looked at the queen. No matter the outcome of the duel, he had to ensure her safety and survival. The composed royal gaze returned to her blue eyes as if she had overcome the horrors haunting her, but Phuran knew how much such resolve must have cost her. She gave him a short nod, and her lips offered one silent syllable.

Run!

He hesitated. The oath he had made required nothing less than a sacrifice of his life in the queen's service, and he would never question to fulfill it, but Cahala's stare made it clear she was giving an order. It took him only a heartbeat to understand: the mage killer wanted her alive, so she wasn't in immediate danger.

Duty demanded he stayed, but having pledged his life to his queen, he had to obey the order and saw wisdom to it. Dead men couldn't rescue anyone.

Before the mage killer could bar the way, Phuran dashed from the chamber, through the mansion, and into the night, never stopping or slowing until the dark line of the trees enveloped him.

AT THE ECHO of footsteps coming down toward the workshop, Kamira tensed, and Koshmarnyk immediately took a fighting stance. She drew energy, but when Veelk entered, both she and the adept relaxed. The two men exchanged nods, and then Veelk walked over to her. The nightfly tucked under his belt freed itself and made for her wrist, coiling.

"Almost everyone except the queen is dead," he said while she looked him over in search of wounds. "But I fought a skilled warrior, and he ran away."

"Phuran," Koshmarnyk muttered. "He's trouble."

Veelk nodded. "We have to go. The woods are crawling with Gildya's people. It seems that they are looking for you." He inspected the prisoners, his eyes skimming the dead woman and stopping on Pelina, who shrank under his gaze so much that she dared not make eye contact with Kamira. His hand flinched as he hesitated before reaching for his keshal.

"She could be our eyes in the High Towers," Kamira said.

"Didn't know we needed eyes," Veelk muttered, but she could swear she caught relief in his voice. "Are you a servant there?" he asked Pelina.

"A student," Kamira replied before the woman could choose to lie.

Veelk's expression hardened. "That's a risk we don't need. Besides, leaving one person alive could raise questions."

"Or satisfy them," she said. "Pelina could weave the story that would put all the blame on the Devanshari queen and ensure anyone who asks that a certain adept was never here." She threw a glance at Koshmarnyk. "And neither were we."

"And you'd trust a high mage?"

She couldn't blame him for asking. No matter how scared or innocent Pelina might look, the High Towers corrupted teachers and students alike, and anyone faced with the prospect of death would make promises that could save their life. But, in the end, she had to make a decision. "I trust she has reasons to help us. If not"—she eyed Pelina—"I doubt the archmages would be delighted to learn she made a deal with me, no matter what kind of information she could promise them." If the woman turned on her, she could only confirm suspicions Yoreus already had, so as long as Kamira was careful with the knowledge she shared, Pelina couldn't do much harm.

Pelina swallowed and nodded, but didn't try to convince Kamira that she would never betray her. Such reassurances would only spark suspicions, since anyone would find it hard to believe a mere student like her wouldn't break under a magical interrogation or would have unyielding loyalty toward an arcanist she just met.

"Here's what I offer you," Kamira said. "In a while, you'll receive a letter with... instructions. You will follow them without question. I'll know if you don't." She smirked, thinking of what she had planned.

"And that's all?" Pelina narrowed her eyes.

"Other than that, you'll study and serve the fourth archmage as you did before, keeping your eyes and ears open, but don't risk running around and spying on purpose," Kamira replied. "When I'm back from my travels, I'll send another message."

The mage's first response was a bitter smile, but then she nodded. "Fair enough. I suppose the less I know, the less danger I pose to your plan."

Even if trust was out of question, Kamira had to appreciate Pelina's insights. With a little luck, this unexpected ally could turn out more than useful.

Veelk regarded the chained woman. "If we want to make others believe she was lucky to survive, she'll have to be wounded. As if someone didn't have time to finish you off.

Don't worry." He threw her a reassuring glance. "The Gildya's near, and they'll want answers, so they'll make sure you live."

Koshmarnyk shifted. "There was another woman as well. Phuran took her upstairs."

Veelk tensed and shook his head. Kamira knew that he'd left no one alive, but when they devised their plan, they didn't expect the previous captives to be alive. Killing servants might have been a step too far, but they, at least, had a choice to leave. If they didn't, it meant they willingly partook in Cahala's plots.

"I could..." Kamira brushed against the nightflies on her wrists. She doubted Veranesh would be concerned about killing a human, let alone simply wounding one.

"I don't trust... the precision of these things." Veelk's voice made it clear he didn't trust Veranesh to let Pelina live.

After a quick consideration, Kamira had to agree. They had no time for arguing with the demon, especially not in front of a high mage, and as much as Veranesh was willing to help her, she wouldn't put it past him to make his own decisions. And in his eyes, letting a stranger live must have been nothing but a foolish risk.

"I could give you more of the sleepseed extract," Koshmarnyk said.

Pelina shook her head. "I'd rather be awake. I'll have to call for help."

Her attention was on the adept, so she missed Veelk's movement. Before she looked at him, the mage killer's keshal pierced her torso. Pelina let out a scream of pain and covered her mouth, eyes wide with fear as she stared at Kamira's nightflies. Relief flashed on her face when the crystal creatures didn't move to finish her off, and she crumpled the bottom of her shirt, pressing it to the wound instead.

"Let's go," Veelk said. "The sooner we leave, the sooner she can start calling for help."

Koshmarnyk nodded, but walked over to one of the dead guards and dragged his corpse closer to Pelina. Then he slipped the key to the shackles into the dead man's pocket. "If no one comes, you can still free yourself."

Kamira said nothing, but appreciated his gesture. If he cared enough for an insignificant woman, he had enough of humanity within him left, no matter the amount of stones in his body, and it put some of her concerns to rest.

Veelk's rushing gesture made them both head for the stairs, and Kamira threw Pelina one last glance before departing. It might have been her Tivarashan heritage, or perhaps she'd spent too much time plotting with Veranesh, but she enjoyed the thought of adding another pawn to the game she played with high mages and demons. A pawn that could think for herself, and her actions could yet change many plots. At the same time, she couldn't resist a smirk at the thought that her demon was as likely to disapprove of her choice as he was to join her in the excitement of the unknown outcomes of such a decision.

"Are you keeping the queen alive?" Koshmarnyk's voice brought her back to reality once they reached the top of the stairs.

Cahala was unconscious, tied up and slumped against the wall. She was nothing like Kamira had expected: a middle-aged woman, still beautiful, but her face spoiled by the downward crease of her mouth, telling of many possible flaws the woman could have. Having spoken to Prince Allyv, Kamira thought his mother would be more composed and truly royal, but instead she seemed like a petty and capricious person.

Veelk hefted and slung the queen over his shoulder with both ease and lack of care for her wellbeing. "Kamira thinks she might be useful before she dies."

They made their way through the mansion, and Kamira paid little attention to its interior and did her best to ignore bodies on the floor. Veelk's work was thorough, and the sooner they left Cahala's den, the less likely she would succumb to feelings of guilt and remorse.

"You did bring him along, didn't you?" She already knew the answer, since Veelk had kept the queen alive, but the question could distract her from unpleasant thoughts.

"He should be waiting nearby," Veelk confirmed.

As they walked outside, Kamira caught Koshmarnyk's curious glance. "I apologize," she said. "There is one more matter we have to... see to, and then you can have all your questions answered." She hesitated. "Unless, of course, you'd rather meet with us later."

In the light of the waning moon, she almost missed his arched eyebrow, as if he was questioning whether she was truly ready to let him leave. But since they were rushing through the clearing toward the dark line of the forest, it seemed hardly a good moment for explanations.

"I admit, you got me curious," he replied. "It'll be easier if I stay."

She offered a smile of gratitude, but the adept wasn't looking at her anymore as Veelk gave him a nod of approval. She could only guess that her request would have held much less weight if not for the mage killer accompanying her, and in the end, this was all she needed. Koshmarnyk didn't have to trust her if he trusted Veelk.

8

Ryell paced on a small clearing and listened to every sound in the dark. Veelk hadn't told him much except for a half-barked order to wait for him, and the more time passed, the more unsettled Ryell grew. Part of him regretted agreeing to that strange offer, but at the same time, he couldn't pass on the promise to learn of Cahala's whereabouts. No matter how he despised the mage killer and the idea of accepting his help, after weeks of fruitless inquires and dead ends, he had little choice, unless he wanted to waste his life away between Atissa's embrace and Yoreus's menial tasks.

Desperation bred his acceptance, but when he departed alone with Veelk, suspicions got the better of him. Kamira wasn't with them, so Ryell might have been walking into a trap devised by the mage killer. Yet if Veelk wanted to get rid of him, he didn't have to travel so far to the north, where the fields and plains shifted into a rich forest, reminding Ryell almost painfully of his lost homeland. A quick blade to his heart in some dark alley or a snap of his neck would have done the deed quick and easy enough, and with Kaighal offering a plethora of thugs and killers, the blame could easily be shifted... If Kamira even inquired about him to begin with.

Bitter thoughts swarmed his head, and he chased them away as the nearby bushes rustled. Ryell stepped back into the shade of trees, letting the darkness conceal his presence and regretting the idea didn't come to him earlier. No matter what Veelk had said, staying in the open was inviting trouble. At some point, Ryell had to stop thinking like a royal guard and get used to acting the way a vagabond would. How low he'd fallen! But then, few of the Devanshari fared better in Tyorane, and it was foolish to cling to a title and pride that meant nothing to local people.

"It's me." Veelk entered the clearing, holding a woman by her arm.

Ryell brightened at the sight, but when they stepped into the moonlight, he realized it wasn't Kamira who accompanied Veelk. Instead, Cahala qi'Devanshari dragged her feet across the grass in vain resistance to Veelk's strength. When her eyes met with Ryell's, she froze and almost fell to her knees. Veelk yanked her forward. Her mouth was gagged, but a whimper rose nevertheless.

"Whatever you want to say or do to her, be quick about it," Veelk said. "The forest is swarming with Gildya adepts."

Cahala fought to tear herself away from Veelk's grip, but her eyes stayed focused on Ryell, and the expression on her face made it clear that she recognized him. He allowed himself a small smile of triumph—a bitter one, perhaps, when he thought all the lives lost, but satisfactory nonetheless.

"I'll take her to my people," he said, feeding on her expression of dread. "To be tried for treason."

Veelk shook his head and refuse to relinquish his grip. "She'll die tonight."

"That's for the Devanshari people to decide." Ryell tensed. He was no match for the mage killer, but he wouldn't allow his queen to be butchered in the middle of a forest, no matter her crimes. "In a fair trial."

"Do you really believe that such trial will be fair?" Kamira walked into the clearing, adjusting her coat. Her hair lacked the typical tribal adornments and was woven into a braid instead.

If the circumstances were different, he would have enjoyed her innocent looks, but her voice remained cruel as she continued to speak.

"Do you really believe she won't find a way to make you the one judged? A royal guard who disobeyed his orders? Who ran away from the falling city? Who went mad from the lack of essence and sought someone to blame?"

Ryell took a step back, his hands shaking. "That's not true!" His blood rushed, and so did his thoughts. How could she? How dare she?

"No, it's not." Kamira stayed calm. "But it could become the truth if you let her speak to others. There will be no judging, no squabbling over how big or small her treason was, or giving her a chance to find excuses for however she wronged your people."

He held back words of denial. As cruel as they sounded, Kamira's arguments rang true. Cahala had many devoted followers among the Devanshari, and he had nothing but his own account as proof. If the trial even came to pass, it would be a farce, and in the end, she would walk free again. His shoulders slumped.

"Then why did you have me come here?" His voice was quiet and solemn.

"So you can sate your need for revenge." Kamira's voice softened. "It might not be what you dreamed of, but it's better than living the rest of your life knowing that you missed your only chance."

Ryell swallowed and nodded. If they had time and Veelk wasn't around, he would ask her how she knew so much about revenge. Maybe, after all was done, he'd have that opportunity. Until then, he could only appreciate Kamira's thoughtfulness, so he shifted his attention to the queen.

Cahala's eyes, widened with fear, looked so different from the last time he'd seen them. The memory of her smug face as she gazed at him from afar while Ryell listened to the order forcing him to fight a battle already lost resurfaced, and with it, his anger.

His simple dagger caught what little light there was just right, like a glimmer of justice in an unjust, treacherous world. "For the fallen city. For all the people who died there because of you. For the treason against your own kingdom," he said as he stepped closer. "On behalf of those who fell and those who survived, for your crimes, I sentence you to death, Cahala qi'Devanshari. May your name be forgotten."

She raised her bound hands, but Ryell didn't care whether it was an instinctive defense or a plea. His blade dug into Cahala's stomach, and then he ripped through her bowels. The sight of her face twisted in pain and her muffled scream brought unexpected satisfaction. Veelk let her fall to her knees, and Ryell grabbed Cahala's hair, forcing their eyes to meet. Even though he wanted her to suffer, to suffer forever, torture wasn't in his nature. He cut clean across her neck and didn't look away until the gurgling and coughing died out and the last spark of life faded from her face.

Cahala's blood, black in the moonlight, stained her

bright skin, and her body slumped onto the grass. Ryell stood motionless over it until Kamira placed her hand on his shoulder.

"It's not how I pictured it," he whispered into the silence.

"Revenge is rarely what we expect it to be," she said. "It comes at the wrong time and never the way we wanted it."

"Garivan." The word slipped out of his mouth before he thought about it. It wasn't Kamira who'd shared that story with him, and mentioning a man who betrayed her and Veelk couldn't be a good idea. It could remind her she couldn't trust Ryell either.

Veelk shifted. "We need to go." He glanced at Ryell. "I hope you'll find your way back to the city." He looked over his shoulder. "Head south first, not east, unless you want to answer Gildya's questions."

Ryell nodded absent-mindedly, his eyes on Kamira. "You're going away again, aren't you?" He couldn't hold the bitterness at bay. Veelk's words made it clear that Ryell wasn't invited to travel with them.

"We can't take you," she replied quietly.

"Demon's rot you can't! I won't let you leave me behind this time." Not after she helped him get revenge, and not after she almost died in the desert while he... Memories of the pleasant times with Atissa swarmed him with guilt.

Veelk stepped quickly between them, but Ryell ignored him, staring at Kamira, and the mage killer sighed. "Make it quick," he said, turning away.

Ryell gritted his teeth, and his fist clenched on the dagger he still held. One strike, one attack his opponent could hardly foresee, and he'd never have to suffer Veelk's presence again. But killing him meant also killing any chance of building a friendship with Kamira. Ryell took a deep breath, even though it couldn't cool his boiling blood.

Kamira waited in silence.

"You're pushing me away." Ryell scrambled for words, any words, no matter how petty or pitiful they might sound. "You always talk about how you can't trust me, how I'm too close to Yoreus, but you never give me a chance to prove you wrong."

Her face changed, but knowing his stab had reached its mark didn't offer Ryell any satisfaction.

"It's not the best time to argue." Her words barely carried through the night.

"Of course it isn't!" He raised his voice. "But it never is. You're stubborn and refuse to listen to reason. You won't talk to me, and you won't talk to the high mages, stuck in your pretty grudge. And go on, tell me I have no idea. Of course I don't. Not only are you leaving me behind again, but you're keeping secrets, too."

She said nothing. Her chin trembled, but Ryell couldn't tell whether he'd brought her to the verge of crying, or whether it was a sign of quenched fury.

"I'm sorry." He reined in his anger. If he pushed her too hard, she'd just walk away. "I just don't want to sit in that inn waiting for you to come back wounded and battered again, and think that I couldn't help." He put his hands on her shoulders and forced Kamira to look into his eyes. "I won't let you leave me again."

Silence fell between them.

"I have no choice," she said eventually. "I'm going to Veelk's tribe, and I can't even be sure they'll allow entry to me, let alone someone else. And they're the only ones who might be able to help me."

He could swear a note of desperation rang in her words. "Help you with what?"

By the look in her eyes, she must have been fighting with

herself, so he swallowed the bitter words forcing their way to his lips.

"There's a demon who wishes me dead," she replied. "I'm only alive because I deceived him, but my time is running short. Veelk's tribe has ways to help me."

The way she said it left no doubt she wasn't offering him all the truth, but he took refuge in the fact that she'd finally shared something with him. He wanted to learn more, to understand how and why a demon might be after her, but something told him his time was running short. If he wanted to gain something, *anything*, he had to go straight to the point.

"What about the high mages? Don't you think they could at least try to help?" Ryell fought to keep his voice calm. If he let his emotions speak, he could push her away again.

A grimace spoiled her face, but no anger accompanied it. "The archmages would kill me without a second thought and give the demon exactly what he wants. Besides, they know little of demons. But if I can't find help with Veelk's people, I'll have to risk talking to them anyway."

He took it as a sign of hope. No matter her grudge, she was at least considering asking the high mages for help. "Why not now? I can speak to Yoreus on your behalf, and I know he'll be reasonable. Not all of the high mages are as evil as you see them."

"Kam!" Veelk called out from the darkness.

His voice, muffled, carried only enough to reach them, and it reminded Ryell that the Gildya's people were close. But when Kamira looked over her shoulder, his anger resurfaced and he dug his fingers into her arms. "No! Answer me first."

Kamira pursed her lips, and for a heartbeat she

resembled a displeased noblewoman, but then her expression returned to normal. "Let's do it this way," she said. "If Veelk's tribe can't help me, I'll seek the high mages' counsel. I'll talk with Yoreus if he wishes to meet." She put a finger on his lips, her gesture between an intimate caress and a gentle order. "And in exchange for your understanding of the delay, I'll answer all your questions when I get back, and not ask how much time you've spent with Yoreus's daughter, be it in the asylum or otherwise."

His cheeks burned. Kamira didn't strike him as someone who'd keep or pay spies, so she must have learned it by chance. Or perhaps she'd made a guess, since the mage killer must have been poisoning her mind all that time. He gritted his teeth. She left him no space for a better bargain.

"All my questions?" He couldn't wish for anything better, but he stalled nevertheless. If only he had more time to talk to her, she'd see reason and seek help in the Towers instead of running off to savages.

"All." A promise rang in that word—a promise he liked. "I'll answer your questions even if I've already found help." She glanced over her shoulder, toward Veelk standing by the tree line. "I should go, and so should you. Better if Gildya's adepts don't find us standing over your queen's body."

He shifted his eyes downward, at the black shape in the moonlit grass. "I never thanked you for..." He indicated Cahala's body.

"No need. I know revenge can be important. It helps to heal festering wounds."

He wanted to reply, but Kamira tore away from him.

"I should be back within two months," she said as she headed toward Veelk.

Ryell didn't chase after her, though all his instincts

demanded he follow. Her silhouette slowly melted into the surrounding darkness when she stepped into the canopy's shade, but before she disappeared from his sight, she turned and waved.

"It's the last time you're walking away from me," he whispered.

That promise brought a sudden warmth to his heart. Enough to help him ignore the nagging frustration at her stubbornness. She would waste two months chasing some questionable tribal solutions when real help was within reach. Ryell had no doubt that Yoreus would know what to do and help her, if for no other reason than to prove Kamira wrong. He sighed, focusing his attention elsewhere.

A bloodstained pendant rested on Cahala's neck: the Devanshari crest. Ryell hesitated. The queen might be dead, but the royal line continued, and regardless of Cahala's crimes, her son deserved to receive the family symbol. Ryell knelt down and closed his fingers around the pendant. He'd find a way to deliver it to the prince in a way that wouldn't raise too many questions, and until then, he had to ensure that one of the most precious of Devanshari treasures wasn't lost.

Before he departed, he looked once more at the trees where Kamira had vanished. The forest around him remained quiet, and he wasn't enough of a fool to hope Kamira would run back out with a change of mind and heart. She was gone, and so he should be.

Pressing the pendant to his chest, safe between his tight fingers, he walked into the dark.

9

K oshmarnyk stood beside Veelk, hidden among the trees. His friend leaned against the trunk in a casual manner, but his eyes remained focused as he watched the scene in the clearing. Once, he called out the arcanist's name, his voice ringing with impatience and ire, but nothing else in his posture or behavior suggested strong emotions.

"I'm guessing Gildya's people aren't as near as you said?" Koshmarnyk asked, more to prompt a conversation than to get the answer.

"Close enough. But we should have enough time, because they're likely to rummage through the mansion first," Veelk replied. He threw a glance at the clearing. "She's nearly done anyway. Then, while we travel, we can sate your curiosity." His lips stretched in a cunning smile. "I'm sure you have many questions."

Koshmarnyk nodded, but said nothing more. Veelk's message was clear enough, and Koshmarnyk was willing to wait for answers a little longer, because he could assume that they were coming. Even if the Tivarashan woman didn't turn out as forthright as she'd promised, he could hope his friend would not hide things from him. Therefore, he ignored his nagging doubts and took time to appreciate his surroundings: the smell of tall pines, the flicker of the stars, the red bleeding of the coming dawn between the canopies. He'd experienced them all before, when Cahala's men freed him, but with the imbued collar as tight around his neck as it was in Gildya's prison, he didn't get to truly enjoy the feeling of freedom. Now, even though obligations to his friend and the arcanist still bound him, he was at least free of his physical binding. And that the arcanist had removed them suggested she spoke the truth about his freedom not being a part of their bargain.

At the same time, he couldn't bring himself to fully trust either of them. Even Veelk... Veelk used to be his friend, but ten years was long enough for things to change. He shifted uneasily as the memory of his former colleagues from Gildya returned. He used to consider some of them friends as well, and it didn't end well. Yet there was a difference between a casual acquaintance with his fellow inventors, no matter how warm they might have seemed, and a deeper bond with an honest warrior and his tribe, built on trust, sacrifice, and shared secrets.

"Did it go well?" Veelk asked all of a sudden, tearing him away from his concerns.

Koshmarnyk looked at him, confused, and then Kamira approached. The question must have been meant for her.

"Well enough. He knows enough to believe me, but whether he passes the information..." She shrugged. "I had to promise I'd answer all his questions when we get back."

"That's risky," Veelk said.

To Koshmarnyk's surprise, she grinned.

"I promised to answer his questions, not to tell him all the truth."

There was more playfulness than cold calculation in her voice, but Koshmarnyk couldn't help reminding himself she was from Tivarashan. The northern women had been playing their games for centuries, and he'd be a fool to believe anything had changed in a mere ten years. And even if she was traveling with Veelk, it didn't mean she had no hidden reasons.

"Let's go." Veelk picked up the bags and handed them out. "We can talk while we walk."

The glance Kamira threw Veelk carried amusement, as if his words reminded her of something they'd shared. Koshmarnyk remained silent, his mind focused. Listening and watching meant learning more about the Tivarashan arcanist and her reasons to be around Veelk.

They set out, and the pace Veelk set pushed Koshmarnyk's still-recovering body almost to the limits. As much as he'd prefer a slower pace, allowing for conversation and getting answers, he had to agree that getting out of the woods—and out of Gildya's people's reach—was more important. Yet, as they made it through the forest paths, soft needles barely making a sound under their feet, he found himself falling behind. Kamira sent him a comforting smile when his pace matched hers. Like him, she was barely keeping up with Veelk, but her face expressed no frustration or displeasure.

"He hasn't changed much through all these years." Koshmarnyk pointed at the mage killer in front of them.

"And you have!" Veelk called out. "I don't remember this speed being so hard on you."

Koshmarnyk laughed. Veelk, indeed, hadn't changed at

all. "Gildya's prison provides little opportunity for training," he replied.

Veelk slowed down and matched his stride with theirs. "I've been meaning to ask what happened. When I heard Gildya forbade the use of imbued stones on any living creatures, I thought you'd left, not gotten yourself captured."

"I was stupid enough to believe they wanted to talk... and paid for it." Koshmarnyk did his best to keep bitterness away from his words. Ten years of loathing was enough, and the volatile mixture of emotions he'd had to bear for the past decade shouldn't spoil his freedom. "How about you two? What brought a mage killer and an arcanist together?" Back in Cahala's cellar, Kamira had mentioned something about bringing the high mages down, but it couldn't be the only reason. The two of them looked like they knew each other better than mere companions with a common goal would.

"She saved my life, instead of leaving me to die in the dirt," Veelk replied. "I stuck around to pay the debt, but whenever I do, she always does something to ensure it's not paid in full."

The mocking tones in his voice allayed Koshmarnyk's concerns. Following unclear rules wasn't like Veelk, but the way he spoke about Kamira made it clear he stayed because he wanted to, debt or not.

"So, how long has it been now?" Koshmarnyk's scolded trust demanded a little more digging.

They looked at each other.

"Some years?" Kamira said after what looked like quite an effort to remember. "Four or five, maybe."

Koshmarnyk arched his eyebrows in surprise. "You must be a remarkable woman to keep Veelk's attention for that long." He hoped his remark sounded playful enough to cover his concerns resurfacing.

Kamira stared at Koshmarnyk, a long moment of silence as his words must have been sinking in, and then she burst out laughing. Veelk—with a wide grin—shook his head.

Koshmarnyk's eyes widened. *What's wrong with you?* He hoped his expression made the question clear, but Veelk didn't react. *Or... what's wrong with her?*

Kamira and Veelk engaged in playful banter, but Koshmarnyk didn't pay much attention. He let his thoughts drift off, wondering what the strange duo had sought him out for. He also wanted to know what really kept them together if they weren't even lovers. The Veelk that he knew a decade ago had a seemingly unending desire for the company of women, and he didn't spend his time with them on witty exchanges. Koshmarnyk's concerns resurfaced, and as he forced half a smile in response to a comment he didn't even hear, he sought Veelk's eyes. Some questions would have to be answered by the mage killer alone, away from Kamira. Until then, Koshmarnyk better stay on his guard.

BY THE TIME the woods shifted into hills, the sun was almost at its zenith, and their pace slowed down. Kamira was dragging her feet, but it didn't escape Koshmarnyk that she kept up with few complaints, and it sounded more like playful teasing than fussing. She might be a Tivarashan, and a noblewoman from what he could tell, but she was accustomed to a traveler's way of life.

In the distance, the jagged peaks of the Spine rose, and the sight of the mountain range reminded Koshmarnyk of the time he'd spent among Veelk's people. Nostalgia stole his thoughts, and even though ultimately those events had led him to Gildya's prison, he would never consider blaming those jovial tribesmen who convinced their demon that Koshmarnyk was worthy of learning their secrets.

He huffed, amused—even his own name, Koshmarnyk, was their choice. In his own mind, the man he was before, Alluvendran, was long gone, and escaping—from both Gildya's and Cahala's power—made him all the more eager to forget that name.

Before Kamira collapsed from exhaustion, Veelk picked a narrow valley shielded by the hills to make camp. Shadows crawled in the tall grass, and several trees above allowed little light through, making broad daylight seem like dusk. Lush green at the valley's belly told of water, and soon enough they found a small pond.

They set up a small campfire, and Kamira shared food. Koshmarnyk bit into cured meat and dried cheese wrapped in a bread-like dough, enjoying the simple flavor. Cahala's servants had kept him fed, but travel rations always had a distinct taste of freedom for him, enhanced even more by the decade in prison.

"First watch?" Kamira asked Veelk as soon as she was done with her portion.

When the mage killer nodded, she laid her head on a bag with a sigh of relief.

"I suppose my questions can wait a bit longer," Koshmarnyk remarked, not without amusement. For a Tivarashan, Kamira surely wasn't fussy about things.

"You can ask Veelk," she said in that tone used to dismiss anything and everything when one was already half-asleep.

Of course he'd ask Veelk... all the questions not meant for the arcanist's ears. But that had to wait until he was certain she couldn't hear them, so he fished out another ration from a bag to stall.

"I let her sleep first," Veelk said with a broad smile. "Otherwise she falls asleep during her watch."

"I can have the nightflies scout if you keep complaining," she murmured.

Veelk shook his head. "I could do without the demon's company tonight."

Kamira's sleepy response made no sense to either of them, and they exchanged smiles. Then Veelk became serious.

"If I knew you were Gildya's prisoner all these years, I would have come sooner," he said.

Koshmarnyk stared at the flames licking the wood. He had no doubt Gildya had made sure he disappeared without trace. "I got what I deserved for trusting them. You warned me."

"I did."

"What about you?" Koshmarnyk asked, and glanced at Kamira, but her steady breath suggested she was deep asleep. "Running around with an arcanist? And not even a lover, from what I understand?"

Veelk snorted at some thought, but his reply was serious: "She saved my life, and I want to pay the debt the tribe's way."

Koshmarnyk nodded as the memories of Veelk's brethren returned. The honor and life debts always proved hardest to repay, since it mattered not what was done, but how.

"That still doesn't explain why you didn't..." Koshmarnyk cleared his throat. "It always seemed to me you wouldn't overlook a sheep, let alone a fine-looking woman."

Veelk's eyebrow arched, but the trembling corner of his lip betrayed his amusement. "I have some standards."

"And which part of 'a fine-looking woman' doesn't fit?"

"All of them." Veelk grinned. "Women should have curves and pleasant personalities. And a man should not mix work with pleasure."

That remark sparked Koshmarnyk's curiosity. "Mercenary work?" If someone else was paying the duo to go after the mages, it would be good to know before he got involved.

To his relief, Veelk shook his head. "We explore old ruins, bring back artifacts... mostly risk our lives for naught."

"And you still haven't paid your debt? Or is she more of your type than you care to admit?" It would be so like Koshmarnyk's friend to conceal any deeper feelings.

But Veelk laughed and shook his head. "She became a friend. We work well as a team, and we make decent coin, which means the best room in the inn, the best food, and the pleasant company of women with a less... bitter sense of humor."

Koshmarnyk watched him intently, but Veelk's behavior offered no signs of deception. Part of him wanted to tease his friend a bit more, but reason reassured him all jabs would miss in the end. Veelk really must consider Kamira a friend, and a really good one at that. Unless... Another thought sent a chill down Koshmarnyk's spine. Unless she knew a way to manipulate him. There was one thing that the elders of Veelk's tribe had warned Koshmarnyk about, one thing all those who carried imbued stones within their bodies could fall prey to. With a powerful demon behind them, mage killers had little to be afraid of, but Kamira could be skilled and knowledgeable enough to overcome such obstacles. With those nightfly trinkets of hers, she seemed to have tapped into the forgotten arcane knowledge.

He rubbed his chin. "So, why come and rescue me now? I'm sure you didn't seek me out just for the sake of old times." Even if the answers he got were part of the deception, he had to ask questions if he didn't want either of them suspicious.

Veelk looked at him, clearly surprised. "She didn't tell you?"

"Only that you need help bringing the high mages down. Nothing that would explain why me in particular." Of course, reasons were limited. Kamira had to be after his knowledge or skill, because finding simple muscle would have been much easier... if Veelk even needed help with the fighting side of the task to begin with.

His friend shifted uneasily. "I'd prefer her to be awake for that conversation. Get some rest, and we'll talk in the evening before setting out. It's been a long night."

Koshmarnyk took his bag and lay down, searching for a comfortable position. "Wake me up for the second watch."

"Courteous as always." Veelk grinned. "Very well."

A hint of guilt stained Koshmarnyk's thoughts, because courtesy wasn't the reason for his offer. Yet he kept his mouth shut. Until he knew the truth, the last thing he would do was let Kamira watch while they slept.

Koshmarnyk played with his long knife and watched Kamira brush her hair. The tentative manner with which she moved her left arm told him of a recent injury. Veelk repacked their bags nearby, and then they would likely be on their way again. With a little distraction, this could be Koshmarnyk's best opportunity.

"I believe there are some stories to be told before we set out again," he said.

Kamira looked at Veelk, and after the mage killer nodded, she said, "I'll try to make it short, so ask if something is unclear. Recently, we came across a powerful demon. It's the one I have a pact with now and who controls the nightflies. He put a spell on me, and if I don't find a way to free him from his prison, I'll die, and the world will suffer another Cataclysm."

He arched his eyebrows. After Veelk had claimed they weren't working as mercenaries, Koshmarnyk expected a story of personal vengeance, maybe spiced with some wrongdoings of the high mages to appeal to his heart. To weave such an improbable tale meant that either she was confident in her lies, or she actually spoke the truth. He found no hints of deception so far, but his skills were nothing in comparison to any Tivarashan woman.

"And what do you need me for?" he asked, already expecting what the answer would be.

She rummaged through her bag and then stretched a hand toward him. Even from this distance, Koshmarnyk sensed power flowing through the imbued stones—power no ordinary demon had.

"I need you to put these in my skin and make it look like Veelk's tribe did it," she said. "In return, I offer more of these stones for you to use as you see fit, or anything else you wish as payment."

As soon as she finished speaking, Koshmarnyk dashed forward and grabbed her hand. The stones rolled into the grass, and he pulled Kamira off balance. Surprise and fear took hold of her, and before she could react, he locked his arms around her body. One hand clenched her crossed wrists and held tight around the nightflies, while with the other he held the knife to her neck.

"If you say a word or try to use magic, I'll kill you," he said. He could only hope she was smart enough to take the threat seriously, so that he wouldn't have to act on it.

Veelk was already standing nearby, hesitant but ready. He must be deciding whether attacking was worth the risk, and Koshmarnyk tensed. One wrong move or word could change this confrontation into a bloodbath, one that likely only the mage killer would survive.

"Let her go," Veelk said.

"First you and me talk about *geharash*."

Veelk's eyes widened with understanding, and he looked at Kamira. "Do as he says, and you'll be fine." His voice lost the dangerous edge. "I'll answer his questions, and then you'll be free."

Kamira gave a cautious, slow nod. With her body so close, Koshmarnyk would sense if she tried to use magic, and the tales told by the tribe's elders claimed that arcanists couldn't manipulate their victims without their magic. He hoped that the knowledge passed over the centuries was true.

"We could have talked about it when she slept." Veelk squatted with his arms resting on his knees, and Koshmarnyk had no doubt that, despite his earlier reassurances to Kamira, the mage killer was readying for a fight should the need arise.

"Not with these bracelets of hers."

"Fair enough." Veelk pulled a lizard-shaped dagger from his boot. "You'll need this one, too." He casually threw it on the ground in front of Kamira.

Koshmarnyk didn't dare to reach for the crystal weapon,

but it should be close enough to alert him of any magic flows.

"I speak of my own will, and Kamira told you the truth," Veelk said. "We need your help because you're the only person outside the tribe who knows how to blend the stones with flesh."

Such words brought relief, but there were more questions to ask before Koshmarnyk was satisfied. "And what if I refuse?"

Veelk sighed. "I'd plea with the elders to make an exception for her. Suzhaul granted her audience once and seems to be on good terms with her demon."

The tale had taken another improbable turn, and Koshmarnyk's freshly discarded concerns surged once more. "Suzhaul? I find it hard to believe she managed to summon him." He remembered well the time he'd spent with Veelk's brethren, and how adamant their demon was in ignoring outsiders. If Koshmarnyk hadn't been accepted into the tribe, he'd never have gotten even as little as a glimpse of Suzhaul.

"She didn't. We sought out a kallan to do the summoning. Her demon spoke with Suzhaul as well."

"I take it you were present when this happened?"

Veelk nodded, and Koshmarnyk weighed his decision. Kamira didn't move nor use magic throughout the conversation, and he didn't notice anything odd in Veelk's behavior either. Also, Suzhaul wouldn't allow any arcanist to control one of his mage killers in his presence.

Koshmarnyk moved the blade away from Kamira's neck and loosened the grip on her wrists. "I apologize for the discomfort. You're free now."

She scampered away, and Veelk was by her side instantly with his hands on her shoulders. "It's fine now."

Her expression conveyed her lingering distrust as she glared at Koshmarnyk, but no anger. "I don't suppose you could tell me what that was about?"

"He wanted to make sure he can trust us both," Veelk replied. "That you aren't manipulating me."

A grimace spoiled her face, but then she nodded and looked straight at Koshmarnyk. "Is it all settled now?" Her fingers flexed in what had to be instinctual readying for combat.

Avoiding sudden moves, Koshmarnyk sheathed his knife and reached into the grass. The magic flow guided him, and he picked up the stones she'd dropped. "It is. I apologize once more. And, of course, I'll be happy to help you."

She arched an eyebrow, but didn't say anything, and Koshmarnyk couldn't help an inquisitive glance. He expected some display of emotion, even accusations of how he himself was not worthy of trust in return, but she got over the situation quickly.

"Is something wrong?" she asked.

He smiled and shook his head. "Nothing. You just don't seem... particularly upset about what happened."

The curve of her lip could be considered a smile, but when she replied, her voice carried residual coldness. "I can understand distrust. At least you were open about it." She glanced at Veelk. "And you owe me some explanations about this *geharash*."

Veelk laughed, shaking his head. "It's something arcanists are *not* supposed to know."

"According to the legends, arcanists of the past knew how to control someone through the demon within imbued stones." Koshmarnyk hoped the truth would be enough of a peace offering, and Veelk's playful response suggested he didn't mind sharing that secret. "You seemed like someone who could know, and Veelk... usually doesn't stick around any woman for too long, so I got suspicious."

She rewarded his last remark with a short chuckle, and he hoped that he heard some warmth in it. "That'd get me suspicious too," she replied, throwing a glance at Veelk.

Veelk ignored her teasing. "Time to go. I want to get to the mountains as soon as possible." He picked up their bags and retrieved the dagger from the grass.

"Someone's after you?" Koshmarnyk frowned.

"Demons, high mages, common thugs... Take your pick." Veelk shrugged. "We can tell you on the way."

"Sounds like a story I shouldn't miss," Koshmarnyk replied.

Before they set out, he offered the imbued stones back to Kamira. She hesitated before reaching out, and she watched his face. He didn't twitch a muscle until she moved away. Even though she gave him a somewhat apologetic smile, she kept away from him as they made their way through the hills. Once or twice, he caught her glancing at him as if she was making sure he still posed no threat. He held back a sigh. If he was to help her, he had to put the knife to her body again. *What I did today isn't going to help.*

KAMIRA GAVE the ledge a look of doubt as Veelk began climbing. The mountain range towered over them, its gray rocks beautiful and threatening at the same time. She hadn't expected that her friend was planning to actually venture into them. They might need a discreet place away from known trade routes and human settlements, but the woods surrounding them provided enough seclusion without the need to risk breaking their limbs or necks for a bit more distance.

Uncertain, she looked at Koshmarnyk.

"I'm not about to follow in his footsteps," he reassured her. His usual half-smile accompanied the words, and during the week-long journey, she'd learned to recognize the humor in his dry tone. "I was born a man, not a mountain goat."

"I heard that!" Veelk scaled the rocks will all the ease needed to substantiate Koshmarnyk's comment. He soon disappeared over the ledge, and a rope unraveled down the rock face.

Kamira glared at it with contempt. Any other time she'd claim to be unable to climb, only to make Veelk's life harder when he'd have to carry her up, but Koshmarnyk's curious and rather scrutinizing expression made her abandon all thoughts of complaining. Not that she would climb the entire way on her own...

Without delay, she woke up the nightflies and gently pushed away Veranesh when he tried to take control. The creatures readjusted their sleek bodies along her forearms, and as she began her ascent, their wings fluttered to support her efforts. Her muscles burned and ached with the strain, and Kamira clenched her teeth while Veelk peaked from above, blatantly enjoying the sight of her sweating.

At least he spared her another remark about physical exercise, and when she got close, he reached out and helped her over the edge. She slumped onto the ground and massaged her sore arms.

Within heartbeats, Koshmarnyk joined them, proving that his years of imprisonment hadn't taken quite the toll he claimed. As he stood nearby, the gentle magic of the stone in his body teased Kamira's senses and reminded her that he, too, had help climbing.

The grass-covered platform on which they stood stretched wider than Kamira expected. The black mouth of a cave in the mountain's face promised both shelter from elements and that they wouldn't be climbing more. The treetops of the forest below rocked in the wind only a hand's reach away, welcoming sunlight to the ledge, but keeping it concealed from travelers' eyes.

"In the past, mage killers used to stay here when traveling," Veelk said. "You two will be safe here."

Kamira looked at Veelk, ready to demand explanations, but it was Koshmarnyk who spoke first.

"If I'm to do stone blending, I'll need specific tools and supplies," he said. "I took some from the queen's place, but there are a few more I'll require to do it the tribal way."

"We'll get them for you." Kamira took the chance to ignore Veelk's previous remark. He couldn't be seriously thinking of leaving her alone with a man who was ready to kill her not so long ago, no matter his motives. "There's a town to the north."

Veelk eyed her. "I'll get them. You two are staying here." He pointed at Koshmarnyk. "You better not show yourself where someone from Gildya might recognize you. And you" —his finger moved to Kamira—"will stay here, because you're supposed to be with my tribe. If someone sees you wandering and brings the message to the mages, that story won't hold."

Kamira opened her mouth and then closed it. As much as she wanted to argue, Veelk was right. The two months in hiding were a necessity if she wanted to make it look like she'd traveled far to the southwest and back. She fought off a grimace, feeling Koshmarnyk's eyes on her. Throughout their journey, the adept had done nothing that would validate her concerns, and at the same time, he respected the distance she couldn't help keeping, so to express her distrust seemed unfair.

Veelk arched his eyebrow, waiting for her to say something, but as silence lingered, he headed for the cave. "I'll check on the food supplies and whether the water from the underground stream still runs fresh. Make a list of what you need."

Kamira tore out a page of her journal, then fished out a flask of ink and quill for Koshmarnyk.

He looked at her with a sly grin. "Can he even read?"

As he began scribbling without waiting for a reply, she let out a chuckle to show her appreciation for his attempts to put her at ease. She'd hate to admit it, but trust issues aside, he sparked her curiosity. A man to befriend Veelk's tribe and openly adorn his skin with imbued stones had to have interesting stories to tell and intriguing insights to share. Like her and Veelk, this was someone who lived his life on his own terms, ready to face the consequences of his choices, good or bad. She had to appreciate that.

"Everything is as my people left it." Veelk came out of the cave. "There's a place to cook, but try to not use fire too much. Smoke can carry. Your magic will be better for light."

Koshmarnyk stood up and passed the list to Veelk, who read through it.

"That's an awful lot of sleepseed extract," the mage killer muttered.

"Is it now?" Koshmarnyk asked.

They exchanged stares, and the silence that followed drew Kamira's attention.

"Maybe you're right. It might be the right amount," Veelk said, and she couldn't help thinking he wanted to avoid her questions. He sent her a smile. "Don't fight any demons while I'm away, and don't annoy your own demon."

Her clenched throat offered no sarcasm in return. "Come back soon."

"Three weeks, maybe four," he replied. "That note of yours will make it longer."

Kamira nodded. Of course, she could change her mind about delivering it, but in the end, if she wanted to have reasons to trust Pelina, she needed to get instructions to her as soon as possible, and Veelk would ensure it reached her hands without drawing too much attention.

Veelk's wide arms closed around her, offering warmth and safety, but then he stood up, exchanged nods with Koshmarnyk, and climbed down the rock. She watched after him, lost in the realization it would be the first time they were apart for such a long time, and Koshmarnyk clearing his throat made her jerk.

"I'll sleep outside," he said it in a casual way, but his expression made it clear that Kamira's reaction didn't escape him.

"That won't be necessary," she replied. "I have my nightflies." She might as well be open about her distrust. And no matter how quick the adept was, Veranesh would keep her safe.

"Works for me," he replied. "So, shall we see what kind of a primitive place our barbarian friend left us in?"

Part of her, ingrained in Tivarashan's nature, remained suspicious at his casual remarks, ready to see it as deception and an attempt to blindside her, but at the same time, she saw his efforts at making the mood pleasant. After all, they were to spend the next weeks together, and hostility wouldn't help in such a limited space. With that in mind, she gave a nod and a cautious smile. Koshmarnyk did his part, so she could be amiable as well.

They entered, and the cave turned out bigger than she'd expected. A narrow stone corridor led to a bigger opening. Several baskets stood by the walls, and stones marked the central fire pit. Two other tunnels led away, and the sound of running water echoed from one.

"I'm surprised no wild animals claimed this place." Kamira inspected the tribal symbols on the walls, but none of them bore any trace of magic.

"I think Veelk's brethren buried imbued stones at the entrance." Koshmarnyk looked over his shoulder. "And the grass outside has a distinct aroma, one that keeps rodents away. I wouldn't be surprised if they sowed it there."

She gave him a surprised look. Information that magic could ward off animals wasn't new to her, but something else had caught her attention. "You can sense imbued stones?" Even with the sensitivity to magic all arcanists had, she had to make an effort to sense stones, and they had to be nearby or powerful. "Is that because of the ones you have?"

"A particular one I made for that very reason." He indicated his shoulder. "I never thought Gildya would turn on me openly, but I expected some might want to deal with me in a less forthright manner: hired assassins, Tivarashan fanatics..." He paused. "I apologize."

It took her a moment to catch on. "No need. I've seen how... *passionate* our priestesses can get about what they think is right."

"Is that why you wander the wilderness with a tribal warrior instead of holding the position of a respectable arcanist somewhere in your homeland?" The question was equal parts serious and playful.

The lumisphere followed her when she walked over to

one of the corridors and peeked into a small, empty niche. "Arcanists aren't exactly respected in Tivarashan," she replied. "Considered useful, yes, but not respected, if they turned down priesthood. Our Temple of the Four closely watches every single one of them and is quick to judge any misconduct, be it real or not."

Memories resurfaced, and she leaned against the cool stone wall, giving in. The Temple was one of the reasons she'd never decided to go back home. Most Tivarashan had no issues with bowing and praying to the four demons that protected their land in exchange for worship, and the priestesses and priests used the power given to them, but as an arcanist, Kamira couldn't bring herself to treat demons as something more than they were: creatures from another world who could grant magic through pacts but otherwise had no power within the human realm. And without pursuing the path to priesthood, she'd be stuck forever in a servant's role, like most other arcanists in her homelands.

"How ironic," Koshmarnyk replied. "They use imbued stones for everything, and even Gildya envies their techniques and inventions, but they treat the arcanists as a necessary evil."

"Doesn't everyone else also?" Kamira asked. "If you have no one to blame, find an arcanist... or a demon."

"Nothing has changed in the last decade, I see." He lifted the baskets' covers, revealing grain and what looked like rations wrapped in soft leather. "One would think the Cataclysm happened yesterday, and not centuries ago."

She couldn't help cringing. "And we don't even deserve that."

Koshmarnyk abandoned the basket inspection. "You know something, don't you? There's more to that High Towers plan." Then he stopped and laughed, shaking his head. "I apologize. You don't owe me answers like that. My curiosity got the better of me."

He was right, but at the same time, it could be a way to work on mutual trust. They might have traveled together for a while already, but Kamira was cautious to not reveal anything important in their scant conversations, and she'd avoided summoning Veranesh. Veelk respected her choice, even though he didn't seem pleased with such an approach, and she couldn't keep this going forever. With Koshmarnyk's decade-long imprisonment, she had little fear that he could be involved with high mages and demons. Of course, Veranesh would be against sharing such information with anyone, but if she wanted her own distrust gone, she needed to talk to the adept instead of avoiding him. That also meant sharing secrets. Besides, he was going to stay around for at least a couple of months, until the blending was done. It only seemed fair he knew what the real stakes were.

"It's dangerous knowledge," she replied. "It almost got me and Veelk killed."

"I spent ten years chained to a wall. I wouldn't mind a bit of danger." His tone might be lighthearted, but his expression suggested he took her warning seriously.

Kamira offered a smile. With small steps, she could wipe away the unpleasant memory of his knife at her neck. "Then let's bring the bags in and get some food. I can tell you the story while we eat."

10

For the rest of the night, Phuran tended to his wound hidden in the trees and watched Gildya adepts swarm the mansion. While they carried the corpses out, he dreaded spotting Cahala's body among them, but the mage killer must have taken her away. How and when, Phuran couldn't tell, but if the savage warrior sided with the demonologist and the treacherous adept, they likely had means to sneak away from the Gildya.

Time passed, but Phuran couldn't make his move with all the scouts scattered around the woods, and in the dark, he wouldn't be able to search for tracks anyway. With no other choice, he watched the bodies being carried out, all of the people dead. The mage killer left no one alive... Even though their lives mattered little in comparison to Cahala's survival, such savagery and waste made his blood boil.

At sunrise, most of them departed, but some were left on guard, and Phuran cringed. They must have found the treasures. His hands locked into fists as he counted his opponents. The need to spill their blood, to defend what little was left of Devanshari heritage, urged him to act. He took deep breaths to steady his heartbeat and flexed his fingers, forcing them to uncurl. He could take Gildya's men on, but fighting was always a risk. He was already wounded, and he needed all his strength and skill to save the queen. All the wealth in the world meant nothing if she died.

With that in mind, he checked his wound again, but he couldn't hasten its mending. If he confronted the mage killer, he'd be at a disadvantage again. At the same time, as much as he wanted to draw that savage's blood, he didn't need to fight him to save Cahala. Either sneaking in and carrying her away or taking a captive on his own to make the trade, it should be easy enough to ensure the queen's safety. And the mage killer... Phuran would take care of him when the right time came, and this time he wouldn't lose.

He lowered himself from his hideout among the branches and made his way around the clearing, not drawing the attention of the men posted around the mansion.

Gildya's men scouted in pairs, so the tracks of four people leading deeper into the forest didn't belong to them. Picking up the trail in the soft ground proved child's play, and Phuran followed it without hesitation. Two men and two women traveled together. He recognized the queen's slipper, so the others had to be the mage killer, the adept, and the demonologist.

The longer he pondered the events, the more convinced he became of a carefully laid trap. Somehow, the demonologist had led the mage killer to them, letting herself to be captured. Alluvendran's role in the foul play remained unclear, since he had no means of sending a message out, but his acquaintance with the woman left no doubt. Phuran gritted his teeth. He would have killed the adept if she hadn't interfered. He focused on following the trail. The time to right all the wrongs would come soon enough.

The sun sneaked through the foliage and teased his eyes. The fight and sleepless night had taken their toll on him, but Phuran pressed on nonetheless, and before noon he came across another clearing. The lighter of the men—it must have been Alluvendran—stayed behind while the mage killer and two women made it into the open.

A figure lay in the grass, and Phuran's eyes widened as he uttered words of denial. The sight of familiar golden silk rising and dancing in the breeze made him dart through the clearing to the queen's body. Dewdrops shone like imbued stones on her pale skin, and the pool of darkened blood told Phuran he was too late.

I never should have left!

He trembled as he knelt by Cahala. He relived every moment of the previous evening, every strike of the sabers, every step, every decision, including the one to obey his queen's order. The image of the mage killer haunted him, never to be forgotten. There would be blood for blood, that much was certain, even if Phuran had to devote the rest of his life to it. He had failed his queen, but revenge remained within his reach... All of them would suffer: the adept, the demonologist, and, most of all, the man who took Cahala from him. His resolve brought renewed integrity, but then Phuran spotted a line of single tracks. *Someone else came here...* The footprints indicated a man, and judging from where the others stood, it was the newcomer who'd struck down the queen.

Phuran hesitated. Blood lust urged him to follow the three people, but he already knew their faces. They could only run for so long before he found them, while the fourth assailant remained unknown. If he wanted revenge and justice, he had to find him too.

But all that had to wait a little longer. He had one more thing to do.

The ground, soft and moist, didn't resist as he dug with hands and blades alike, and it left dark smudges on his face when he wiped the sweat away. When he was satisfied with the depth of the grave, Phuran stroked Cahala's hair and shifted her body with care, every move tearing his heart apart over again.

"I swear I'll find them," he said before the dark soil hid Cahala from him forever.

11

The excruciating pain in her chest made Pelina snap her eyes open. She gasped for air and lifted her hand to defend against an unseen foe, but instead of some brute on the verge of untold offenses, she stared at a painted ceiling high above, and her arm rested on soft covers as she breathed out her relief. The room itself looked like the teachers' bedrooms in the High Towers, furnished simply but comfortably, and her heart skipped a beat, responding to surging hope. She'd made it back home.

"Lie still," said a man. He sounded familiar, but she couldn't place it in her memory. "You've been wounded and lost a lot of blood."

Despite the recommendation, she moved her head. "Where... where am I?"

A man in mage's robes stood nearby, but it wasn't Kerl, and it took her a moment to recognize his face.

"Back in the High Towers." The second archmage, Yoreus, offered a gentle smile. "Gildya's people found you during their raid against rogue adepts. Seemingly, you managed to utter that you were from the Towers before passing out, so they brought you here. We did promise them answers once you woke up."

Pelina sighed with relief. Back in the cellar workshop when the blood loss had slowly taken her consciousness away, she doubted whether she'd survive. She hardly remembered Gildya's woman leaning over her, asking questions, and her own insistence to speak with high mages. Yet, under the scrutinizing glare of an archmage, she didn't have time for recollections, and a single twitch of her face could betray thoughts she'd rather keep hidden.

"I was kidnapped by some Devanshari people. I was there for days, maybe longer, and there were more women there. They did... things with imbued stones. Then a fight broke out, and a man came, killing everyone." As she spoke, she let her voice become a whisper, and the pain helped to squeeze a tear out of her eyes.

The archmage leaned closer. "Did you see who it was? Who attacked?"

"It was too dark, and when he stabbed me, everything became a blur. I thought I was done for. But... I do remember his arms as he struck, thin and marble-like," she lied smoothly. It wouldn't hurt to direct suspicion toward the Devanshari, suggesting it must have been an inner feud.

Yoreus sat at the edge of the bed and brushed her cheek. His gesture had nothing to do with the predatory behavior she'd experienced with Kerl, and then she remembered that the second archmage had a daughter. She must have been roughly her age. At the same time, she couldn't put it past him to use displays of compassion to ensure she trusted him. Archmages played games constantly, undermining each other, and didn't hesitate to use students in their deception. Pelina tried to keep a mixture of relief and uncertainty on her face, an expression one would expect from her.

"You're safe now. You were very brave." His voice seeped into her mind like honey. "Now you need to rest and heal. The adepts might come later to ask you more questions, but I'll ensure they don't bother you too much."

"Thank you, second archmage." She relaxed. "Could I pass a message to Fourth Archmage Kerl?" she asked with little hope. The old drunkard had likely already found someone else to torment.

Yoreus's features hardened. "That won't be necessary. The fourth archmage failed to even inform anyone of your disappearance, and we decided it's best if you receive further schooling from someone else. When you're able to go back to your duties and studies, you'll report to Third Archmage Loktra."

"Thank you. It's an honor."

"It's the least we can do for such a brave woman." Yoreus smiled again. "Rest now."

When he left, Pelina closed her eyes. The pain assured her that the memories and the deal with the arcanist weren't a dream. And she had just told her first lie on that account. The part of her that wasn't terrified enjoyed the feeling of cautious excitement. She might be no one, but she had just joined the archmages' games, and Yoreus's arrangement opened new possibilities. Pelina doubted Loktra would prove much more of a teacher than Kerl was, but being around the third archmage meant secrets to be uncovered. In two months, she might have something to help that crazy arcanist. But Yoreus's decision could also mean that the archmages suspected more to the supposed raid against Devanshari and wanted to keep a closer eye on her. Kamira made it clear that above all Pelina shouldn't draw attention to herself, so before she went hunting for secrets, she had to convince Yoreus and others she was an obedient student who wished for nothing more than to forget the dreadful events and return to her studies.

Yet, as she pondered possible outcomes of the plot, her thoughts ventured into the dark shadows of failure. Doubts set in, and her survival instinct urged her to call for Yoreus to come back, so that she could confess her deception, but she discarded it. The chance of achieving something, of becoming part of something bigger outweighed her loyalty to the Towers, already stained with the bitter disappointment in lack of proper schooling and Kerl's abuse of power. No matter what Kamira intended, if she succeeded, things would change for all the high mages and students. Besides, the arcanist had taken the risk of trusting Pelina, and if she wanted to prove her worth, she couldn't fail by submitting to her own fears.

The door closed in the distance, and that sound sealed her resolve. Calm and determined, she drifted off to sleep.

WHEN PHURAN WALKED into the Jagged Swordsman, several heads turned toward him, but the patrons' curiosity died quickly, and no one bothered him as he made his way to the counter. He took in the solid wooden tables and benches, along with several smaller tables with few chairs around each of them, clean floors and lamps powered by imbued stones. He had to admit that the inn wasn't at all what he had expected from a place that offered shelter to a demonologist and a savage. If that was the right place to begin with. After losing track of the stranger from the woods, Phuran had spent a lot of time searching for the three others and avoiding meeting his fellow Devanshari. He wasn't ready to answer questions about what happened, about the queen. It was better they believed she was still out there, working on the promise to give them their Hajihali back. After all, simple people didn't need the truth—they needed hope. His mind took a turn toward Cahala's son, but that spoiled and ungrateful brat with no political cunning and a heart too soft was hardly suited to be the king. Yet, when his revenge was done, Phuran would find him and offer him the same loyalty he gave his mother. If nothing else, this would be something that the queen might have wanted.

A young woman poured the drinks, and while Phuran waited for his turn, he studied her pleasant features. She smirked at him, and any other time he'd be wondering whether she could get friendlier, but the memory of Cahala's death stained his mood. Maybe later, after he'd spilled enough blood to wash the images of the queen's lifeless body away, he could return and find out.

"Are you Ryell's friend?" she asked as she returned to the counter burdened with a tray of empty mugs.

"Ryell's?" Phuran's eyebrows arched, but he discarded the thought that there could have been another Ryell around, since the name was of Devanshari origin. It seemed that the troublesome royal guard had avoided the thugs Phuran sent after him. "No."

"Oh, I'm sorry!" Her voice was pleasant, but too emotional for Phuran's taste. "I just assumed you two might be friends, since you're both Devanshari."

He chose his response carefully. No matter his thoughts of Ryell, making a scene would gain him nothing. "I know that Ryell you speak about, but I'm looking for someone else. I've been told he visits this place."

The woman smiled. "Ask away. I know all the patrons."

"The man's tall and broad-shouldered. A warrior. Copper skin and a bald head."

"No doubt it's Veelk!" Her face brightened, but then her smile faded. "He's not around now. He and Ryell left some days ago."

Phuran instinctively leaned forward at her words, but then fought to keep his calm. No need to scare the woman away or give her a reason to warn his mark. But... the mage killer and Ryell? If they'd left together, it might mean that the lone tracks Phuran had seen in the woods belonged to the royal guard, and he was the one to strike down the queen. Phuran held off a smile. He'd come to the Jagged Swordsman with little hope of gaining information, and he'd found more than he could have dreamed of.

"Do you know where they went?"

She shook her head. "But Ryell came back the other night. He comes here often to visit Kamira and Veelk, so he might know where they are."

Kamira must be the name of the demonologist, so Phuran committed it to memory. "Veelk's not back yet?" he asked, though if he'd read the tracks correctly, he already expected the answer.

"He said they'll be away for at least two months, if not longer. He never tells me where they go. Probably because I'd worry too much," she added with a forced smile.

A new thought took root, so Phuran looked at her with a compassionate expression, warmed by a slight curve of his lips. Women like her, sweet and gullible, were easy to play. A smile and display of empathy should be enough. "You care for him deeply, don't you?"

With her blush, she looked even more innocent, and she nodded. "He'll be back for sure—he always is." It sounded like she was reassuring herself. "If you visit often, you're bound to meet him here. Or I can pass on a message if you're not staying in Kaighal that long."

Excitement flooded Phuran's veins as his plan solidified. "No need for a message. I'll visit again. You've been most helpful..."

"Lefna."

"Lefna. A beautiful name." He flashed a smile. "I'll be happy to talk to you again."

The next time he talked to her, he would have everything ready. His adversary's two-month absence would delay his revenge, but it also gave him enough time to prepare it. With dangerous and treacherous opponents like a mage killer and a demonologist, he needed to ensure that he had the upper hand. The memory of the wound he'd received that forced his retreat and led to Cahala's death reminded him he couldn't risk a rushed confrontation. He paid for his ale and drank it hastily to wash the bitter taste of failure from his mouth. This time, things would be different.

He left the inn with a reinvigorated sense of purpose.

I'll strike him where it hurts the most... just like he did to me. As he stepped into the shade of a side alley, his ugly smile ensured no beggar nor thug bothered him, and he ventured into the bowels of Kaighal. *And later, I'll get Ryell, Alluvendran, and that Kamira.*

Thoughts of the tortures to come replace his grief with joyful anticipation.

MIZENA SIGHED, taking a sip of water from her hip flask. With the sun high, she'd rather be resting in the shade, watching people pass by, instead of actively searching for them in the sweating crowds that filled Kaighal's streets. Yet there was no coin in the shade, because she couldn't count on her quarries strolling by. Besides, she'd have to get up to follow them anyway. At the same time, aimlessly roaming the streets wasn't much better. It seemed that the two people the archmage was after had left the city, and Mizena wasn't fool enough to search for them in the wilderness, even if she knew the direction they'd set out. And if she wanted to know when they returned, it was enough to watch the Jagged Swordsman.

At the same time, Mizena couldn't help trusting her instincts. Sure, the odd duo left and returned often enough to make it look commonplace, but something about this time seemed different. Perhaps it was the fact that she didn't see them both leave Kaighal; the Tivarashan woman had disappeared, and the broad-shouldered tribal warrior left the city on his own, accompanied by one of the Devanshari refugees. That meant a change in their habits, and such things stood out to a spy. Perhaps the woman was still around, free of prying eyes, having convinced everyone she'd left. But to learn of her whereabouts and plots meant walking in the heat of the day, hoping to find a clue.

Mizena grimaced. The archmage—or rather the lackeys he used to communicate with his spies and informants—didn't pay enough for her to follow people who didn't want to be found and frequently ventured out of the city. It wasn't her kind of work. Yet he did pay more than her other patrons, and she didn't have any other work lined up. Free to search and roam, she gave in to her instincts' insistence.

Every now and then, another person would catch Mizena's attention, a shady figure exchanging coin with a merchant or a young woman sneaking away from her mother's guidance, but information had only as much worth as what the one who sought it was willing to pay for it, and she knew better than to chase all of those tidbits. The best spies, among which she counted herself, chose only the best-paying information to pursue... like the whereabouts of two people the archmage was interested in.

She grimaced, ready to ignore her instincts. The two were long gone from Kaighal, and seeking them within its walls meant wasting time. The best spies also knew that sometimes it paid better to chase the smaller fry.

A commotion by a smaller alley drew her attention. She only caught the end of what seemed a pickpocket attempt, but when a hood slid off a tall man, a glimpse at his bald, copper-hued head was enough. With as much caution as she could muster in a rush, she made it toward the alleyway. At least in daytime, within the crowd, her hastened passage raised little attention. The man, already hooded again, was disappearing into the alley, but at the sight of another one following him, Mizena slowed down.

Her acquaintance with Rolof stemmed from their profession, but it was hardly anything more than knowing each other's faces. She didn't owe him any courtesy, let alone the favor of getting out of his way, but three people in such an empty alleyway would be a crowd, and Mizena liked attention focused on anyone but her. Yet, after wasting her whole morning on the search her instinct demanded she wouldn't give up that easy. If she couldn't stay close to the tribal man, at least she could follow Rolof. With as lousy a spy as the scrawny rat was, he likely wouldn't notice he had a tail himself. Then all she'd have to do was get to the archmage's men first to collect the coin.

When she made it to the alley's entrance, her mark was already taking a turn into another one, and Rolof rushed after him. Such foolishness would get him killed one day, of that she was certain, though her own instincts tugged on her to hurry as well. She ignored them. A good spy knew to keep a distance, and the man, so tall and broad-shouldered, could not easily disappear. And if he did, it meant he was aware of someone following him—a situation Mizena would rather not find herself in.

Slowly, she made it to the turn. If Rolof's skills were worth anything, he'd keep on his mark, so all she had to do was not lose him.

"You've been following me."

Her heart jumped at the deep, confident voice, but a glance reassured her no one else was with her in the alley. Slowly and quietly, she made her way to the edge of a building, its wall offering hardly any concealment on a sunny day, and peeked around the corner.

The tribal warrior stood in the alley, his hooded cloak on the ground, and his posture made it clear he was ready for a fight. Mizena didn't miss the elongated shape wrapped loosely in fabric. He must have been holding the weapon in his hand so it wouldn't be spotted easily in the crowd. That meant he had to be aware someone was after him, and Mizena's blood turned colder.

Rolof stood in the middle of the alley, and even with his back toward her, she could read his uneasiness. Confronted like that, he could either lie or flee, but neither guaranteed survival.

"I... What? No. I live nearby. Three streets down."

Mizena scoffed at the lousy attempt, but at least he could use his own fear to his advantage. Any innocent person would be scared of a thuggish tribal.

"Oh." The man relaxed. "I didn't know. In that case, pass my greetings to young Salgie."

"I sure will," Rolof said in a shaky voice.

She didn't envy him. With the lie he chose, he had to pass his quarry now, pretending that he indeed was heading home. If the tribal warrior had any wits at all, he'd check if Rolof was telling the truth. The followed would become the one who follows.

The man took a step to the side as Rolof passed him by. No matter his response, he clearly hadn't fallen for the spy's lie. Unless... Her eyes widened. There was no girl named Salgie living around, and Rolof's words betrayed the truth. The man she considered a threat because of his muscle and mass had just become a bigger one if he also used his brain.

She flinched when the man lunged at Rolof—a strike unexpected even for her. With so many years in her trade, she'd learned to read cues, yet somehow she'd missed this one. With her heartbeat faster than moments ago, she watched, mesmerized. All it took was three moves, and Rolof collapsed to the cobblestones with a numb thump. His crooked neck left no doubt the attack was lethal.

The man knelt by him and searched his belongings in a quick, composed manner. He unfolded the paper from Rolof's pocket and studied it with an arched eyebrow—an expression that did not convey inability to read or even a struggle with it. Mizena took a deep breath. This man was smart enough to devise a trap that revealed Rolof's lies and did it on the go, likely as soon as he noticed the spy. The more she thought about it, the more likely it seemed that he wasn't simply on his way somewhere but had chosen the small and empty alley on purpose. Mizena was better than Rolof at everything, from following her marks to devising plans and weaving lies, but was she good enough? If she overplayed her hand, if she slipped... She clenched her fingers to stop her hands from shaking. This man left nothing to chance. If he caught her, there would be no wriggling out or pleas. The memory of his quick and efficient kill returned unwanted. If she failed, she'd be as dead as Rolof was.

With that in mind, she turned away and rushed out of the alley, into the crowd that would help her vanish. No wonder the archmage paid so much for the information, but the coin was not worth the risk. She wouldn't be able to spend it rotting somewhere in the dark alleyways of Kaighal.

The wide street greeted her with sun and people's chatter, but Mizena didn't slow down or relax. A cunning opponent like that might have noticed there was someone else following him and Rolof.

The more distance she put between her and that man, the better, and for the first time in her life, Mizena considered leaving Kaighal.

12

K amira's sigh echoed in the cave as she stared at the page covered with symbols. While Koshmarnyk spent time enhancing his martial prowess on the ledge outside, she leafed through Gayabal's journal, but the high mage's notes provided only vague information. A week had passed with nothing to show for her studies but frustration.

"This makes no sense." She looked up at Veranesh hovering by her head. "It looks as if they made two circles in one."

"It's possible," the demon replied. "I was trapped as soon as I stepped into this world, and if we assume the pactees had no part in devising the prison, some of the symbols might be the high mages' doing."

"But even if the high mages used Hauhan's Graver to alter the circle, someone would have to have noticed. The most skilled arcanists performed the summoning."

She scratched her nose. She'd only used the Graver several times when studying under Master Tijhran, but each time the added symbols, though invisible to the eye, emanated faint magic. At the same time, she could come up with many reasons that prevented the arcanists from discovering deception. Changes could have been done in the last moment, or the old Towers were simply brimming with magic enough to muddle individual flows. Not to mention that back then, no one would have expected such subterfuge, though her Tivarashan nature doubted that there weren't various factions interested in seeing the failure of the grand summoning. She discarded that thought. If any of them discovered the high mages' tinkering with the circle, they wouldn't have notified anyone if they wanted to see their opponents fail.

Yet she couldn't help thinking she was missing something.

"Can you see all the symbols clear enough? Can you tell me if some are etched in a different way than the rest?" It seemed like a long shot, but such a difference could have manifested after the trap was sprung.

The nightfly froze, only its wings beating the air, so Veranesh must have focused on his prison.

"It's going to take time," he replied. "There's dust and rubble around, and I have no means of clearing it unless I lure a creature and change it. My magic is barred from leaving the crystal in its pure form."

Kamira circled several of the symbols. "These look like altered barrier glyphs. When used in a normal circle, they block magic from getting inside." She paused. "But the flow in these seems reversed, directing the barrier inward. That could be what keeps your magic within the prison." Another thought struck her, and she narrowed her eyes. "If it can't pass the barrier, how did you manage to put a spell on me?"

Veranesh laughed. "Do you doubt I did? Or are you looking for ways to free yourself?"

"Neither," she said. She'd promised to exercise trust, and after Veranesh had saved Veelk, she couldn't bring herself to think of betrayal anymore. Even if the world was to remember her as the one who freed an evil demon or caused another Cataclysm, she'd keep her part of the deal. "The way you did it might help us find the solution."

The silence that fell made her wonder whether Veranesh wanted to answer her question at all, but then he said, "You have traces of what they call high magic within you. If you were only an arcanist, I wouldn't have been able to cast it." He let out a dry laugh. "I'd still have broken your pact and tried to convince you to help me."

Kamira openly snorted at the idea of Veranesh being able to convince her without any leverage. Now, when she had more pieces to the puzzle and enough trust in his truthfulness, she might have agreed, but back then she'd laugh and leave. Giving up her magic seemed a small price compared to making a deal with a demon she had considered evil and treacherous. Besides, as soon as they got far enough from the ruins, she'd make a new pact. There were always demons ready to offer one.

She focused back on studying the page in front of her, and then tore another one from her journal. She copied the symbols, this time breaking them into groups. "These are the markings of that powerful reverted barrier, so I guess they've been added by high mages. These make up a summoning circle."

The tip of the nightfly's body pointed to several of them. "These would be part of the original circle too."

Kamira looked up at him. "They don't look familiar."

"And they shouldn't. It's my name," Veranesh said. "A necessity to bring a higher yalari through in the flesh."

While copying the symbols to the other page, she couldn't help pondering their shape. None of them resembled the arcane drawings, suggesting that either the art was not as related to the demon world as some claimed, or that demons kept a lot of the knowledge to themselves. Seeing as Veranesh didn't mention the order the symbols should have, she would bet on the latter. Keeping curiosity at bay, she focused on the task. One day, perhaps, he would be willing to lift the veil that concealed the many secrets of his kind.

"Do you recognize anything else that could be part of the initial circle? Little knowledge survived, and after what happened, another attempt at bringing a high demon into this world was considered a bad idea, to put it lightly." She grimaced at the memory of the grievances still alive and well after all those centuries. "Some surely still try, and some must have succeeded, since your kin are here. But it's not something anyone would announce as a success."

She shook her head when another thought distracted her. *What would make an arcanist agree to such a deed? Besides pacts, what else do demons have to offer that would blind weak-willed arcanists with greed?* With all she knew about demons, how foolish those arcanists had to be to believe the demons would keep their part of the bargain once summoned to the human world. The pact might be of mutual gain, but it didn't protect the naïve ones from death should the summoned demon decided that slaughter was easier than the payment for the services.

"I recognize some of the symbols. They come from our language," Veranesh said. "But I have a limited understanding of how arcanists used them."

Koshmarnyk entered the cave and picked up the water flask. Patches of sweat stained his shirt, but he drank slowly, taking controlled sips, with his eyes on the nightflies.

Kamira almost smiled at the memory of how the introduction between the demon and the adept went, with mutual curiosity. Koshmarnyk expressed interest in the nightflies' origin and workings, while Veranesh inquired about the stones in the adept's body. Since then, they'd treated each other with little distance and cordiality. She would have never expected such an outcome, not after Koshmarnyk treated her with suspicion. At least now she didn't have to worry that he'd try to stab her on account of her demon.

"How fast are these creatures?" he asked.

"Fast enough," Veranesh replied. "Why the curiosity?"

"I need to regain my strength and speed, and I lack a challenge. I'd like to see if I can catch them in flight." Koshmarnyk looked at Kamira. "That is, of course, if you don't need his assistance."

Kamira thought of all the unanswered questions and the tangle of arcanist symbols left to decipher, but she smiled. Questions could wait if she had a chance at making the adept amiable. "Care to oblige?" She woke the other nightfly.

Both creatures circled her and then darted toward the cave's exit.

Koshmarnyk followed, looking over his shoulder. "Maybe you should join us outside. Pulling your thoughts away from the riddles might bring some fresh ideas."

"As long as you don't expect me to join." She gathered her notes and followed him. The nightflies hovered over the circle marked with several rocks the adept had been using.

The grass within was bent and pressed into the ground—a testimony to Koshmarnyk's intense training.

"The rules?" Veranesh asked.

"Every time my hand reaches you, I score a point. Every time you cut my skin, you score a point." He took his shirt off and stepped into the circle. "Whoever steps or flies outside the marked area loses."

"A competition. I like it," the demon said excitedly. "Let's make it even, then." One of the nightflies left the circle and flew over to Kamira, who sat down with her back comfortable against the mountain stone. "This will be interesting."

She gave him a nod, but the imbued stones encrusted into Koshmarnyk's body had drawn her attention. Most of them didn't exceed the size of her thumbnail, but their colors stood out against his skin. The small ones marked the muscle lines from his shoulder down to his wrist, and the bigger ones were by his collarbone. When he turned, Kamira spotted two more on his shoulder blades, and their slightly crooked placement suggested he must have done the work himself. Uneven lines of stones also ran down the sides of his chest, and she wondered whether his legs were enhanced similarly.

Koshmarnyk gave a nod, and the nightfly darted at him. He dodged, his arms following the creature's flight, and his fingers missed the target by a hair several times. Both the demon and the adept picked up the pace, and Veranesh counted out the points through the other nightfly when it became more and more difficult to spot the hits.

Kamira watched the blur of flesh and crystal with fascination. *He's even faster than Veelk.* Her friend's reflexes had no match, but the mage killer used his speed only for the moments necessary to act or react, while Koshmarnyk maintained the pace longer. She drifted off in thought, comparing the ways the two men had used the magic within the stones, and only refocused when Veranesh's voice died out.

The adept stood within the circle, and his chest, glistening with sweat, heaved with heavy breaths. He nodded to the nightfly and walked over to Kamira.

"So, who won?" she asked.

"The demon, of course." His skin bore the marks of multiple cuts and grazes.

"By the time we part ways, it might change," Veranesh said. "You've made good use of the knowledge Suzhaul's people shared with you."

Kamira pointed at several deeper gashes in the adept's skin. "I better have a look at these." She wouldn't mind an excuse to see how they differed from Veelk's powdered-stone-filled scars.

Koshmarnyk shook his head. "No need. They'll heal soon enough." To her relief, it sounded more like a lack of concern than distrust. "I appreciate your time." The adept looked at Veranesh. "I'd be glad to repeat it when you are willing."

"That can be arranged."

Koshmarnyk picked up his shirt and entered the cave.

Kamira glanced at Veranesh, a smile dancing on her lips. "You seem to have enjoyed it." The demon must have been truly bored to engage in such an activity and cater to a human who, in the end, meant nothing to him.

"Didn't you? You watched the game quite absorbed."

"It was entertaining." Kamira hoped a blush didn't show on her cheeks. At least Veelk wasn't around to make light of it, because he'd have undoubtedly caught that it wasn't the sport that absorbed her attention, but one wiry body.

Unwilling to reveal too much, she forced her thoughts into another direction, and as she stared at the circle marked with rocks, an idea struck her. "Maybe we should put the symbols on rocks or pieces of wood. This way we can move them around and rearrange them, maybe find a pattern to sort them."

"This might help," Veranesh said. "Work on it while I see what I can do about the circle in the chamber. There might be a few more to be added."

The nightflies descended, and Kamira stretched her arms, letting them coil around her wrists. As they froze into bracelets, she looked at the page again. It was going to take a while.

KAMIRA STIRRED THE STEW, but the steam carried no distinct aroma. The dried meat and grains they'd thrown into the pot offered little flavor, and the arcanist inspected the food with growing doubt.

"I've seen you eat worse will less fuss." Veranesh hovered over the pot.

She snickered at the memory of her and Veelk's return to Kaighal after the battle with Uganel. "We had little choice, didn't we?" To hasten their journey, the demon did most of the hunting, and the memory of the nightflies carrying small desert creatures and bugs resurfaced. With their food supplies gone, she was happy enough to sink her teeth into anything that was put to flame long enough to stop moving.

Yet she wasn't in a rush to explain to the demon how things were different this time. Instead, she glanced toward the cave's exit, but Koshmarnyk was still outside. He trained every day, and his body had regained some flesh, while his skin took in the sun, losing its pallor. The changes didn't affect his stern expression, but as his silhouette lost its famished features, he looked younger, and Kamira realized he must be closer to her and Veelk's age, and not the aging man she'd taken him for. Every other time, she found an excuse to watch his training, and day by day, her curiosity grew.

"Trying to put the adept in a good mood?" Amusement rang in Veranesh's voice.

She really hoped the man in question wasn't within earshot. "Can't hurt, can it?"

The way the adept behaved in her presence drew Kamira to him. The one incident with the knife aside, he hadn't shown any distrust, and one thought kept coming back to her: Koshmarnyk didn't care that she was an arcanist and had a demon flying about. That alone made his company much more pleasant than any meeting with Ryell. The Devanshari's endless arguments rang in her ears again. He was more interested in making her a high mage than anything else.

Koshmarnyk walked in; his shirt, soaked with sweat, revealed the muscles beneath and the odd shapes of the imbued stones. As she tried not to stare, Kamira had to admit that her interest in the adept's body wasn't only of the scholarly nature, and she scolded herself for such distractions.

"You two come up with anything new?" Every time he asked, it seemed that he was genuinely interested in their progress.

She shook her head. "Veranesh is still working through the rubble in the chamber."

"It's taking more time than I'd like," the demon added.

"Next time you take a break, let me know. I'd like a

rematch," Koshmarnyk said. "But now, I'm going to wash that sweat off."

Kamira pointed at the stew. "The food won't be ready for a while. The meat was quite hard, which makes me think mage killers have demon powder in their teeth too."

Koshmarnyk laughed and went into the smaller niche that served as the bathing chamber. She liked when he laughed and his features lost the roughness of a man who'd suffered through too much.

"Maybe I should let him win next time, so he can show off." Veranesh kept his voice down, though the murmur of water flowing through the small niche would muffle any sounds from the main cave.

"Maybe next time you should cut deeper, so that I will have to treat his wounds," Kamira muttered, only half in jest.

"I like the way you think, pactee."

A grin came to her face. "Too much time around you."

The demon said nothing, but the nightflies hovered around, and Kamira wondered what he was thinking about. Pardayi had mentioned of his interest in the humans, but how much could a being from another world actually understand of friendship or romance? Demons expressed passion and hate, and they suffered from the same pride and cruelty that plagued humankind, but they seemed to lack any deeper attachment to others.

"Do demons ever fall in love?" she asked.

The nightfly spun in the air. "Sometimes, yes. Though most are wise enough to avoid the passion."

"Is it considered a weakness?"

At first, no reply came. The nightfly froze, and only the steady beat of the crystal wings kept in in the air. "It can be dangerous when the feeling is not mutual. It can also be dangerous when it is," Veranesh replied. "I suppose the ones who do not take part in the power struggle fall for it more often. And I see you grin, pactee. I won't answer the question you're about to ask."

She chuckled. "That's answer enough for me." She couldn't resist teasing, though in fairness, more than in Veranesh's possible romances, she was interested in demons as a whole. If love was so rare, and their violence culled their numbers, they could be a dying species already. Yet nothing indicated they were.

"What is?" Koshmarnyk stepped back into the chamber, wet clothes clinging to his body.

"Kamira has taken a sudden interest in yalari culture," Veranesh replied, his voice dry and emotionless, as if indeed they were discussing mundane topics. "One would think pactees would be more educated on this matter."

The adept walked over to fire. "Don't stop on my account. I'll gladly listen." He served himself a bowl of stew.

"I'm done for today." The nightflies hovered over Kamira, and she lifted her arms, letting the creatures rest. The demon surely knew when to disappear.

Kamira gave the stew another doubtful glance as she took the pot off the fire and poured it into her bowl, but Koshmarnyk seemed satisfied with the food. No matter how bland it tasted, it must be better than what Gildya served in their prison.

"So, what do you do when you aren't arguing with your demon or putting your life in danger?" Koshmarnyk asked between bites.

She thought for a moment. It seemed best to match his lighthearted tone. "I argue with Veelk or treat his wounds... or both. I practice magic too, but I've let it slide lately."

"Practice magic? I thought arcanists had easy access to it

through the pact." Koshmarnyk leaned closer. "I know high mages have to memorize the spells, but you don't seem to need to. I saw how quick you could react in a fight, too."

She took the remark as a veiled compliment, especially given that Veelk rarely commented on her battle skills in a positive manner. "It's to master the energy manipulation." She paused, looking for an analogy he'd understand. "It's like fighting: the more you practice, the faster you are, and your precision grows."

"So how does an arcanist practice her magic?"

"I can show you, but we have to go outside. I'd need more space." She put her bowl away.

Koshmarnyk lost interest in his food instantly and headed out, making it clear he was up for a demonstration. By the time she got outside, he was already sitting by the cave entrance, and Kamira made her way to the middle of the ledge, picking a spot he often trained at for its lack of thicker grass.

"No circle?" he asked as she made herself comfortable on the ground.

"A circle is good for stable barriers or when you're dealing with a demon, but it's not necessary for practice." Of course, practicing drawing them was a whole other matter, but she wasn't about to bore him trying to get perfect lines in the rough ground.

She closed her eyes and relaxed, lifting her hands out of habit. He couldn't sense magic the way she did, so it had to be something visible. Like a beginner student, she started with a lumisphere above her head, and as it spun, streaks of energy separated from it and reached out toward the ground, forming a cage made of light. She exhaled slowly, then moved her fingers and let the magic flow and change. Motions weren't necessary for the art, but they could help in directing her powers, and she'd never gotten rid of that habit. The lumisphere erupted with light into a tangle of lightning cracking around with the sound of a hundred whips. Ice or water? Arcanists considered both transitions difficult, and even though Koshmarnyk wouldn't tell the difference if she used something else, she couldn't resist a little challenge, and forced the energy circling to slow down. The lightning arcs wavered, but she held the flow steady, and a smile of triumph danced on her lips when the crackling cage around her became a construct of ice.

As the energy was easier to control in such a state, she allowed herself to open her eyes. Koshmarnyk approached, sliding his hand along the frozen shapes. Kamira released the energy, letting it change again, and instead of touching ice, his fingers sank into water. Multiple streams followed the patterns drawn previously by the frozen construct.

"Amazing," Koshmarnyk said, his hand still submerged in the flow.

He didn't look at her construct anymore, but directly at her. *I better not mess this one up.* The thought of them both soaked in water and sharing a laugh had its appeal, but she wanted to keep that fascinated expression on his face. The water stopped flowing at her will, and she changed it into air, sending wind in all directions to disperse the energy. The strong gust pushed on Koshmarnyk, but he kept his footing.

"I've never seen a high mage perform something like that," he said.

"They rely on their incantations to cast spells, so they don't need to control the flow." Kamira got up and brushed the dirt of her pants. "But they are also limited by the words someone else scribbled. Once the energy is drawn in a certain shape, there's no changing it. But they don't need a pact, so their power comes purely from their skill, while a talented arcanist with a minor demon will never reach the heights of his or her ability without seeking a pact with a better demon."

Koshmarnyk arched an eyebrow. "So having a pact with Veranesh...?"

"Yes, it's every arcanist's dream come true," she replied. "Except that most would fear entering a pact with a demon of his stature. They're powerful beings, and one can never know what they really intend. It took me weeks before I trusted Veranesh, and I still can't help worrying a bit about what happens once he's free."

"You'll be remembered as the arcanist who brought the high mages down."

She couldn't help smiling. Not only was Koshmarnyk not bothered with her pact or demon, but he seemed to have confidence in her abilities, and with Veelk away, she appreciated that bit of comfort. But then, as she looked at the horizon, her calm waned. In the distance, beyond the hills and forests, the challenge awaited her. *Once I get the stones blended, and we figure out the circle, there'll be little left to do.* A colder gust of wind made her shiver, and she rubbed her arms, but the thought of confronting the high mages, even as indirectly as it was through freeing a demon, sent another jolt down her spine. *Is one ever ready for something like that?*

Koshmarnyk stood beside her, and he would probably offer enough reassurances to chase doubts away, but she didn't dare to ask the question out loud.

~

THE MORNING'S crisp air prickled Kamira's skin as she drew an elaborate circle outside the cave. The ground resisted, and the lines were far from perfect, adding frustration to her anxiety. Veranesh hovered in the nightfly's body, but spoke little, letting her work. With weeks spent in the cave, they'd had enough time discussing the plan while they worked on the circle, so all there was left was to test it.

"Can you control the demonling once I summon it?" she asked. "I saw Uganel doing it."

"Uganel was here, in this world, in flesh, and unrestricted," Veranesh replied. "But I should be able to manage one long enough."

She sighed. Recreating the ritual from centuries ago had proven more of a challenge than expected, and her lack of knowledge brought a whole new array of emotions. The thought that she was about to attempt a spell designed for several high mages with nothing but the meager help of a demon-controlled nightfly made her blood run cold. Even if she wasn't about to trap an actual higher demon, settling on a demonling instead, there were still so many ways an attempt could go wrong.

She moved to the other circle, the one she'd prepared for herself. There was an irony in an arcanist recreating the spell that pushed her arts into obscurity and elevated the ones she hoped to bring down. Even with Master Tijhran's detailed notes and her own guesses as to what happened during the Cataclysm, she still didn't fully understand how the circle worked.

"Begin when ready," Veranesh said.

His voice forced her to focus, and she summoned a demonling into the other circle. At least this part she'd had a chance to practice before, though the memory of saving the children of the Devanshari wasn't what she needed now.

The creature, resembling a winged, disfigured opossum, stared at her, and its claws scratched the ground, but it didn't move. *By the pact, these things are ugly.*

She inhaled sharply at her control over the demonling slipping away, but then Veranesh said, "I have it."

"Now the harder part." Without knowing what words the high mages might have used for such an elaborate spell, all Kamira could do was to channel the energy and hope the markings on the circle would do the rest. At the same time, if all their power indeed came from Veranesh, their chants would result in hardly anything, let alone trapping a powerful demon. She sneered at a new thought. She wouldn't put it past the first high mages to have made pacts with their demon allies to ensure the spell's success until they could draw power from their prisoner.

Energy condensed around the demonling, and Kamira constructed a barrier anchored within the circle. Several symbols flashed in response, and the tug of power made her fight for balance, but the magic solidified into a crystal-like growth trapping the creature inside. Regardless of the cool air, droplets of sweat trickled down Kamira's face.

"That was quick," she said with surprise.

"It's a small asayalari. And it didn't fight back."

"What did you do back then? What caused the Cataclysm?"

She could almost hear him smile, as if he'd expected her questions. "I destroyed three demons that had a pact at the time and channeled the energy through their pactees into this world." His voice carried no emotion. "But it didn't break the spell woven around me, as it turned out it was cast in another place."

Silent and grim, she stared off into the distance. The world still suffered the consequences of what Veranesh had done. The chronicles mentioned the demise of the arcanists present that day in the High Towers, and the destruction of the vast lands that followed. *All that death caused by demons' and high mages' greed.* Her imagination painted the picture of Veranesh entering the human world for the first time, invited and welcomed, and finding himself in a trap instead. She could only imagine the shock, betrayal, and maybe even panic he must have experienced, but she knew better than to ask such question. Besides, she still related to the survival instinct that pushed him to resist regardless of the consequences. She smiled, recalling their first conversation. They indeed were somewhat alike.

The nightfly flew over to her face but said nothing more, waiting.

She finally looked at it. "You destroyed the demons using their connection with their pactees? Can other yalari do that too?"

"It's unlikely," Veranesh replied. "Most have too little understanding of what pacts really are, and the few who might know enough lack the means and motivation to do what I did."

"Sometimes I wonder if you're really as powerful as you claim you are."

Veranesh laughed. "Yalari suffer the same pride humans do. But if I wasn't powerful, I'd have been destroyed, not trapped. And a bunch of yalari wouldn't be shivering at the mere thought that you might set me free." Cruelty rang in his last words, as if he was enjoying the prospect of revenge.

"Speaking of which," she replied before the uneasy feeling that his voice had woken up took hold of her. After experiencing Uganel's torture and destruction, she had a good idea of how cruel Veranesh could become in his pursuit of revenge. "We should get back to the task at hand.

I want that thing out of my sight." She pointed at the demonling still motionless within the crystal. Only its eyes shone with immense hate, as if the semi-sentient creature was preparing to retaliate.

"Begin, then."

She fixed her eyes on the crystal, and while she channeled the energy toward it, her own circle activated. She increased the flow steadily, testing both effects and her own abilities. Even if there was no need to use it all, Veranesh's magic was at her disposal, and the feeling of power that accompanied it was almost overwhelming. With that sensation, she could understand why so many arcanists fell prey to demons' schemes. The promise of such resources could drive one mad with greed.

The energy flowed, and at the first crack of the demonling's prison, she let out a triumphant shout. Her voice drowned in Veranesh's sudden shriek, and the nightfly spiraled down. Kamira took control over the creature and called it back to her wrist. Her eyes blurred when the nightfly's vision overlapped what she saw with her own eyes.

The crystal crumbled and the accumulated energy dispersed in a sudden outburst. The wave of power threw Kamira into the mountainside behind her, leaving her breathless at the impact. Her head hit the rock, and she collapsed, half dazed, but stared at the broken crystal with satisfaction. And then her eyes met those of the demonling. The creature stretched its body with curiosity, as if testing its boundaries of freedom. Even with her head spinning, it became clear to Kamira that Veranesh no longer controlled it.

As if responding to her thoughts, the demonling leapt. Instinctually reacting, Kamira released the energy burst in an uncontrolled stream, hoping it would be enough. At the same time, a blurry figure ripped into the creature, and her magic caught them both. Koshmarnyk tumbled to the ground, wrestling with the demonling. The sound of cracking bones made her cringe, but it was her magic coiling and sizzling around the adept that caught her attention. He must have put protective stones in his body, though more crude in their working than Veelk's intricate scars.

He stood up, while the creature twitched on the ground until it curled and froze. "Experiment gone wrong?"

She stretched carefully, checking for injuries. "Just... some unexpected results." She didn't bother with a remark about getting in the way of an arcanist's magic. He must have been confident in his stones to protect him.

"Maybe you should wake me up next time you plan something like that. When I heard the scream, I reacted instinctively, but it seems you had things under control." He glanced at the stone above his wrist pulsating with the magic it absorbed. "That was somewhat painful."

She chuckled. "I expected a lecture about being careless and putting myself in danger. Veelk wouldn't let it slide."

He massaged his forearm with a slight cringe, and even at this distance, Kamira sensed energy spreading through his body. His stones might have protected him against magic, but unlike Veelk's scars, they didn't make him invulnerable to it. "One would think that for someone who tries to pay a debt of life, he'd be wishing you constantly in danger," he said.

His good mood was infectious. "I think he doesn't want to pay his debt, because he'd have to search for a new purpose in life."

Koshmarnyk smiled and looked at the dead demonling. "I better get rid of it before it starts to stink."

"I'll do it." She walked over, her moves stiff with promises of bruises, and let the flames envelop the creature's carcass. The odor of burned flesh forced her to press her sleeve against her mouth, but she maintained the spell until the demonling turned into heap of ash.

"So, did you make any progress?" Koshmarnyk asked.

"I think so," she replied. The memory of the magical disruption at the end of the spell came back to her, and she woke up the nightfly again. It uncoiled and hovered in front of her, obedient to her will, but the demon didn't take control as expected. "Veranesh?"

No response came, and Kamira gave Koshmarnyk a worried glance. She waited a little longer before recalling the nightfly to her wrist. She'd rather keep it awake, but controlling it would quickly become cumbersome if she was to do other things as well.

"Whatever made a demon scream like that had to be serious," Koshmarnyk remarked.

Kamira shivered, remembering the last time she'd heard a demon shrieking. But she still had her magic, so Veranesh had to be alive. As the sunrise brightened the treetops, she couldn't help reminiscing about the violent magical outcome of Uganel's death. If something similar happened to Veranesh, the whole world would know.

Koshmarnyk lifted his hand as if ready to comfort her, but he never made the move. "Let's get some food," he said. "Let the demon do whatever he's doing. He'll be back sooner than you think."

Kamira nodded, though she couldn't muster a smile. She broke the crystal prison, but the feeling of triumph faded with Veranesh's lack of response. *Something must have gone wrong.*

~

KAMIRA GAVE up on another attempt to communicate with Veranesh and looked at the notes instead, even though with each passing day since their experiment, doubts and fears had settled deep within her thoughts. The lumisphere filled the cave with bright light, but they'd still set up a small fire. A chunk of meat roasted over its flames. Koshmarnyk's hunting venture into the woods had been an unnecessary risk, but the smell of fresh meat filling her nostrils argued otherwise. After weeks of eating grains and dried meat, she longed for some real food. Yet even a feast like they were preparing couldn't draw her away from grimmer thoughts for long. She stared at the pages covered with symbols and searched for the mistake within.

Koshmarnyk sat nearby, sharpening his knife and checking the blade on his skin.

The knife reminded Kamira of how he was ready to use it against her, and she tasted the bitterness of regret in her mouth. Over the weeks spent together, they might have been amiable, and he was always courteous and considerate, but she would be a fool to hope that the adept had any warmer feelings for her. Yet, with the seeming openness their conversations carried, she could at least ask. "You still don't fully trust me, do you?"

"Why do you say that?"

"The knife." She pointed at it. Even back when Veranesh guarded their sleep, he had kept it close. "And you seem to watch me often."

A confident smile stretched his lips. "I watch because you're a fine-looking woman," he replied. "One who's neither chained to a wall nor Cahala."

Her eyes widened at such blunt honesty, and her heart

skipped a beat. Koshmarnyk was the first man in a long time except Veelk who didn't seem bothered by her profession. With his forthright reply, she couldn't help the curiosity and attraction, wondering whether he'd be interested in something more.

"And the knife..." He glanced at the blade. "If you're still set on having the stones blended with you, it'll have to be sharp. Speaking of trust... Do *you* trust me enough to let me put a blade to your body again?"

Kamira bit her lip. She trusted him enough to not worry that one night he'd attempt to murder her, but at the memory of the last time he'd held that knife to her... "Veelk trusts you," she muttered under his insistent gaze.

"It's not Veelk who's getting the stones." He put his knife away and moved closer. "But I understand. Let's see if I can put some of your concerns to rest. Tell me more of why you need them."

She didn't hesitate. Even though Koshmarnyk had already agreed to help her, they'd never really talked about what was going to happen. With Veelk being secretive about his tribe's ways, she had little idea of what the blending looked like. "I'll need them to channel a lot of energy. A lot more than my body can endure on its own." She hushed the tiny voice whispering that, after the recent fiasco, she couldn't be sure what she would need.

"Arms should be enough, then," Koshmarnyk said. "Unless you want them all over, just like Veelk."

She shook her head. "The less the better. I need to conceal their real purpose. If anyone asks about the scars, I'll say Veelk's tribe tried to help me and failed. No one will know you did it."

Koshmarnyk took the meat off the fire, placed it on wooden plates, and passed one to Kamira. "I can copy the markings close enough, but it means the powdered stones will blend with you forever. And the scars will stay as well."

She picked at the meat, distracted by their conversation. "I have little choice, but arcanists can have scars. I already have more than I care to count." The newest addition on her leg still reminded her of the fight with Uganel, along with heightened soreness when she strained her muscles too much.

Koshmarnyk leaned closer, and for a heartbeat she thought he'd ask where those scars were, but instead he held her wrist and lifted her arm.

"The powder will go here, on the top side." He traced his finger along her skin, and she drew a deep breath, as his touch proved more pleasant than expected. "Your skin is too thin on the inner side, and the veins are too close." He moved behind her back, and his breath brushed Kamira's neck. "If you're fine with it, I'd go as high as your shoulder." His finger followed the trail set by the words. "And onto the shoulder blades, but far enough from the spine. This should help you control your limbs while the energy flows."

"Why not the spine, then?" Her attention was split between the conversation and his presence behind her.

"I'd have to go all the way along your back. Otherwise, a sudden tug might snap it." Koshmarnyk's fingers moved slowly down her spine with enough pressure for Kamira to feel his touch through her clothes. "And then it would be wise to do similar with your neck."

When his lips traveled along her neckline, Kamira twitched in surprise. It seemed he wasn't a man who wasted opportunities.

"Should I stop?" Koshmarnyk asked, his mouth by her ear and his breath tickling her skin. The tone of his voice made it clear he was ready to continue his... demonstration. "Or do you still have some concerns I could help with?"

She hesitated only a moment, as her heartbeat had already decided. The actual questions could wait a little longer. "Does it involve letting me have a look at the stones you have?"

"All of them." Koshmarnyk pulled her closer and kissed her neck again.

13

P elina ensured the storage room's door was closed before she ventured between the crates and baskets creating a maze within its walls. Dust filled her nostrils as she brushed against the wood to find her way in the darkness. She kept the candle unlit, as the fire's flickering could draw the attention of servants or guards to the seemingly unoccupied room, and only when she reached the far corner of the narrow room did a spark of flame by her will jump to the wick, offering meager light.

Once settled, she took out two sheets of paper. The first one contained a note written in a steady hand—unsigned, but she had no doubt who'd written it. *I'll still meet you when the time comes, but in the meantime, I need you to do something for me.* She read it once more, even though the letters had already sunken into her memory. The instruction said nothing about secrecy, but it didn't have to. Doing an expelled student's bidding openly was asking for trouble, and whatever Kamira had in mind, it surely wouldn't please the archmages.

That thought brought Pelina to focus on the second sheet again. It contained a detailed description of a ritual and a circle for Pelina to copy. At the very bottom, several words were listed, and Kamira had advised to try one first, and if the ritual failed, repeat with another one. No explanation of its purpose or effects followed. Pelina stared at the text, speculating all the possible outcomes, but the markings on the circle and the words of the spell remained foreign to her. It looked every bit like she would expect an arcanist ritual to look, but they required a pact... Once more she pondered a visit to the library, but if someone noticed she'd taken interest in demonology all of a sudden, questions would follow, and Kamira was adamant that Pelina was not to draw attention to herself.

Staring at the parchment any longer would bring no more answers than it did when she first read it, so Pelina sighed, faced with a choice. Either she trusted the arcanist or put both notes to the candle's flame, pretending she had never gotten them.

Curiosity pushed her past her doubts. If she proceeded, she'd have answers soon enough. The piece of coal in her hand made lines across the floor as Pelina copied the circle drawn on the paper, and only a voice of reason whispered that discovering the ritual's outcome could be the last thing she ever learned.

The circle's preparation took longer than Pelina had thought, and the result hurt her sense of accuracy. She scrutinized the most crooked line and corrected it several times until satisfied. With little else for an excuse, she recalled the memorized words and, giving a final sigh, let them flow. Her voice, no louder than a whisper, wavered at times, but she didn't stop the incantation.

The high mages' training didn't make them sensitive to energies around, so her eyes snapped open when magic condensed around her in ways she'd never felt. She allowed herself a moment of wonder, though no visible outcome accompanied the phenomenon, and then she took another breath. Before she could continue with the incantation, a shuffling sound reached her ears and made her freeze stiff.

"This isn't something I expected upon entering." First Archmage Irtan stepped into the narrow ring of the candle's light. "I don't suppose it's a part of your official schooling?"

Pelina stared at the archmage, and all the thoughts hid away in the corner of her mind like a bunch of scared children. No answer seemed good enough to save her, and pretending she was performing the ritual of her own accord seemed the best option, but the note from Kamira lay beside her, a silent witness of the lie to be told. Irtan would likely seize it, and destroying it meant admitting she had something to hide.

He studied the circle with a meticulousness of someone knowledgeable in the matter, and his amused expression never waned. "I think I know that ritual. It's one of those better not interrupted, so by all means, continue." His tone was ever so slightly tainted with sarcasm. "We don't want some side effects to lure more onlookers, do we now?"

Her shoulders slumped with the burden of the inevitable. Irtan was playing a game, but she remained at his mercy. At least it seemed that he wanted to keep it quiet. Curiosity of his motives overshadowed her fear for a moment, but wherever the archmage's game led to, whatever agreement was to be made between them, it would come after she finished the ritual. At least she knew now that it wasn't something that would kill her in some spectacular way... Or maybe it was? The archmage, after all, looked amused.

Pelina let the spell flow again, her voice shaking more than before, but she finished the ritual. When she spoke the last word, the energy thickened in front of her into a mist and took a manlike shape. As his features became clear, Pelina gasped at the feathered eyebrows and long, crooked nose that made her think of a beak. And the small but strong-looking wings at the creature's back left no doubt what he was. Only the archmage's composure prevented her from scampering away.

The demon stared back with matching curiosity. She didn't expect any conversation, but then he suddenly said, "I accept the pact."

She had no words to reply, and her heartbeat drummed in her ears for a last moment.

The demon turned to Irtan standing off to the side, still smiling. "Back in the past, one ensured at least some training before allowing their student to summon for a pact," the creature said.

"Back in the past, many things were different," Irtan replied, unmoved. "You can't expect much nowadays."

The demon nodded. "But I do expect you to train her, so that she brings no shame to the pact she made." He looked at Pelina again. "And I expect next time we speak, you'll be truly worthy of my time," he said, and then disappeared.

The magic tingled Pelina's skin when it dispersed. She blinked, all of a sudden having gained a new sense, which made her aware of the magic's flow, and the High Towers were full of it. When she focused, she found a link leading to a distant place, and to the demon who'd just spoken to her. She sat motionless in the middle of the circle, letting the truth and accompanying sensation set in.

She'd become a demonologist.

For some reason, the demon had not only accepted the pact, but also believed Archmage Irtan to be her teacher.

Irtan moved and picked up the pieces of paper before she could dispose of them. "Interesting note. Unsigned, but I'm sure you know who sent it."

Pelina's lips trembled when she looked at him, and the first archmage's face lost the softness of an amused man.

"We can do it two ways." No threat echoed in his voice, but it carried the gravity of the situation clear enough. "You can come to my chambers and tell me everything you know. In exchange, I won't notify the others of what transpired here, and I'll offer some knowledge on how to benefit from the pact you've made." He paused, as if letting the words sink in. "Or you can choose to keep the truth from me and answer the other archmages' questions. I can assure you they won't be as forgiving."

Pelina hesitated. Refusing Irtan meant she'd be interrogated and expelled, and the archmages would likely use any means necessary to make her speak. That wasn't a choice.

"I'll tell you everything." One chance encounter not only had rendered her useless to Kamira, but also put the arcanist in danger. As she gathered herself up from the floor, she took time deciding how much she could tell Irtan and at the same time convince him she had divulged everything. She had to reveal the true events leading to her regained freedom, but at least she could pretend she didn't know Kamira's name. Or she could tell the archmage it was a man that struck a deal with her.

If the archmage noticed her inner struggle, he didn't show it. Instead, he pointed at the crate. "Take some items from here. It'll make it look like you're doing a chore for me."

She picked up a basket and filled it with various fabrics while Irtan waited. The smile of amusement returned to his face, and she thought that no matter what game the archmage played, taking chances with him was a better choice than putting herself at the others' mercy.

Irtan put out the candle and summoned a lumisphere instead, the words of his spell soft and quick. She followed him, but before he opened the door, he spun in place and caged her with his sharp glare.

"And let's make one thing clear before we start," he said. "You'll keep Kamira unaware of our agreement."

The name he mentioned must have been nothing more than a lucky guess, but he caught her unprepared, and her own face betrayed her before she could control her response. Tears filled her eyes, and Pelina bent her head low to conceal a bitter grimace. She hadn't even joined his game yet, and the archmage had already outsmarted her.

LOKTRA STEPPED into Yoreus's chamber, making an effort to conceal her curiosity. With how the second archmage perceived her, the invitation must have had nothing to do with discussing theories of magic. He loathed her almost as much as he did Irtan, but he had significantly less respect for her insights and studies. Yet the second archmage wanted to talk, and Loktra was not a fool to refuse. Playing politics and maintaining her position in the High Tower meant that, on occasion, she had to suffer a conversation with him.

"Come in," Yoreus said. "I hope I didn't pull you away from anything important."

Loktra could swear there was a hint of sarcasm in his tone, but the other archmage's face revealed nothing except for courtesy. She sat down, and Yoreus's daughter served wine and candied fruit.

"My research can wait, and I'm sure you wouldn't ask to meet if it wasn't important." Loktra forced a smile.

Yoreus gestured Atissa away, and she left instantly. Loktra had to admit that Yoreus had trained his offspring well, though the gossip of Atissa being spoiled to the limits also reached her ears. In the end, though, Atissa's whims or how she treated others mattered little if she had enough wit to always obey her father.

"It's more to discuss recent events than share new information," Yoreus said. "With Irtan's approach to matters, my hands are tied."

Loktra arched her eyebrows in polite interest. Undoubtedly, the other archmage was speaking of the secret meeting with the demon, the mysterious eruption of magic in the desert, and Veranesh's prison trembling, but she wouldn't deny herself the pleasure of forcing his hand. If Yoreus wanted her support, he could at least sweat a little for it.

"How so?" She feigned surprise and lifted her cup to her mouth. The wine tasted good, and if nothing else came from the meeting, she could at least indulge herself. It seemed that either Yoreus had access to more coin than she did, or his suppliers were superior to hers.

"The first archmage is getting old, and his actions are those of an old man," Yoreus said, keeping a neutral tone. "Young men don't fear what's unknown, and they're ready to make decisions that require courage while elders cling to what's known and become defensive. Irtan's leadership brought us prosperity and stability, but it means his time as the first archmage lacked real dangers and challenges. And now that they have come, he doesn't know how to proceed."

She almost burst out laughing when the meaning of his words dawned on her. "You want to replace him." She didn't bother pointing out that Irtan was only two decades older than Yoreus, and that the second archmage himself could hardly be considered young with over half a century weighing on his shoulders.

"I want to ensure the Towers survive," he continued. "With Irtan's indecisiveness, we risk being outrun in the race for power and control, be it by our dear 'allies' or the ones who seek to free..." He stopped abruptly and glanced at the door that must lead to his daughter's room. "To free what we cannot allow to be freed."

It didn't escape Loktra that Yoreus didn't trust his own daughter with the secrets of high magic, but at the same time, it was reasonable. A mind of a feeble young woman could break under such revelation and cause a lot of trouble. Loktra herself shivered every time Veranesh's name was brought into a conversation, even as indirectly as the second archmage did it, reminding her of the burden she had to carry, of the high mages' most guarded secret. The image of Irtan revealing the truth about the demon still haunted her. Back then, Loktra didn't expect advancing from the fourth to the third archmage's position would be anything more than a formal change. She took a deep breath. If they removed Irtan, they'd have to deal with the consequences.

"I'd agree that in light of current events, Irtan doesn't seem the best leader," she chose her words with caution. Refraining from clear declarations and resorting to vague statements had served her well in the past. "But forcing him to step down would mean changes in the Towers' structure. Kerl would take the third's place." She was already suffering because of the fourth archmage's habits, forced to take on an additional student. That Pelina girl might be bright enough, but teaching was always a hassle rarely worth the time invested. If anything, it led to creating another potential rival rather than a useful lackey, because ambitious students were eager and compliant only for as long as they had to be.

"I thought about it," Yoreus replied without concern. "If we decide to act, I'll visit the fourth archmage myself and make him aware that if he doesn't sober up, he'll be stripped of his position and privileges. If he's not willing to work with us, I'm sure Varessa will."

Loktra grimaced at the mention of the fifth archmage. The woman was righteous and always following rules to the letter, but every bit of a great mage, and she probably deserved the title more than Kerl. At the same time, Loktra couldn't even begin to imagine how Varessa would react to the truth about high magic and what she would do. Elevating her to the position of the third archmage could bring even more trouble than they already had. At least maybe the threat of Varessa taking his place would force Kerl to finally become a real archmage.

"The plan sounds reasonable," Loktra said under Yoreus's insistent gaze. "If Irtan sees us both support you, he'll have no choice but to step down."

Yoreus's smile stretched. "I'm glad we see eye to eye on that matter. I'll arrange everything, and we could meet with Irtan tomorrow. The sooner we put things in motion, the sooner we'll be able to focus all of our resources on matters that threaten the Towers."

And the sooner you'll brandish your new title. Loktra kept the comment to herself and offered another smile. If Irtan refused to step down, the situation could end with blood, which meant either way she'd receive the second archmage's title. As she shook Yoreus's hand, exchanging pleasantries and goodbyes, another thought crossed her mind. The two archmages could also kill each other during the fight for power, leaving the leader's position vacant. When she closed the door behind her, a cold shiver went down her spine. Of course, who wouldn't want the first archmage's title? But in troubled times, such a burden was too much for Loktra's liking. The second's position provided nearly as many opportunities and posed much fewer dangers. For her own sake, she hoped Irtan would step down and give Yoreus what he wanted.

With second thoughts plaguing her, Loktra was ready to knock on Yoreus's door again, but pride and fear pulled her away. They'd made an agreement, and trying to dissolve it mere moments later would damage her image and paint her as the coward she didn't want to be. And she knew Yoreus well enough to have no doubts that he would never let her forget. Besides, many of the second archmage's opponents had suffered mysterious "accidents" in the past, and that ultimately made her withdrawal out of the question. As she walked back to her chambers, she regretted not asking for time to think. Swept by Yoreus's daring plan and blinded by the prospect of advancement, she had broken her own rule of keeping her responses vague enough to avoid commitment. And the payment for that would be doubts, destined to haunt her until the confrontation with Irtan.

YOREUS HAD trouble concealing his excitement as he walked into Irtan's chamber, but made an effort to act as casually as always. Behind him, Loktra fidgeted as sweat gathered on her forehead. Sometimes he couldn't help wondering how a woman like her could have made it to the rank of the third archmage with her constant lack of firm opinions and reluctance to act. At the same time, because of that, she had outlasted several other archmages who'd chosen the wrong side in the subtle political struggles in the Towers, and here she was, with the title of the third archmage secured. At least if Yoreus got what he wanted, she'd be easy to manipulate and control, and would likely support him out of the desire to avoid confrontations.

The first archmage poured three cups and indicated the chairs. "Have you learned anything new?"

Yoreus shook his head. "We're here to discuss another matter."

Irtan's eyes narrowed, and his face lost much of its jovial friendliness. The subtle aura of authority enveloped the old man and reminded Yoreus that one didn't become an archmage only through politics.

"I see." Irtan put the bottle away and approached. "One that keeps you from taking a seat."

A shade of doubt clouded Yoreus's confidence, but he reeled it back in an instant. *Looks like the old man still knows how to play the game.* He hesitated. He could sit down and discuss any trivial matter regarding governing of the High Towers, but Irtan had enough experience to guess the confrontation was coming. *I've waited long enough, and I won't be able to catch him any more unprepared than he is now.*

"We think it's time you stepped down from your position, first archmage." Yoreus put all his effort into making his own voice confident. Until he'd walked into the chamber, victory seemed inevitable, but confronted with Irtan's stern face, his resolve wavered. "You've become feeble and detached from current events. In turbulent times, the Towers need strong leadership, decisive and ready to act."

"It isn't time to ponder every possibility or remain defensive, allowing the demons to gain the upper hand," Loktra chimed in, repeating the very words Yoreus had told her earlier. At least the nervousness wavering in her words made the remark sound somewhat genuine rather than a rehearsed slogan.

Irtan smiled. "I see." He walked over to the table, picked up a cup, and took a nonchalant sip. "I understand you're ready to challenge me, then?"

Yoreus's thoughts raced. Irtan's response was unexpected and required consideration. It could only be a desperate attempt to discourage him, but Yoreus couldn't discard the possibility that the first archmage's old body maintained enough skill to pose a threat. "I have Loktra's and Kerl's support, and I'm sure others will see reason in it too. You can't take us all."

Irtan nodded, but the smile never left his face. "No, I can't. But I'm sure Fifth Archmage Varessa will be wise enough to avoid a fight she might not win, especially with the prospect of being promoted to the second archmage when I'm done with you two and Kerl."

Yoreus kept his face straight, even though Irtan's voice carried every bit of the gruesome promise. With the archmage being a lifelong title, mages had only three ways of climbing the ladder: when an archmage died, stepped down—often through other archmages deeming him or her unsuitable for real or made-up transgressions—or through a challenge, and Irtan seemed ready to fight for his position. Yoreus clenched his teeth and fought to keep his hands relaxed. *I'd rather take the challenge than back away now.*

Irtan stared at Yoreus as if he knew every thought and every emotion going through the second archmage's mind.

"I think this concludes the power demonstrations," Irtan said. "Now Loktra will leave, and the two of us will discuss the matter until we find a satisfactory solution. Unless you prefer to follow through with the challenge, entertaining all the mages and students in the Towers with our duel?"

Yoreus exhaled, then looked at Loktra. "Let's give the first archmage a chance to retire on his terms."

The third archmage nodded, and as she mumbled courteous apologies and farewells, relief was clear on her plump face. Yoreus withheld a cringe, even though her behavior didn't come as a surprise. Yet the thought that she'd turn on him in an instant if the first archmage offered her a way out poisoned whatever satisfaction he might have had from Irtan's possible acquiescence.

"Now that the onlookers are gone, let's talk seriously," Irtan said as soon as the closing door announced Loktra's retreat. "I've been waiting for your move for quite some time now."

Irtan indicated chairs again. Yoreus swallowed his pride and took a seat. This might not be how he'd envisioned his ascent, but as long as he got what he wanted, he could later bury this memory forever.

"That was quite skillful play on your part," Yoreus said. "But it makes me wonder why we're talking now."

The first archmage took a sip of wine. "I've been watching you. You're not only ambitious but also quite ruthless in your pursuits. I could force that challenge to take place, but it's possible that we'd kill each other. I think such an outcome is unappealing to both of us. Or I could let myself be satisfied with putting you in your place now." He looked Yoreus in the eye. "But we both know I'm getting older, and you'll get me one day by poison or some other underhanded means."

Yoreus relaxed and leaned back in his chair. "So what do you propose?" With the promise of his own desires fulfilled, he could be generous, as long as Irtan stayed reasonable with his demands.

"I'll announce that, due to my old age, I'm passing my responsibilities onto you, along with the first archmage's title."

Yoreus arched his eyebrows, as such a declaration had to be only a prelude to a list of conditions.

"I'll remain in the Towers, though," Irtan continued, "with the title of an honorary archmage given in similar circumstances. I'll teach the students I choose, and I'll take part in the discussions you, Loktra, and Kerl will be having on certain events. The final decisions will be yours, of course, but I won't be kept in the dark and taken by surprise if something was to... transpire. I also have no desire to move from my chambers."

Yoreus nodded. Irtan's terms seemed almost too reasonable, and even though they fitted well into the tale of resigning due to old age, the second archmage couldn't resist suspecting ulterior motives. Despite the declaration, Irtan would likely undermine his authority whenever possible, but with the first's title to his name, Yoreus would have the upper hand, including removing Irtan from the picture entirely. At the same time, since Irtan mentioned poison, he must be aware what Yoreus did with inconvenient rivals, so maybe he indeed was looking to unload the burden of leadership while keeping the privileges he cared about.

"Is that all?" Yoreus asked.

Irtan was about to nod, but then lifted his hand. "Actually, no. That woman who studied under Kerl, the one Loktra took in. Have her assigned to me."

That request made Yoreus narrow his eyes. "You haven't been interested in women for quite a while. Why the sudden change?"

To his surprise, Irtan shamelessly grinned. "Being a first archmage doesn't leave much time for pleasures. With you taking over, I plan on enjoying life a little bit."

Yoreus burst out laughing. *I didn't know the old man had it in him.* The thought of Irtan being no more than a man with all the usual mundane urges and desires brought sufficient satisfaction. "That can be arranged too. If you get bored with her, I'll be sure to send another one."

"Yes, that'd be good." Irtan leaned back in his armchair. "I'll make an announcement tomorrow. Do act surprised and honored. Smug expressions are not suitable for first archmages."

Yoreus got up from his chair, hiding his reaction. This was the last time Irtan would use that condescending tone with him, so he could let it slide. "In the end, you played it well. Very well," he said as he walked to the door. As much as it stung to admit it, all that mattered was that he was about to become the most important man in the High Towers... even in all of Kaighal.

"I wouldn't be where I am if I didn't know the game better than anyone else," Irtan replied with his usual amusement.

As Yoreus left the chamber, the echo of Irtan's last words sowed seeds of uncertainty. Irtan's clear suggestion of having won their confrontation forced Yoreus into searching for what he might have missed. Then, as no answer presented itself, he shook his head.

He was just trying to get back at me... to have the last word. Admitting that he was too old to play the game was likely too much for Irtan's pride.

Yet, walking through the hall of the High Towers, Yoreus still cursed Irtan for having so skillfully planted the doubt in his mind. Its roots grew thicker regardless of what explanations and reasons Yoreus could conjure, and spoiled the taste of victory.

14

The night was Veelk's ally. Even if his tall, broad-shouldered body stood out as much as in the daytime, with the darkness promising more threat than safety, both honest people and ne'er-do-wells knew better than to bother a cloaked figure, so at least he had a chance of leaving Kaighal unnoticed as long as he kept to the back alleys. A grimace spoiled his face at the memory of the encounter earlier in the day. The scrawny little rat couldn't have been anyone important, but he must have known enough of Veelk if he'd decided to follow him. At least Veelk handled the matter before the informant slipped away, but there was always a possibility that someone else saw Veelk in the streets.

He shrugged that thought off. Until he walked into Yoreus or Ryell, neither would believe some opportunist spy, and once Kamira was back, she'd have scars to turn the lie— their trip far to the southwest—into truth. In the end, it wouldn't matter if either the archmage or the Devanshari man had their suspicions. They would be too busy realizing that Veranesh was a step away from freeing himself.

Veelk snorted at such a hopeful thought. For all he knew, he'd be back at the cave with Kamira and her demon still none the wiser on how to break the crystal prison.

Thinking of Kamira made Veelk pick up his pace. With all her magic and Koshmarnyk around, Veelk didn't have to worry about her much, but after years spent together, this journey was unpleasantly void of her caustic remarks, depriving him of the enjoyment in engaging in their usual banter. Having spent time traveling alone and with accidental companions, he appreciated one that, despite her frequent complaints, was neither a burden nor a nuisance to be around.

"I told you, look for someone else!"

A woman's words brought him back to reality, and he slowed his pace as he approached the alley's turn. The northern part of Kaighal was the poor district and home to many shady characters, so a distressed voice wasn't uncommon, but such a shout could just as likely be a ruse used by a pack of thugs waiting for naïve passersby.

"You don't get to change your mind in the middle of a job," a gruff man responded. "You got paid already."

"I got paid for what I brought you last time," the woman said. "And I don't work for you. Find someone else to risk their skin."

Veelk took a step back, caution winning over curiosity. Their argument wasn't his, and though he didn't mind helping, the less attention he drew, the better. After all, he wasn't supposed to be in Kaighal in the first place. And he wouldn't be, if only the alchemists and herbalists in the smaller towns were better stocked! But then, he also had to deliver Kamira's message to that rescued high mage, and even if he wouldn't be able to do it in person, he could at least ensure a reliable messenger to carry it. He scoffed.

With the decision long made, revisiting it would change nothing. It only brought distraction he didn't need.

The man and the woman still argued, but Veelk paid them attention no more. He did, though, hear the footsteps, and turned in time to see a man with a lantern emerging from an alley. The stranger wore simple trousers and a tunic, with a loose cloak over his shoulders, likely concealing more than one weapon. He stopped and gaped at Veelk, his face longer and longer as recognition flashed on it.

"All demons curse it!" He looked back into the alley. "She brought him here!"

That single remark pushed all Veelk's caution aside. If the man recognized him and somehow tied him to whoever the woman in the alley was, Veelk couldn't leave. He sneered. He couldn't let the other man leave either.

At least the thug had enough instinct to drop the lantern and dash back into the alley, but Veelk was already at him when the lantern hit the cobblestones, oil and the flame bursting as it shattered. Within the alley, another man stood close to a woman who wore a merchant's outfit, but they were far enough away for Veelk to ignore them in favor of his first target. Keshal's thin blade could imitate a dagger's thrust well enough, so he struck without hesitation, piercing the running man's back. As the victim gurgled his dying protest, the other man took a step forward, reaching for a club by his belt. A motion forever to be unfinished, as the woman slit his throat in one swift move.

Veelk eyed her with caution. The way she disposed of her quarry suggested she'd severed enough arteries to know where to strike. She didn't have an assassin's moves or eyes, so the killing must be but a side to her actual profession.

As he took a step forward, she took one back, spreading

her arms wide, as if she wanted to make sure he didn't take her as a threat.

"Thank you for your help with those two." Her voice was pleasant and sounded genuine enough. If she was playing, she knew how to make the role of a grateful victim convincing, but Veelk would have none of it.

"I don't know you," he replied. "But you know me." He couldn't be sure, of course, but the men had recognized him and thought he was with her. "I usually don't bother asking questions, so you have one go at explaining what happened."

To Veelk's surprise, she smiled and shook her head. Casually, she slid her knife back into the sheath. "I'm a spy."

He would not admit it, but she'd caught him by surprise. This must have been the first spy to be so open about her profession. Or it was a game as well. He almost smiled at the thought that spending so much time with Kamira had left him too suspicious of everyone and everything. His grumpy companion's unhealthy distrust was rubbing off on him, but this once, he wasn't about to discard it. "Hoping that a confession will save your life?"

She shrugged. "Can't hurt trying, can it? I saw your work earlier today, and you're not one to swallow lies like sweetbread." She huffed as she glanced at the dead body by her. "I figured if I wanted to live to spend coins, I better earn them in another way than spying on you. And this is what got me into this situation." She pointed at the dead. "It's just my cursed luck that you had run into us when I was trying to turn down the job."

"Aren't you too honest for a spy?"

She looked him straight in the eye. "You're too deadly to risk lying to."

He burst out laughing. "So what now? You expect me to

let you go?" The more he talked to her, the less he wanted to do the deed, but he needed more time to determine whether mercy would be his undoing.

A thought must have brought her amusement, because a smile flashed on her lips. "You could pay me to stay quiet... or to make sure that my patron hears the right information."

Veelk grinned. "I take it your earlier remark of my wits was an effort to dim it through faint praise?"

The mean glare she gave him reminded him of Kamira. "If I wasn't trustworthy, I wouldn't have stayed in the trade long enough."

It would be easiest to kill her and move on, but Veelk couldn't help appreciating her honesty. And in the end, he'd done the damage himself by simply arriving in Kaighal. No matter what precautions he took, two people had spotted him, and there could have been more. If the woman was as truthful as she claimed to be, she could ensure there was enough conflicting information circling to conceal the truth.

He eyed the two dead bodies. "So, who were they working for?"

"An archmage," she replied without hesitation. "Which one, I don't know, and if you're trying to stay out of sight, it would be unwise to try finding out."

Honest *and* smart—that was a rare combination, and he would welcome someone like that working for him. Inadvertently, an image of the young high mage from Cahala's den came to his mind. Kamira had taken a chance with her. Perhaps he should follow her steps. Besides, he was growing to like that little spy.

"What's your name?"

"Mizena." The way she was eyeing him made it clear she still expected a blow to come.

"Well, Mizena, you found yourself a new employer, then.

Take whatever money they had on them and use it to make sure... the archmage or anyone else interested knows that we've left Kaighal. If someone else has seen me today, spread some gossip. Maybe that we paid someone to make it look like we're still around." As he spoke, she kept nodding. "And I pay you when we get back... if I like your work."

"Fair enough," she replied. "If you need to find me, leave a message at the Old Maiden tavern in the port."

She squatted down by the body. The way she relieved the corpse of the purse and several valuable trinkets suggested she was not beyond stealing.

Veelk took a step back, and when she gave him as little as a glance, as if ensuring he wasn't going after her, he left the alley. Guard patrols were a rarity in the northern district, but with all the bad luck going around, he'd rather not risk one would stumble upon him in the same place as the bodies. He had no doubt that Mizena would disappear quickly as well, leaving the guards to believe the two unfortunate men had met particularly bloodthirsty thugs.

He stopped only for a moment, to clean the blood off his keshal. The city's tall walls were nearby, and as much as he hated the idea of climbing with his packs full, reason demanded he leave Kaighal immediately rather than at dawn, when the gates opened.

The sooner he left all that mess behind, the better.

HER BELONGINGS FIT into one basket, and Pelina carried it through the High Towers corridors led by a guard. Teachers and other students glanced at her, and whispers filled the air as she walked past. They tried to cover their jealousy with contempt, as if earning one's advancement by sleeping around—which they most assuredly believed she had—was a scandal in the High Towers. No one had ever had three mentors in such a short time, so the gossip would circle about them giving up on her, but such blabber would be meaningless. With each new teacher being a more powerful archmage, Pelina had no doubt that every single student would gladly swap places with her if they could.

She held off the bitter smile accompanying those thoughts, and kept a smug expression of satisfaction on her face to deceive everyone around. If only they knew what was really happening... Given a choice, she'd go back to Loktra in a heartbeat, not because she was a better teacher than Kerl or Irtan, but because she was too self-absorbed to pay close attention to her new apprentice. Pelina could play her as easily as she played Kerl, but Irtan was another matter. Sharp and suspicious, within a night he'd learned more than Pelina ever wanted to reveal.

The memories of their conversation came back to haunt her again, threatening the mask she had on. With no choice, she had to tell Irtan everything. To her surprise, the archmage took the news calmly. She expected questioning on Kamira's whereabouts or the arcanist's plans, but Irtan just nodded as if he'd expected the revelation. She still tried to understand why instead of exposing her, the archmage simply asked her to inform him of anything new regarding Kamira.

What game are you playing? The question returned time and time again, but when Pelina thought of Irtan stepping down and Yoreus's smug smile, she had to consider that Kamira could have been nothing more to Irtan than a way to debase a rival. It seemed unlikely that the old mage would risk the High Towers' future only to make sure Yoreus didn't win, but archmages' motives were rarely transparent. Either

Irtan didn't believe Kamira posed much threat, or something else was at play. If Pelina figured it out, maybe she could still help Kamira with a useful piece of information or a warning.

The long climb up the stairs led to Irtan's quarters, and as the guard left, she pushed the thoughts away and knocked.

"Come in," Irtan called.

The receiving chamber had four chairs and a small table, and Pelina admired lush tapestries on the walls. Tall windows let in the light, and as Irtan had claimed the highest of the towers for his quarters, the only thing behind those windows was blue sky. The view alone must be worth all the climbing, and she looked forward to having a peek or two when the archmage wasn't around.

The archmage pointed to the east window with a smile. "There's a balcony overlooking the city. But get settled first. Your room is small and a bit dusty, but you should be comfortable there."

He indicated the door to the left. The room, bigger than Pelina expected, was decorated with the same taste as the main chamber. Compared to the closet she had in Kerl's chambers, this one seemed worthy of an archmage's apprentice. Pelina's eyes widened at the sight of a wide bed, her own desk, a table with two cushioned chairs, and a massive chest in the corner, but it was the shelf filled with countless books that captured her interest.

"I prepared some reading for you." Irtan's voice sounded right by her ear, and Pelina almost jumped. The archmage moved like a ghost. "I'm guessing you didn't pay much attention during the arcane arts class. No one ever does."

"Arcane arts?" She looked at him in surprise.

A grimace was his first response. "I believe students call it 'demonology.' The fundamentals of your new path."

Pelina shivered. Part of her had hoped Irtan would demand the pact be severed, maybe even instruct her on how to do it, but instead he had surprised her again. The more she thought about it, the more convinced she became he had reasons that went beyond getting back at Archmage Yoreus. "You'll teach me?"

The chuckle he let out contrasted with his domineering pose. "Your demon surely expects me to do so, and I'd rather ensure no one discovers what you've become, so I'll instruct you how to hide it. The rest you'll learn from books and through practice."

"Why?" she asked. A high mage had no reason to help a demonologist—an arcanist—to become better. Even with as little attention as she had indeed paid during the obligatory lectures, she still knew that, centuries ago, high mages were the ones to clean up the mess the demonologists left the continent in.

"That, my dear student, you'll learn only when you prove worthy of such knowledge." Irtan smiled, and she thought of all the ways he could use her to his ends. "I expect you to be done with the list I left on your desk within the week. I also expect that you won't skip any of the regular lectures you're supposed to attend."

Pelina let out a sigh. Irtan might have other reasons for becoming her mentor, but nevertheless, he took teaching seriously. And with the amount of work to be done, she'd hardly have enough time to cause him trouble or collect information.

"There is a lock on your room's door," Irtan said as he walked away, "and you're free to make use of it. But to keep you out of the other archmages' reach, I suggested to Yoreus that my interest in you is not of the scholarly type but more... carnal. It would be good if you kept the tale alive even if it means gossiping about me."

He walked through the door on the opposite side of the main chamber—it must have been his bedroom—and left her alone.

Pelina put her belongings down on the bed and looked through the list Irtan had prepared, but her mind kept coming back to his words. To keep her out of the other archmages' reach... For some reason, he wanted to protect her and even teach her, or at least provide enough guidance to ensure she learned on her own. It didn't seem a plot to confuse her, but Pelina had learned that trusting archmages brought nothing good. He'd likely kept her away from others not out of care, but as a way to ensure he controlled the information she had on Kamira. She needed to find a way to outsmart him before he forced her to betray the arcanist and her companions.

With a sigh, she pulled out the first of the books on the list. Playing along required a lot of studying, but the thought of learning how to use her new power woke the excitement she'd forgotten a long time ago. The prospect of actually studying magic, even the one frowned upon, compensated for the concerns, and when she sat down to read, her mind focused on nothing but the text.

A WOODED path weaved between the trees and hid in the grass like a playful child, but Yoreus never lost his way. After two days of journeying with merchants, pretending to be a low-ranking high mage, he'd left the caravan claiming to have relatives in the nearby village, but as soon as the last wagon disappeared into the green and yellow blankets of leaves, he ventured into the forest. There were easier and faster ways to his destination, but taking known routes would mean meeting people, and Yoreus couldn't risk someone recognizing him.

The canopies shielded him from the sun's blaze, but even in their shade, the journey took its toll on him. Every muscle complained about the strain and reminded him of how little he'd traveled in the recent years. Too afraid to miss anything important in the High Towers, he'd rarely ventured far from Kaighal, focusing instead on politics and avoiding backstabbers who craved his position.

A courier brought news every month, so Yoreus had little desire to visit the mansion, as he called his old family home, but recent events had made him reconsider the journey. Within the two weeks of his ascension to the highest position among the archmages, he'd found no reasons for concerns, and Irtan behaved suspiciously senile, but Yoreus couldn't shake the doubt sprouted from their confrontation. The old mage must be plotting something, and his complacent act was nothing but a way to dull his opponents' awareness.

As Yoreus walked, his soft shoes, perfect for High Tower appearances and strolls through Kaighal, made him pay with every step. Every stone and twig dug into his feet like a toll to pay for his desire of discretion. Years earlier, he would have avoided making such a childish mistake and prepared better for the trip, but nowadays his mind was focused only on High Towers games. Besides, he reasoned, if he wanted to leave as he'd left, he couldn't have taken much time getting ready. An archmage wearing an outfit of a traveler was bound to draw attention, and the last thing Yoreus needed was someone following him. It was better if his fellow archmages believed he was still in Kaighal, perhaps in secret meetings with Gildya or preparing a complex scheme, even if it meant sore feet and ruined shoes.

His thoughts wandered toward what waited for him at the end of the path. It'd been a decade, maybe more... He could hardly recall whether he'd bothered with a visit since his father's death. Yoreus still cringed at the memory of the disappointment on the old man's face, as even with his last breath he scolded his only child, his only heir to the family's wealth, for choosing such an unsuitable path as that of a high mage. Even the archmage's title—the sixth or the fifth at the time, if he recalled correctly—couldn't have lifted his father's displeasure. And the birth of his granddaughter, a child of a woman of questionable reputation, was a reason to complain. Alone in the woods, Yoreus allowed himself a bitter smile, since because of his father's stubbornness, Atissa had never gotten to meet him or see the place that would be her inheritance one day.

The last stretch of the journey pushed him to the verge of giving up and spending the night in the woods, but the prospect of a warm bath to ease his sore feet and a decent meal made Yoreus continue the journey. The first archmage in the High Towers would not be beaten by a half a day of a hardly strenuous trek.

The trees became less dense. Overlooking a curve of the path, high upon a hill and surrounded by solid walls, stood a two-story building. Vines crawled among the stones, clinging to decorative reliefs and masking the old fortifications, and the tiled roof towered over them. Yoreus's family had acquired it nearly a century earlier. It had wasted away as its previous owners moved to Kaighal, and Yoreus couldn't blame them. Hardly anything happened in the quiet woods, with only few small villages nearby. Yet such a place was a perfect spot for a wealthy nobleman fleeing the tumultuous politics of the Western Kingdom. They meant to rebuild their power and return to reclaim their position, but they never did. The remote house, tranquil and safe, dulled their ambitions and desires, condemning the family's name to oblivion.

Yoreus grimaced, as even from the distance, the fog of stagnation seemed to linger over this old house, rivaled only by the ghost of his father's constant displeasure. Both reminded the archmage why he'd left.

A single guard stood posted by the cast-iron gate, though his posture and alertness left much to be desired. Only when Yoreus approached did the man stretch lazily to a mostly upright position and offer a lousy bow. The gate sang the years of neglect, or perhaps voiced a wordless complaint to its rightful owner never visiting. It was still more of a greeting than he got from the guard, and Yoreus walked the pebbled path to the building, where his butler already waited. The archmage couldn't resist the thought that the gate was left creaking to alert Dynar when guests were coming.

"My lord, we didn't expect your visit." Dynar bowed. He was a man in his fifth decade. His receding hair and the first wrinkles on his forehead and around lips betrayed his age, but his moves were confident and demeanor robust. "Were the reports not detailed enough?"

"They were fine." Yoreus entered, and his shadow slid across the floor while a maid dutifully lit the many lamps. Most of the upper corridor drowned in darkness, speaking of Dynar's thriftiness. With Yoreus's absence, the butler saw no reason to waste lamp oil for those rooms. "But there are things I need to look into personally."

"Of course."

The entrance hall was like Yoreus remembered: spacious enough to greet a few guests, but nothing like the reception area of the High Towers, vast and always bustling with high mages, students, servants, and visitors. With only a few people around, the whole place would seem as empty, but he noted with satisfaction no dust or other signs of neglect.

"Have supper prepared. No need for anything special. I'll be in my study." His body demanded a bath first, but he preferred to work while his mind was still sharp.

No words came, just another bow, and Dynar left Yoreus alone. Such a butler, quiet and resourceful, was a true treasure, and the archmage once more congratulated himself taking time to find an appropriate man in Kaighal. His father would not have approved, of course, but it hardly mattered when his ashes were already scattered to the wind.

With that thought, Yoreus ventured into the maze of rooms. Over the centuries, his family had made adjustments to the house's layout, which often resulted in odd corridors with too many corners and rooms without windows. The study at the back of the building looked as if he'd left it a few days ago. A book about high magic still lay open on his desk, and a bottle of wine with a clean glass waited for him —a testament to Dynar ensuring everything was always ready, even though the study's owner visited so rarely. Yoreus smiled, putting together words of praise for his servants, and reached behind the curtain to pull a hidden lever. With the quiet song of a well-oiled mechanism, the shelves parted to reveal a passage and stairs. A few words were enough to summon a lumisphere, and Yoreus descended into the darkness.

The underground workshop bore signs of dust that reassured him no one had entered since his last visit. The narrow tables by the wall still bore scarce tools and alchemical equipment he hadn't used since the rituals. His memory drifted to the time he'd spent there in the company of the best arcanists he could buy or lure, performing complicated spells and trying to marry two schools of magic. Yoreus had little interest in the superiority debates, and publicly loathing arcane arts was nothing more than a means to an end, so when he was allowed into the High Towers' biggest secret, he took it calmly. The revelations of what high magic had become after the Cataclysm didn't shake him at all. In the end, the first high mages craved power, and they took it, at the same time ensuring their rivals' fall. If anything, they should have been praised for not only what they did, but how they did it. As long as magic served his ambitions, where it came from was a secondary matter, but Veranesh being the weak link always worried him. Should he break free, or if someone altered his prison, all high mages could lose their power.

Yoreus smiled with satisfaction as he strode through the workshop. All but him.

Even with the partial knowledge Yoreus had at his disposal, the ritual proved successful. The partaking arcanists, of course, died soon enough to ensure the secret would remain unspoken. Yet the archmage couldn't help thinking of what he could have missed. He had hoped that Gayabal's journal would provide him with more insights into how Veranesh was captured, but in hindsight, sending Kamira out to the old Towers might have been a mistake. Back then, he considered having someone familiar with magic exploring the ruins beneficial, as she could recognize and bring back valuable items and books. Only later, when he remembered that Kamira had always been too inquisitive and defiant for her own good, did he consider the consequences. He gritted his teeth. She might have claimed that she had never reached the ruins, but she could have ventured inside and discovered secrets not meant for her... or anyone else, for that matter. Recent events, both demons' sudden interest in the stability of Veranesh's prison and the strange surge of magic in the desert, had made him believe Kamira was involved more than anyone suspected.

The lumisphere cast a long shadow on the empty floor as he left the worktables behind and approached three crystals grown into the floor. They were wide and reached all the way to the ceiling, as if threatening the integrity of the building. Inside them, demons wavered incoherently as their magic flowed to Yoreus, and he smiled. No matter the consequences of sending Kamira to the ruins instead of mindless henchmen, he wouldn't be unprepared. The demons' combined power couldn't match what he had at his disposal when he manipulated the energy coming from Veranesh, but it ensured Yoreus could still use magic should the worst come to pass.

He inspected the dazed creature. Perhaps the next time, he should bring Atissa along. His daughter might not have been appointed an archmage and was not permitted the secrets, but keeping her in the dark wouldn't help Yoreus's ambitions. She needed to know the stakes, and she needed to use magic in case Veranesh broke free. He hesitated at the thought. His absence from the Towers was only possible because he'd had Atissa see to some matters and watch the moves of other archmages. If he was to take her along, he'd be inviting a possibility of underhanded dealings during their absence. He doubted Irtan would reach for power again, but there were many ways to undermine Yoreus's authority. Besides, the magic he had secured through those minor demons might not be enough. Recalling the old texts and what they spoke of Veranesh's power, the archmage shivered at the thought the stolen energy would be insufficient for himself, should the confrontation come. And Atissa lacked both the experience and knowledge to be of use in battle. Instead of bringing her here, he should write instructions in case he got killed.

He froze, staring at one of the demons. Its birdlike features and hunched body made Yoreus think of a time when he saw vultures feasting on a traveler's corpse. The vision of a demon feeding on Yoreus's own corpse sent shivers down his body, and he retreated upstairs, away from the workshop's gloom.

The next day, he would work on reinforcing the circles making up the prison... At least, he could hope that his efforts would bring such a result. He cursed again at the thought that Gayabal's journal could have all the answers he needed so desperately, but even without certainty, Yoreus had to do something. The odds of Veranesh regaining his freedom remained low, but the archmage couldn't shake the feeling he'd missed something. Once more, his thoughts circled Kamira. He had no doubts that the arcanist had gained some knowledge, and frustration arose whenever he thought of all the failed attempts to make her speak. Perhaps he should have been more forthcoming with the other archmages and had Kamira brought to the Towers for questioning.

He shook his head. Back then it seemed better to let her believe she'd gotten away with her lie. No matter what secrets she might have learned, she was a scrapper greedy for coin, so the artifacts from the old Towers were bound to appear on the market. Yet none did. Yoreus had wasted enough coin for information to know she also hadn't sold anything to private collectors, so whatever her involvement was, it must have come from some other source. Perhaps that mage killer knew more than anyone would suspect from a savage like him. Ryell seemed very suspicious of that man, and supposedly, Kamira was under his influence. Yet Ryell had failed both in pulling her away from the mage killer and gaining any insights.

Yoreus grimaced. Mistakes, all the mistakes he'd made! With Ryell's failure to gain any deeper insights, it could be time for Yoreus to act where Irtan didn't. Using his position, he could order a closer investigation and force Kamira into a confession without revealing too much of his own involvement.

Dynar entered the study without a sound. "Supper is ready. Shall I have it served here?"

Yoreus shook his head. "No, I'll eat in the dining room. Make sure breakfast is ready at dawn. After that, I'll be busy all day." He hoped he wouldn't have to spend that much time on reinforcing the binding spells, but it was better than having to return here later or, worse, to learn one day that he couldn't rely on the power from his demonic prisoners. Afterward he could focus all his attention on the High Towers and ensure that neither other archmages nor the demons overseas threatened his position.

15

Kamira hesitated before waking up the nightfly. After countless failed attempts to reach out to Veranesh, her fear painted a picture of another journey into the desert to talk to the demon again. He had to be alive, since her magic flowed as smoothly as always, but without his guidance and insights, carrying out the plan would be difficult. If nothing else, she needed to know what went wrong before she made an actual attempt at freeing him.

Obedient to her will, the crystal creature rose into the air, but she sensed no demon's presence, and her vision blurred when she looked through the nightfly's eyes.

"Still nothing?" Koshmarnyk asked.

He stood by the entrance to the cave, and she took a moment to admire his sun-haloed silhouette. Thoughts of what his hands and lips were capable of pushed away the concerns, replacing them with much more pleasant memories. It could be so easy to forget about the demon and the archmages, and instead sail away to Juamha. The other continent might be scarred in many ways, just like Tyorane was, but a skilled adept and a powerful arcanist could easily earn their living, and Veelk would get his fair share of both fighting and women's company. She could live her whole life to the full and never think about the destruction her death would bring.

Koshmarnyk watched her with an arched eyebrow. He didn't push her to speak, but his expression made it clear he'd like to hear what thoughts wandered through her head. Yet she couldn't help scoffing at her own foolishness. As much as she enjoyed his company, to believe it was anything more than a pleasant pastime would be making a fool out of herself.

She shook her head. "Nothing." He didn't need to know the direction her mind had wandered to.

He took a step forward, expressing readiness to comfort her.

Kamira's welcoming smile froze on her lips when Veranesh took control of the nightfly. The creature hovered in front of her, beating its wings.

"What happened?" She didn't bother with small talk. "I couldn't reach you for days."

Koshmarnyk moved closer, looking curious but remaining silent.

"I had to recuperate." Veranesh's voice offered no hints to his situation. "And think. What of the crystal and the asayalari... the demonling?"

"The crystal broke, and the demonling survived," she replied.

"I see." A long pause followed, filled with the demon's satisfaction. "Nevertheless, the attempt was an utter failure and—"

"Why?!" The anxiety of the last days broke her self-control. "I managed to break the crystal! We only need to work on the details, and I can free you."

To her surprise, Veranesh expressed no ire at her interruption. "What happened when the crystal broke?" he asked when she paused to take a breath.

Kamira reined in her frustration at the unexpected question. "There was a wave of energy released." She paused when a sudden realization struck her. Veranesh was right to call their trial a failure. They'd trapped only a minor demonling, and the blast's power still sent her flying. "We'd cause another Cataclysm," she whispered.

"That's what I concluded."

The nightfly still hovered in front of her, so she looked at it intently. Veranesh had mentioned the time he'd taken to think, so she could only hope he had a solution in mind. The prospect of being stuck again made her fists curl. With all the preparations almost finished, and Koshmarnyk waiting to put the stones in her skin, they couldn't afford weeks if not months of searching for another way. At the same time, she had to appreciate the comfort of what she'd read between Veranesh's words: he was unwilling to sow destruction and would wait for another solution.

"At least our attempt helped me understand the nature of my prison," Veranesh said. "I have to commend the work of the high mages or the yalari who helped them. I also think I know what we need to break me free without devastating your world."

Koshmarnyk huffed. "Something tells me it's not going to be easy."

She couldn't resist smiling, as her own thoughts were going in that direction too. But in the end, freeing a higher demon from a centuries-old prison had to be difficult. If it wasn't, someone would have figured it out long before Kamira was born.

"You'll have to alter the circle in the High Towers," the

demon said, "and then you'll have to channel your energy there. I'd wager it means only one chance at it. It also isn't something to practice beforehand."

Kamira looked at the uneven surface of the cave walls. After their attempt, she already suspected that she wouldn't be able to break Veranesh free from any place other than the High Towers. Getting in would be easy enough if she pulled the right strings and told the right lies, but the archmages wouldn't let her do what she had to do. The image of Kaighal consumed by the same powers that had destroyed the kingdom froze her. She took a deep breath, forcing her thoughts into focus. Every Tivarashan woman knew that with a crafty scheme, a disadvantage could be turned in one's favor. The spell Veranesh had put on her was a threat to the city she loved, but she could use it to ensure the archmages couldn't stop her.

"I like that expression, pactee," Veranesh said. "You're already making plans, aren't you?"

All her ideas were still vague, but she gave him a nod. "How do I free you?"

"Come."

The creature darted toward the cave's exit, and Kamira and Koshmarnyk followed outside. Veranesh hovered close to the ground, and the nightfly's abdomen spat dirt as it whipped back and forth, drawing symbols in a patch of dry soil.

"These have to be added to the High Tower's circle." The nightfly pointed at the ground. "And then you need to channel energy while in the middle of it. Don't try to direct it or break the crystal."

She narrowed her eyes, inspecting the unfamiliar shapes. "If not directed, magic will disperse. Shouldn't I aim it... somewhere?" Even if she couldn't focus on breaking the crystal, without a goal, it seemed like wasting the energy.

"Not with these." Kamira could swear the demon was smiling. "The high mages devised my trap skillfully. The circle not only draws my energy to channel it to the mages, but also sustains my prison, so while you'd be trying to break the crystal, I'd be fighting against you until either you collapsed or the trap's structure broke. But then, as you've guessed, all the accumulated energy would be released."

Kamira chased away the memories of Uganel's destruction that haunted her at every mention of the Cataclysm. Veranesh's expressed desire to avoid it put her at ease, but she knew that ultimately, had he no other choice, he wouldn't care about human lives lost. "So what do these symbols change?"

"They will create a back flow," Veranesh replied. "Any unused energy will return to me. It'll leak through the crystal and crush it in the process."

"So the energy won't accumulate," she finished.

Koshmarnyk leaned forward, looking straight at the nightfly. "And how certain you are of that solution?"

The crystal creature lifted in the air, to meet him at eye level. "Much less than of the one that requires my pactee's death." Veranesh's voice carried a hint of a challenge, forcing Koshmarnyk to look away. "But there are a few more things to determine, and the odds might start looking pleasantly in our favor." The nightfly shifted toward Kamira. "You still have to find a way to alter the circle without their knowledge and then channel energy uninterrupted."

"I might have someone to do it, before I even set foot in the High Towers," Kamira replied.

"Trusting Ryell with a task would be equal to inviting that archmage to learn your secrets."

Veranesh was open with his doubts, and she couldn't blame him. So far, Ryell had not proved that he was worthy of any trust.

"I have someone else in mind. An archmage's apprentice," she said cautiously. With their focus on other things, she'd never gotten to tell him about Pelina. "She owes me her life."

"The woman you didn't let me kill."

Eerie in its calmness, the demon's voice gave her a shiver. "I expected some disapproval."

"It's as much your game, pactee, as it is mine. I don't suppose I could convince you to bring her to me... or any other high mage, for that matter, and we would have been done with the matter of my freedom in a much easier way, destroying as little as some sands and desert brigands, while you would be in your dear city, shielding it from whatever remainder of magic could reach it."

She shook her head. No matter what lies and deception she had to use, no matter how many people had to die to ensure the demon's freedom, the thought of taking an innocent person against their will to be what amounted to a sacrifice... She curled her fists. "I'd rather go myself."

"I'd rather you didn't," Koshmarnyk said before the demon could reply.

Veranesh's laughter rang through the nightfly's crystal body. "I don't have any desire to run in that circle again. As for the woman... So far, you've been adamant in your distrust toward everyone, so I'm sure you will use both her and Ryell accordingly without risking too much."

Kamira didn't remark that with the plan they were devising, some risk might be necessary. In the end, if her own decisions became her undoing, the demon would still have his freedom.

"I have more things to consider." The nightfly circled down to her wrist. "But feel free to summon me if you have questions or the adept wishes to spar." Its crystal body coiled around Kamira's limb, announcing Veranesh's departure.

Koshmarnyk took a step toward her. "The demon kept mentioning Ryell. Is he someone important?"

Now that was a question to fill her day, but it wouldn't be a pleasant conversation. "He's a Devanshari refugee and the one whom you saw killing Cahala. He might be useful if everything else fails, but he's not an ally, and considering him one would be foolish."

He studied her. "Until now, I didn't ask about that event in the clearing, because it felt irrelevant. But Veranesh's remarks suggest he's more involved."

"A chance meeting made our paths cross, and the events led him to side with archmage Yoreus. The same man who started it all when he sent me to the old Towers."

"But that's not all, is it?"

Of course it wasn't, and Kamira bit her tongue before making a scathing remark about prying. Not so long ago, she was fantasizing about escaping to Juamha with him, so if she really wanted to consider him someone more than a pastime pleasure and a man who agreed to do her a favor, he deserved to know more. "He seems to have taken an interest in me, though I'm not sure how genuine his feelings are. He's addicted to magic and sleeps with the archmage's daughter, which means it might be nothing but a game."

"I see." He leaned closer, trapping her with his gaze. "And what about your interests?"

Her lips curled upward at the thought of how they'd spent the last days when Veranesh wasn't around. "My interest should be quite clear to you," she teased, but then became serious again. "I owe Ryell some answers, nothing more. If I could, I would try to pull him away from Yoreus, but not... at the cost of lying about my feelings." She could only hope that Koshmarnyk wouldn't ask about her feelings for *him* next. Even though their time together brought her much enjoyment, and a thought of inviting the adept to join her and Veelk for longer crossed her mind, she wasn't about to rush into confessing any deeper feelings that had yet to grow.

"Good." Koshmarnyk pulled her closer, and his lips brushed her neck. "Because unlike Veelk, I don't like to share. Are you done with the demon? I have plans for the rest of the day," he murmured. It seemed that he also didn't like the idea of hasty declarations, but there was a promise of possibilities in his voice, and they weren't only the ones regarding immediate pleasure.

She welcomed his embrace. "I think he doesn't have to know I'm not working all the time when he's not around." Besides, with the plans for Veranesh's release clarifying, she had little left to do.

Koshmarnyk led her back to the cave, the hunger in his eyes clear, and with her own body responding likewise, Kamira was certain no work would be done... for a while.

KOSHMARNYK DIDN'T KNOW whether his instinct woke him or the intruder had made a sound, but the moment his eyes snapped open, he pulled Kamira closer, providing as much protection as possible with them both lying naked under several thick furs. His thoughts raced, and many were directed at the demon. He cursed himself for trusting that Veranesh's watch would be enough. Kamira stirred in her sleep, and Koshmarnyk held her tight, trying to assess the danger.

As sleep's blur left his eyes, he stared at a tall warrior standing in the cave's entrance.

"The nights here must be colder than I remember." Veelk approached. "The demon suggested I should wait outside till you awoke. Now I understand why."

Kamira shuffled under the furs and freed herself from Koshmarnyk's embrace. "Of course, you didn't consider taking his advice."

Koshmarnyk snorted at her grumpy tone. Not bothering to cover herself more than necessary, she picked up her clothes, and her gray skin flashed as she retreated to the bathing niche. He entertained the thought of joining her, but Veelk's presence reminded him that the time for pleasures was up. With the mage killer's return, they were about to focus on more important matters. With some regret, he pulled his pants and shirt on.

"And this is the man who spoke to me about standards." Veelk dropped his travel bags to the side and squatted by the fire.

"She fits mine just fine." Koshmarnyk smirked. Kamira had caught his eye the first time they'd met, but he preferred to make sure he wasn't about to get in his friend's way—or hers, for that matter, if she had any hidden feelings for Veelk —but the last weeks together had put all his concerns to rest.

Veelk arched an eyebrow, telling of a jab to come. "If I knew you were so desperate from your years in prison, I'd have arranged some pleasant company for you."

Koshmarnyk fed the fire with more wood and placed the water pot over the flames. "If I'd been desperate, I could have seduced the queen." He showed no ire at such crude remarks, confident that his friend was testing him rather than trying to insult him or Kamira.

Veelk nodded, and the mocking smile faded from his face. "I figured that's not your way." He stared Koshmarnyk in the eye, his mood shifting once more from playful to serious. "But if you hurt her, I'll rip every stone from your body."

The adept endured his friend's gaze. He knew better than to challenge such a declaration, or mention that if it should come to that, Kamira would likely leave little for Veelk's vengeance. Instead, he nodded then looked over Veelk's shoulder. "Veranesh not coming?"

"The demon has a talent for avoiding difficult situations." Veelk snorted. "He'll likely wait to see if we kill each other and intervene only if Kamira's in danger."

Koshmarnyk laughed. "I wouldn't expect anything else."

"So, how have things been here?" Veelk asked. "I see you two have... made friends, but did they find a way to free the demon? All that putting stones in her body makes no sense if they don't have a plan."

He watched the flames, recalling the few past days, and the scraps of her conversations with the demon he'd caught. Kamira might have not kept him out of those exchanges, but wasn't very forthcoming about the details. "They do, and you won't like it."

"How can you tell?"

Koshmarnyk swallowed a bitter smile. "It involves altering the High Towers' circle and casting a spell there." A general answer seemed better than sharing his own concerns about the risks he could only suspect.

"You're right. I don't like it."

The water boiled, and Koshmarnyk threw in handfuls of grain. "Me neither." He trusted Kamira to come up with the best solution, the one that gave her the greatest chance of success, but it didn't mean he liked the idea of her being in danger. His growing attachment, something he hadn't expected to develop, gave rise to concerns, worries of the plan's outcome... and growing fear for Kamira's safety. And Veelk, so used to being by her side, must feel the same.

Kamira walked out of the bathing chamber dressed and with her hair done. Nightflies darted into the cave and coiled around her wrists as she approached the fire. To Koshmarnyk's regret, focus and determination had returned to her face, and he thought of the nights when in the faint light of the dying flames, Kamira's expression softened under his touch. For a moment, he allowed himself a dream of taking her away, far to the south and into the jungles, where she'd be safe from demons and mages, but then he turned to Veelk.

"Did you bring everything I need?" he asked.

"Took me some time, but I got it all," Veelk replied, and turned to Kamira. "I also got your message delivered, but whether that mage gal even bothered reading..." He shrugged.

"We'll know soon enough." Her voice remained emotionless, as if she'd already considered alternatives. "We know what to do to free Veranesh, so once the blending is done, we should head back to Kaighal. No reason to delay anymore."

Koshmarnyk kept his face straight. He could find excuses to prolong the blending and stay with Kamira longer, but in the end, she had to go, and he wouldn't stand in her way.

Veelk slowly nodded. "Getting into the High Towers will be difficult." His fingers moved as if he was already reaching for his keshal.

"Not that way," she said with a smirk. "We'll use deception... I'll go openly and on my own."

"How's that deception?"

Koshmarnyk held off the laugh rising in his chest. It seemed that no matter how serious or grim the situation was, the two would engage in their usual squabbling. "I think that's quite the deception if they expect her to sneak in," he added.

"I'll pretend to seek help from the archmages," Kamira told Veelk. "I promised Ryell I'd do so if your tribe couldn't help me, and we can use it to get inside. The spell I have to perform will take too long to try anything else. I need to make them think they have the upper hand, even if it's risky."

Veelk shifted in his seat and displeasure emanated from his posture. "It's unlike you. Trusting Ryell is even more stupid than trusting that high mage."

Her stare became cold. "I trust him to do what he thinks is best for me."

Koshmarnyk's eyes widened when he understood the meaning of her words. "You expect that man to betray you. You're planning that he will." When he looked at her, he saw a Tivarashan noblewoman, calculating and deceitful, and he chased that image away. She was only doing what she had to, and it didn't mean that was her nature.

"I'm sure he won't see it that way," she replied with a hint of sadness. "Though it doesn't matter whether he'll get me into the Towers willingly, leading me into a trap or believing he's helping to cure me of my evil arcanist ways." She stepped closer to the fire, but didn't sit down by the men. "I wish you two could be there, but if the high mages suspect anything, all will fail."

"I don't like this plan," Veelk said. "I'd prefer one that

doesn't hinge on so many possibilities. On that girl's loyalty, on Ryell doing his part, on you and the demon getting everything right."

She chuckled. "You mean, you'd like the one where you go into the Towers alone and clear them out for me?"

Veelk's grin was enough confirmation. "I could take Koshmarnyk with me. I'm sure he likes my plan better too."

"I'd prefer something more discreet," Koshmarnyk said in a lighthearted tone, though his thoughts were heavy with the possible outcomes of both approaches. "Something that gives us a chance of survival... Like getting in there quietly and defending the entrance while she does magic."

Kamira's lips curled downward, and her serious expression made it clear that banter time was over. "The one I put together with Veranesh is the best, and it doesn't include you two dying heroic deaths."

Koshmarnyk held her arm as she turned toward the cave's exit. "Does it include *you* dying a heroic death?" he asked. She had the right to decide her path, but if it led to her death, he'd offer his own life first.

She looked away, and only the cracking of flames disturbed the silence. When her answer finally came, it wasn't louder than a whisper, and Kamira tore away, retreating outside before uncomfortable questions chained her in place. The three words she'd spoken still hung in the air after she was gone.

"I hope not."

~

Koshmarnyk waited while Veelk tied Kamira's limbs to wooden stakes secured deep in the ground. She lay facedown, shirtless, and her eyes became blurry as the sleepseed extract took control of her body. With Kamira determined to go back to Kaighal as soon as they were ready, he'd found no reason to delay the blending, though he wouldn't have objected to a few more weeks of peace filled with training and Kamira's presence. Not to mention that he had yet to decide how to proceed. The duo had found him for a particular reason, and despite his friendship with Veelk and—he was hoping—shared affection with Kamira, he was hardly a part of their lives. Perhaps the time they would go their separate ways was nearing.

"Is it really necessary?" Kamira's words melted into a slur. "The extract will knock me out anyway."

Veelk didn't answer, and Koshmarnyk just sighed. Kamira's eyes closed, and her head finally rested on the folded cloak when the drug won.

"Don't you think she's right?" Veelk finished with the last bind. "You drowned her in the extract. She won't feel a thing, let alone twitch." He lifted Kamira's head enough to open her mouth and insert a piece of wood between her teeth. Then he secured her head with his hands.

"She's an arcanist, and magic is already within her," Koshmarnyk said. "I can't be sure how she'll react to blending."

He moved all the tools closer and checked the powdered stones mixed into a paste with the blending ingredients. He'd rather put full stones in her body, like he had his own, since they could be removed later with few scars, but Kamira had insisted on making it look like Veelk's tribe markings, and Koshmarnyk had lost the battle. With a last look at the pattern they'd designed, Koshmarnyk corrected the knife's grip and leaned over her body.

During his own first blending, the elders insisted on him being conscious, and he saw the wisdom in it until they started the ritual. He gritted his teeth at the pain he'd endured back then and later, until he found a way to ease it while still awake. Sometimes he suspected that Veelk's tribesmen did that to discourage him from seeking the knowledge, but once he left, he had to do it alone, so he would have to be conscious anyway. At least he could spare Kamira the same experience.

Drops of blood blossomed like flower petals on her gray skin when he pulled the blade across, ensuring the cuts were deep enough to receive the powdered stones. When the first lines marked her arm, he put away the knife. As long as he could see the pattern, he didn't need to bother washing off the trickling blood. He scooped the paste while in his other hand held a small imbued stone at the ready. He then pushed the ingredients into the wounds and pressed the edges together before moving the stone back and forth over them as he whispered the words the elders had taught him. He always wondered about the chant's purpose, but they kept their explanations scant.

Contrary to Veelk's predictions, Kamira twitched, and a muffled scream escaped her clenched jaws. Veelk freed one of her arms and pressed it to her back, but Koshmarnyk shook his head. She should have been unconscious and unable to move, but it seemed the magic within her had overpowered the sleepseed extract.

"Once I'm done with this part, I'll finish with the rest of the cuts, and then insert the mixture." He sighed. Blending more of the powder at a time meant greater pain, but with her reaction so severe, doing it bit by bit meant extending the process for days. Even if they didn't run out of the extract by then, they'd risk her never waking up. "I'm sorry," he whispered.

"She'll manage," Veelk said.

Koshmarnyk couldn't help remembering all the scars he'd discovered on her body. She must have been through a lot, and was no stranger to pain, but it didn't mean he was happy to add to her experiences. Yet he proceeded. Kamira's screams rose as she writhed violently. Veelk held her head firm, and the adept worked until all the wounds had been sealed with magic. The scabs' vibrant red contrasted with the gray of her skin, and Koshmarnyk hoped the marks would fade over time, just like Veelk's.

They worked steadily throughout the day, accompanied by Kamira's repeated screams.

Veelk dripped more sleepseed extract into her mouth, and she relaxed more with every drop, offering short stints of silence, but once Koshmarnyk moved the imbued stone closer to work on the blending, the groaning and wailing would soon follow.

By the time their shadows stretched long and the sun dipped behind the mountain, thick lines covered both of Kamira's arms, and Koshmarnyk focused on her shoulder blades.

"You should do her spine too," Veelk said. "Otherwise every spell will send her spinning."

Koshmarnyk shook his head, chasing away the weariness of both his body and mind. "That's enough for today. Either she'll learn how to control it, or we'll do more to ground her. And if I do her spine, her legs and neck will most likely have to follow."

"Let's move her inside, then."

They untied the binds and carried Kamira into the cave. Still caught in the sleepseed's grip, she remained serene, and Koshmarnyk hoped she wouldn't remember the pain she'd suffered, but her screams still echoed in his ears, ensuring his own memories would be well preserved. For the first time, he doubted whether agreeing to help had been the right choice. Instead, he should have taken her away from Kaighal, or perhaps even from Tyorane. He could be there, and they could take on anyone and anything in the southern jungles or in the far reaches of Juamha across the sea, and the demon could wait a bit longer... until she died of old age.

"You did what she asked," Veelk said, as if he'd guessed Koshmarnyk's thoughts. "Without telling her it's a bad idea or that you have a better solution for her."

"And that's supposed to be some sort of comfort?"

"She'll appreciate it when she wakes up, regardless of the pain." Veelk offered a huge grin. "Even I don't do that for her."

It didn't lift Koshmarnyk's gloomy mood. He might have done what Kamira asked, but at the same time, it felt like helping her die. "And maybe that's why she's still alive."

"I'd say that's why she's grumpy all the time. Too many people telling her what to do. But I did notice her mood has changed since you've been around. Once this is done, are you going to stay?"

Koshmarnyk arched his eyebrow. Had Veelk noticed that Koshmarnyk's relationship with Kamira was something more, or was he simply hoping for it? Either way, no matter his own feelings, Koshmarnyk also had to take Kamira's into consideration. Reserved as she was, she hadn't shared much so far, and he'd rather give her the time she needed. But Veelk was expecting an answer, so Koshmarnyk said, "If I stay, you might have to leave one day."

Veelk snorted. "It won't happen before you can beat me in a fight. And you're nowhere near doing that."

A smile lit up his face. In Veelk's tribe, a brother or cousin would fight the woman's suitor, so she could decide whether he was a warrior worth her, though Koshmarnyk had always suspected that it was a simple excuse for a good brawl. Women of the tribe were as hardheaded as their male counterparts, and like them, they did what they wanted. Several times he'd witnessed the bride-to-be reject a powerful warrior as not good enough, or approve a man who fell after the first punch as having fought bravely enough. And Kamira wasn't even of the tribe, let alone Veelk's relative. Not that it would change anything, since Veelk hadn't bothered to fight for his own sister, telling the suitor he could fight her instead. Koshmarnyk couldn't help smiling at the memory of Zelna beating her prospective husband into a pulp and insulting her own brother for his laziness at the same time.

He stretched his muscles one by one. After the strain of a long day, a bit of exercise would help take his mind off unwelcome thoughts, and the prospect of sparring against a real man instead of a pair of nightflies, a man of impeccable skill on top of that, only added to the rising excitement. "If you wanted to spar, you should have said so."

Veelk grinned, and they headed outside.

16

Allyv finished talking with his youngest patient, a three-year-old girl whose withdrawal symptoms were less severe than those of many adults. Jesha's reaction to the lack of essence made him believe that Devanshari children had a chance to survive and rebuild the kingdom free of addiction, and he found comfort in that thought. Even if he was the one to fail his people, there would be a future for the Devanshari if his assumption was true, and the addiction to magic developed over one's lifetime spent within Hajihali's power—therefore, children hadn't lived long enough to experience the most severe effects of withdrawal.

He sent Jesha one last smile and left the room. There were other patients to visit, even if he could only offer them a brief examination and words of comfort. Without deep medical knowledge and with no success finding a remedy or a replacement drug, with each passing day he felt more and more useless. Perhaps his mother was right, and rebuilding the artifact was the only way to quench the hunger for magic. The very thought made him clench his fists, but he forced his fingers to relax at the sight of Gulir approaching. No matter Allyv's own shortcomings and frustrations, his people deserved hope.

"My lord, some men came to see you." Gulir panted heavily, proving the three flights of stairs remained a challenge for him. "Hajha told them to wait downstairs."

The only visitors that wanted to speak directly with Allyv were desperate noblemen hoping to find immediate relief or a cure in Allyv's asylum.

"Looks like them Gildya folks, fancy clothes and gear emblems," Gulir added.

"Thank you. Tell Hajha I'll be right there." If Gildya wanted something from Allyv, this had to do with his mother. The queen took her entourage and set out of Kaighal, leaving no information on her destination or goals, but everyone believed he would somehow know. At least he could hope that it was another inquiry about ways of sending a message to her and not a demand of payment. His asylum hardly had enough coin as it was. He wouldn't waste the money his people needed to cover his mother's whims.

With a sigh, he headed downstairs, and the surroundings lifted his mood. The building was as run-down as it was when Allyv first bought it, but, with the efforts of all the workers, necessary repairs were made, cobwebs were cleaned, and fresh paint covered many of the walls. Moreover, word of his asylum spread, and people came offering help or asking for it. Even several mages visited and helped to ease the withdrawal symptoms with their magic, which Allyv knew was Ryell's doing. First, the royal guard brought an arcanist to relieve their people's suffering, and then found mages to spend some time working here as well. High mages might have been the ones to remedy the Devanshari's mistrust toward magic, but

Allyv couldn't help thinking about the Tivarashan woman who came to the asylum offering help when no one else did, likely knowing that her work would not be appreciated. The wounds from the war with the demons were fresh and painful, but perhaps he should invite her to the asylum again, and ensure his people didn't spiral down into unjustified hatred toward all those who had a pact.

He put that thought aside as he walked into the reception area. Six men stood up at his sight, and as Gulir had said, they indeed wore Gildya's attire. Allyv looked them over: four kept to the side and guarded large chests, while the other two stood by the door, and the shorter one held an ornamental wooden box in his hands. It didn't seem they'd come asking about his mother's whereabouts or money.

"Lord Allyv." The tall one stepped forward. A heavy chain and a jeweled pendant spoke to his position within Gildya. "I'm Adept Ervan of Gildya Magna, and I'm afraid I bring unsettling news. Is there any place we could talk in private?"

Allyv bit his tongue before saying the reception area was as private as it got in the asylum, where gossip circulated quickly. His guests expected to be taken somewhere less crowded. He ran over the list of rooms available in the building, from the common dining area to the unoccupied patient rooms, just as Hajha approached.

"I brought the wine and food to your office, Lord Allyv," she said. "But I don't know if our guests wish to carry those heavy chests all the way up to the third floor."

Third floor? Allyv put his memory to work. Several spaces up there were used for storage, but nothing more... Then a picture of the sunlit room came to him. Hajha's face remained as mellow as usual offering no clue of what she meant, but she was resourceful enough to make it look like an office.

"That won't be a problem. My men will stay here with the chests until our conversation concludes," Ervan said. "My colleague, Adept Tekk, will accompany us."

"Let's go, then." Allyv indicated the stairs outside the reception. He glanced at Hajha. "Was there anything more?"

"You received a note from one of our sponsors." She stretched out her hand. "I believe it might be urgent."

Allyv furrowed his brow. He could count the asylum's sponsors on one hand, and an urgent message didn't sound like good news. He kept his composure and nodded. Showing concern to his guest would bring him no gain. Yet the inspection of the note left him puzzled. The letter had no envelope, the paper was of low grade, and it lacked the noble seal.

Inside, there were only a few words scribbled. The handwriting, shaky and rushed, didn't belong to a nobleman, and it said, *Third floor, second door on the right.* Allyv handed it back to the old woman.

"Splendid. I'll send a reply later. Thank you, Hajha."

She bowed, and Allyv led the Gildya representatives up the stairs.

When he entered the room, the clean space made him pause mid-step, but he recovered before his guests could notice. As far as he recalled, the desk at the window and the wide table with four chairs in the middle were there before, but no trace of dust marked them, and the tablecloth looked fresh. A carafe with clear water, a bottle of wine, and light snacks awaited too. He couldn't help smiling. Hajha always surprised him when it came to housekeeping, and sometimes he wondered how quickly the asylum would fall apart without her.

"Please, sit down." Pointing at the chairs, he invited his guests in. As they took their places, Allyv glanced at some of his papers covering the desk, as if he worked there daily. Hajha left nothing to chance, it seemed. "I'm quite surprised by your visit. What matters bring you here?"

Adept Ervan shifted uneasily, and Allyv steeled himself. Whatever the nature of this meeting was, he didn't expect anything good.

"My responsibilities in the Gildya revolve around tracking the misuse of our resources as well as misbehaving members," Ervan said. "And while investigating a report about forbidden experiments, we came across a building in the woods. Many such places were abandoned in the past centuries when their owners moved to Kaighal or even further away, and they were often used for sinister purposes." He hesitated. "Inside, we found many dead, and most of them were Devanshari people. We believe they were the group associated with Lady Cahala." As most in Kaighal, he referred to Allyv's mother as a "lady" and not "queen," a constant reminder what the people of the Free City thought of royalty.

Allyv's heart skipped a beat, and he held his breath. He stared at the wooden box on the table, and a sudden realization of its contents surfaced. As if following his thoughts, Ervan opened the container and pushed it closer. The sun's rays coming through the window flashed across the gold and jewels the prince knew so well: the Devanshari crown.

"Queen Cahala?" The words made it through his clenched throat, but Allyv didn't recognize his own voice.

"We haven't found her body among the others," Ervan replied.

Allyv nodded, busy fighting his own feelings. As much

as he loathed his mother for her wrong choices and disregard of her subjects, the news of her disappearance and possible death turned out difficult to stomach. No matter her deeds, she was his only family, and his people's queen. "Do you know what happened?"

The adept shook his head. "All we know is that there were indeed forbidden experiments performed in the building, but whether Lady Cahala was aware of it remains unknown. The assailants left no trace, but we believe it's the second place they attacked. Weeks earlier, a Gildya prison met the same fate, with all dead and one person missing. Gildya Magna's council is speculating that these might have been carefully planned missions. We have many enemies who perceive all of our work evil, but they wouldn't dare to strike at the heart of Kaighal. Instead, they use sabotage and assassination."

"Anyone in particular you suspect?" Allyv remembered bits of Tyorane's complicated politics and factions, but never had time to refresh his knowledge upon arrival in Kaighal. Too wrapped up in searching for a way to help his people, he'd ignored everything else.

Ervan's face, wrinkled and tired, made him look old. "It could have been anyone. My first guess would be Tivarashan fanatics or the Western Kingdom assassins, but one can't discard the possibility of others being interested. From what we know, before leaving Kaighal, Lady Cahala gathered information about a man held in the prison that was also attacked."

"Why would she be interested in a criminal?"

Ervan shifted uneasily. "It's possible that she thought the man in question might be able to recreate your people's artifact."

The explanation seemed plausible enough. Allyv's

mother would do anything to have Hajihali back, even if it meant the Devanshari would remain slaves to their addiction. "And could he?"

"We don't believe it possible," Adept Tekk said, joining the conversation. "But that adept surprised us many times with unique ideas and inventions that weren't supposed to work. Had he not broken our laws, he'd be one of the most brilliant Gildya members."

It didn't escape Allyv that Ervan scowled at the praise. Their politics interfered even at a moment like this.

"And the criminal you mentioned is missing as well?"

Both adepts nodded, and Tekk continued, "We hired the best trackers, but so far we haven't received any word. Until we find something, we assume both of them are dead."

Such a notion would be unacceptable in Devanshari, but most of the times when people went missing in Allyv's homeland, they were found either dead or alive. Living in a city made it easy to forget how barbaric Tyorane was. They'd never recovered after the Cataclysm, and only Tivarashan survived unscathed. The thought of the kingdom in the north, deeming itself civilized, but still primitive and savage in its culture, as they insisted on demon worship, made Allyv shiver. Stories of their practices circled even back in Devanshari, telling of Tivarashan people mastering the use of imbued stones even beyond Gildya's expertise. They could surely use the skill of an adept dabbling in forbidden experiments, but it remained unclear why would they go after Allyv's mother. He looked at the men in front of him. They likely had no idea either.

"Thank you, adepts. I appreciate that you took the time to deliver the news in person," he said. "I trust you'll inform me of any discoveries."

"Of course!" Ervan opened his mouth just before Tekk

did. "Lady Cahala was Gildya's patron and friend, so we'll do whatever it takes to see the matter to its end."

"Thank you." Allyv regretted he'd never noticed how his father used to finish audiences. Was it the tone of his voice or maybe the particular words he spoke? Without any knowledge of such proceedings, all he could do was to stare at the adepts, hoping they'd understand the meeting had reached its conclusion and he wanted to be left alone.

The adepts didn't move from their seats.

"There's one last thing before we depart," Tekk said. "Our adepts recovered valuable items in the building we mentioned, many of them, we believe, personal belongings of the people murdered there."

Allyv's eyes widened. His mother's wealth... No. Devanshari wealth. He thought of the two chests Gildya's men brought to the asylum. It didn't look like there was much left. His mother must have squandered the rest of his nation's heritage.

"Our laws claim that the belongings of rogue adepts become Gildya's property," Ervan said. "But since Devanshari people were not our members, and we have no proof that they were aware of the experiments or the severity of such a crime, we decided all the items should be returned. We brought two chests with us, but there's more waiting in Gildya Magna."

"I... I greatly appreciate it." Allyv gave a slight bow.

"It's the least we can do in such difficult circumstances," Ervan said. "We cannot rule out that Lady Cahala became a target because she supported Gildya's research."

Allyv held his face straight. It seemed that the return of his people's heritage wasn't a gesture of kindness but one of cold calculation. Mentioning that they had laws allowing them to keep the valuables but decided to return them instead was meant as a way of ensuring Allyv would have no ground to accuse the Gildya of anything. For all he knew, the adepts themselves were responsible for those deaths, but with no proof, such claims would bring no gain to anyone. Gildya wanted the matter forgotten as soon as possible, and he couldn't blame them. Moreover, if he wanted to ensure his people got what truly belonged to them, he had to give the adepts what they wanted.

"My mother was determined to reconstruct our artifact, and this as well might have been a reason for such an attack," he said. "I hold no grudge against Gildya Magna, nor will I burden you with the responsibility for her... disappearance." He couldn't bring himself to speak of her possible death.

"We're grateful for such wisdom." Ervan stood up and bowed, the first sign of respect since Allyv had met him. "I hope the Devanshari people and Gildya Magna will meet again in more joyful circumstances in the future, and the exchange of knowledge will bring benefit to both."

"Lord Allyv." Tekk followed the other adept and bent his head.

"I hope to speak to you again," Allyv said.

When they left, he sat motionless at the table, unable to take his eyes off the crown. The silence was burdened with the weight of his thoughts driving his shoulders toward the floor.

Hajha entered the room, and he looked up. His pain and fear were reflected in the old woman's eyes, but Allyv didn't run to her for comfort like he used when he was a boy. Instead, he straightened his back and said, "Gather up everyone in the reception area and come get me when they're waiting."

"Everyone, my prince?" Hajha asked. In their private

moments, she still addressed him by his old title, abandoning the "lord" everyone else used.

"Everyone who can walk on their own," Allyv replied, fighting with his clenching throat. "I have something to tell them." Later, when all was done, he'd find time to address his own emotions, but he couldn't selfishly see to his grieving while others suffered uncertainty.

Hajha hesitated, but then she hurried away, leaving Allyv alone. He didn't move, staring at the wooden box, awaiting her return.

IRTAN SMILED as Pelina disappeared into her room, and the pile of books in her hands wobbled when she tried to close the door behind her. A sense of pride washed over him when he thought of the young arcanist in training. She was coping with the new approach to magic surprisingly well. Once again he mused on Kamira's choice, or rather what he guessed was following her instincts to make Pelina an ally. Had he not discovered the pact making when he had, Kamira would have had a very resourceful spy in the Towers. That made his thoughts wander toward the unruly arcanist once more. Kamira had disappeared from the city, and even Irtan's new student didn't know where she'd gone. Or she risked concealing that information from him. Irtan held off a chuckle. He could bet Pelina was still trying to find a way to deceive or outsmart him, and he had no doubt that if he didn't keep a close eye on her, she could succeed. He shook his head as he walked into his bed chamber. Neither he nor Kamira trusted the girl as much as she might deserve.

An insane thought flashed through his head—a

temptation to reveal all the secrets to Pelina, to make her tell of Kamira's plans in return, and to make the young woman into something more than a tool. He could use a true ally. He played with the idea for a moment, drawing pleasure from those wild prospects, and then promptly gave up on it. The game had gone too far to risk everything on an uncertain card... Pelina would betray him, of that he was sure. The only question was to whom—Yoreus, Kamira, or perhaps someone else. He couldn't risk finding out the hard way. If he learned Kamira's plots interfered with his, he'd deal with her when the time came, but as long as the rebellious arcanist played against Yoreus, he'd let Pelina help her. His student was useful as a pawn, but to consider her something more was just a spell of weakness.

A cold sea breeze shuffled his short gray hair, and Irtan looked at the window he didn't leave open. He turned to the corner where in his own armchair sat a demon—a very familiar demon.

"Fyertash." Irtan didn't hide his surprise. "I didn't expect you here."

The demon's large body hardly fit in the seat, threatening to burst the wooden frame, and Irtan held off remarking that he liked that chair. After all, his guest was doing him courtesy waiting in his bedroom instead of a less private place. The demon wore clothes resembling human ones, but Irtan couldn't help wondering how it was possible to conceal such huge wings. According to old texts, demons mastered an art called illusion magic, but he knew neither the workings nor the extent of such deception.

"I've been sent to gather information," Fyertash said. "We know Uganel has failed, but we don't know how or who destroyed him."

Irtan shook his head. "You came with your questions to

the wrong place. I'm not the first archmage anymore. I stepped down."

Fyertash's eyebrows arched. "I wouldn't have thought you were tired of the position."

"It was time." Irtan sighed and poured himself some water. Wine would be better, but his aging body demanded he took a better care of it. He needed it strong and capable for a little longer. "And Yoreus offered a good excuse."

"Yoreus? That pompous and arrogant hoyve." Fyertash snorted, and his face, with its crooked, beak-like nose, twisted into a grimace. "Don't tell me he's the first now."

Irtan let a dry laugh. "Pompous and arrogant, but the first archmage nonetheless. You should talk with him if your brethren want to discuss old agreements and new threats."

Fyertash remained seated. "I'd rather hear what you have to say. I'd be surprised if you didn't have any insight on what happened to Uganel."

"Not as detailed as I'd wish, but they lead to interesting places." Once more, Irtan thought of Kamira. If Fyertash's claim was true and Uganel was indeed destroyed, he'd give much to know whether and how she was involved.

The demon leaned forward, his eyes shining with anticipation. "Someone else has been playing around?"

"It seems it's more than just playing around," Irtan replied. "And I think whatever happens, it'll happen soon. But that's not a conversation to be had in daylight, even as receding as it is now." He indicated the twilight skies outside. "Not to mention my student shouldn't overhear it."

"You took on a student? That's quite a risk."

Irtan didn't allow himself to be moved by the scrutiny. After all, the demon had the right to be concerned about an old human like himself possibly willing to give up the game.

"It seemed worth it. She might offer a way to... infiltrate the other interested party."

Fyertash waved his claw, urging him to say more, but Irtan shook his head.

"Not now. Go, speak with Yoreus first. He might even tell you things he's kept from me."

The demon stood up and, with his back straight, towered over the archmage. "And then you and I talk."

"Then we talk."

As soon as the demon was out of the window, Irtan lost sight of him. Only a faint aura of magical distortion marked the spot in the sky where Fyertash might have been, and the archmage couldn't help studying it, though he doubted it would provide him any valuable insights into how demons used magic. So instead, he focused on Pelina. If he sent her away for the night, she'd suspect something, and she could try to spy on him. Once more he played with the idea of letting her in on the secret, as he was curious what Pelina would do with it, but the memory of Yoreus's plots swept the playfulness away. Any other time he'd be excited to make meeting Fyertash part of Pelina's training, as arcanists needed to know how to deal with demons. The thought of how long it'd been since he had a promising student made him long for the risk. At the same time, the experienced player he was, he wouldn't endanger the plan he'd spent years on for the mere entertainment of making his student something more than an unaware pawn.

He swirled the water in his cup, and a solution presented itself. He should still have some sleepseed extract left. His poor student deserved a good night's sleep.

~

SILENCE FELL when Allyv walked into the reception area, and all the heads turned. But no one looked at his face; they looked at what he was holding in his hands. He expected whispers to stir once they recognized the crown, but not a single word arose within the room.

The crowd parted before him, so he stopped in the middle, surrounded by his people and yet isolated from them... alone. He looked at their faces—some he recognized from the Devanshari capital, and others from their sea journey or work in the asylum. Few names came to him. Enveloped in his research, he had lost touch with the ones he'd sworn to cure.

He was everything they had left. He saw it in their eyes, in the anticipated pain mixed with desperate hope.

"My friends, I bring sad news. Our nation has suffered greatly in recent months, and the grief has not yet come to an end. I've received word that people who devoted their lives to serving the queen have been viciously murdered, and my mother, the queen of all Devanshari, disappeared. The Gildya adepts don't believe she's still alive."

He took a deep breath while gasps of horror filled the room. Many people had family members in the queen's service, and the message of their deaths seemed to hit them like a fuldaran eagle striking its prey. Allyv didn't blame them for caring more for their perished relatives than the woman who ruled them.

"My mother was a queen who always put her people first," he said, even though he didn't believe the words. His mother was a selfish gaharra who only cared for herself. "She put all her energy and resources into recreating what's been taken from us." *Just so she could get it back too.* "And although her path was not my own, and I seek another way to end our suffering, I cannot deny her efforts toward restoring our nation's wellbeing." Lie after lie, each of them became easier. His people didn't need bitter words and cruel truths. They needed inspiration and hope. "I can only hope the Light will bring her back to us, and we will rejoice at the news of her being alive. Until then—"

Allyv hesitated, looking at the crown. *Until then—what?* They didn't have a throne room to put the crown in, guarded day and night by loyal sentinels. They didn't have a vault to store it safely. He wasn't even sure his own chest had a lock.

Hajha approached, and when she took the crown out of his hands, relief washed over him. She'd do whatever needed to be done. Hide it, store it, keep it safe, say the right words. She always did what was right.

The wrinkles on the woman's face changed like streams of water when she stood in front of him with a loving expression. "Kneel, Prince Allyv." In the silence, her gentle voice carried the power of thunder.

His mouth opened, but the argument didn't come. Objecting now with all these people around seemed the worst solution, so he went down on his knee.

After a moment measured only by his heart's thumping, Hajha put the crown on his head.

"Rise, King Allyv."

Her simple words concluded the simplest of the ceremonies, and he stood up with the burden of gold on his temples. The cold touch of metal reminded him of his duties, not toward the inexistent kingdom, but toward its people, lost and suffering in a foreign land. He had to succeed where his mother had failed.

Hajha bent her head in a courtly bow, and all the people in the room followed. Allyv watched them, all frozen in servitude and waiting for their ruler to speak. This might have been appropriate back in Devanshari, but not in the asylum where they worked arm in arm every day. Yet, even if the following day he'd be the same "Lord Allyv" who pulled his weight when it came to daily duties, today he was their king. No, he was something more. He was their inspiration.

"I might wear the crown," he said, "but it's only a reminder of the duties a king has to his people. You shouldn't bow before me when I have yet to prove my worth in being called a monarch. There's much to do, and I'll need your help to bring glory back to the Devanshari, but I won't stop until we achieve it."

People lifted their heads. Hope and admiration were on their faces.

"Hail King Allyv!" somebody called out, and more voices joined in, filling the asylum with cheers and shouts.

They rejoiced, and he found comfort in how quickly they adapted. Cahala qi'Devanshari had disappeared not only in Tyorane's wilderness, but also from her subjects' hearts, and though some would still mourn the loved ones they had lost, the grief would be kept private and limited. He understood. With all the death and destruction they had faced, they didn't want to dwell on pain. They wanted to move on, to rebuild. He responded to smiles and waves, a king close to his people like no other before while his mind focused elsewhere.

He couldn't fail them. He had to find the cure.

17

Kamira's stomach churned violently, so she ignored the pain in her arms and stumbled outside of the cave. The retching sensation shook her, dulling her senses, and she leaned against the rock. Veelk and Koshmarnyk were by her side in an instant, and she struggled for clarity against the sleepseed extract's effects as they spoke to her. Their insistent tone shattered what little focus she had left, and she waved her hand at them to give her a moment. She needed...

Magic flowed uninvited, erupting from that single gesture, and hit them both.

Veelk stood his ground, but his scars lit up. Koshmarnyk slid backward, his arms up in a futile defense. Kamira cried out in a desperate attempt to control the energy's outburst before it pushed him off the ledge. Veelk stepped in between them, his scars as bright as sunlight.

Fighting against her own body, she tamed the magic, and its flow ebbed. She took a step toward them, but her body disobeyed, and she fell to her knees, fighting the nausea. "I'm sorry..." she whispered in a raspy voice just before her stomach finally rebelled and she threw up. Every jerk of her body stirred magic, threatening more eruptions of energy, so she took care to avoid any more sudden gestures.

Koshmarnyk knelt beside her and waited while she kept throwing up. "You're taking it better than Veelk did," he said with some joviality. "The elders told me he was sick for a week after his blending."

Kamira spat out phlegm, but it didn't help the taste in her mouth. "I still might do as splendidly. I never thought I'd react to the sleepseed so badly." The smell of her own vomit made her nausea return.

He became serious in an instant. "We gave you more while you were out."

"A lot more," Veelk added grimly. "You shouldn't be awake yet."

Confused, she looked at the sky, and the rising sun teased her eyes. She must have been asleep...

Koshmarnyk followed her gaze. "It's been two nights since we finished the blending."

"Two nights?!" Kamira rose, but the vertigo forced her back to her knees, and the magic within her sloshed violently, like wine in a cup held by an unsteady hand. With deep breaths, she focused on it before another outburst could cause damage. "How much extract did you give me?"

"As much as we could without risking your life," Koshmarnyk said quietly. "It took us a whole day just to finish your arms. You didn't take it well."

Her mind offered no memories, but an echo of pain lingered in her limbs. She inspected the red, swollen scabs lining her skin, and the intricate pattern resembled that of Veelk's tribe. Yet his scars remained barely visible, while her body displayed the knife's work clearly.

"They should heal over time," Veelk remarked.

"Should?" She stared at him and then at Koshmarnyk, but he avoided her eyes. "So you don't know." The words came out harsh, so she softened them with a weak smile. After all, she was prepared to pay the price for the blending. All things considered, it was a low one in comparison to losing her life or causing another Cataclysm, even if scars like that would draw attention she didn't need.

"You didn't take it well," Koshmarnyk repeated. "But you woke up sooner than we thought, and that's a good sign."

"And it worked. I felt magic flow through the markings almost without any focus." It had its downsides if she couldn't learn to keep it under control.

Veelk's expression made her remember what Koshmarnyk had said about using magic before her wounds healed. The phrase he'd used was "strictly forbidden," and her smile faded.

"You'll work on it when you recover," Veelk said. "We can't go back to Kaighal until you control it."

"First, you need to rest," Koshmarnyk said. "I'll take you back—"

With her head still spinning, she risked a gentle shake. "I don't think I'm done throwing up."

"I'll bring soothing herbs." He rushed back to the cave.

Carefully, she moved to the side. Her stomach still twisted like a legless demonling, and the smell wasn't helping.

Veelk kicked some sand over her vomit and kept watching her. "I invited him to travel with us a little longer. Figured you... wouldn't mind."

Despite the vertigo and nausea, she had to smile. He knew her too well, and there was no point pretending that her relationship with Koshmarnyk was nothing more but a pleasant pastime. Besides, she wouldn't like the man in question to walk in on a conversation like that, especially given that she was still exploring her own feelings and had little notion of how the adept really felt. Caring and concerned as he was, she still might be nothing but that pleasant pastime to him.

"It's going to put him in danger," she said more seriously than she'd intended.

As much as she welcomed his company, it meant changes. Koshmarnyk was likely a wanted man in Kaighal, and he wouldn't necessarily enjoy the life she and Veelk had. His martial prowess aside, she had no doubt he was man of research and experiments, not of exploration and travel. But if needed, there would be solutions. She didn't have to wander through the wilds all the time, and Veelk would likely also welcome more time for leisure to spend the coins he so often bled for.

She brushed those thoughts aside. With the upcoming confrontation at the High Towers, it seemed foolish to make plans for the future.

"He cares, Kam," Veelk said softly. "And he knows the risks well enough. Nobody's asking for promises."

Koshmarnyk's return let Kamira avoid replying. She cared too, and it was enough that she had already put one friend in danger. At the same time, it was the adept's decision, and she couldn't insist on protecting him from danger and at the same time not allow him to do the same for her.

Unaware of the conversation, Koshmarnyk offered her a steaming mug that smelled of soothing herbs. While she sipped it, he inspected her wounds.

"It's going to take a long time to heal," he murmured. "Please don't use magic unless your life depends on it."

"What about Veranesh?" she asked. After the demon had admitted that the pact Kamira had was sustaining both his control of the nightflies and the creatures themselves, Koshmarnyk had insisted that they shouldn't be awake during the blending.

"He'll have to wait," Veelk said. "He knows you're alive, and that should be enough."

She gave a reluctant nod. As much as she wanted to speak with Veranesh, a conversation wasn't worth the risk of damaging her arms or slowing down the healing. Either way, she had to wait for the wounds to close, but so close to her goal, the thought of idleness itched her more than the scabs on her skin. The longer it took, the more time she'd have to ponder all the possible outcomes, and hardly any of them promised a victory... or even as little as survival. With that would come doubt, and if she started second-guessing her choices and Veranesh's plan, she would set herself up for failure.

She pressed her lips together and took a deep breath. Then, slowly, she stood up, using the rocky wall beside her for support. Her body was weak, but her stomach was already settling, promising that recovery would come soon enough. "I might not be able to use my magic, but I will walk soon enough. If we travel slow and rest often, I could recover while traveling. The sooner we're back in Kaighal, the less time the archmages will have to come up with something that could ruin our plans."

She expected protests, but both men nodded. Their serious expressions told her that they must have had similar thoughts and concerns: with no other choice but to keep her part of the deal with Veranesh, delays were of no benefit to anyone but their enemies.

"We'll set out once you can walk on your own more than

a few steps," Veelk said. "If I have to carry you all the way back to the city, you won't have enough strength to face the archmages, and you might as well save them the hassle and dive off this ledge."

Kamira sent him a smile. At least he didn't demand they waited until she was able to keep their regular pace of travel.

"Very well," she replied. *Tomorrow. I'll make sure I'm ready to leave tomorrow,* she thought.

18

The evening had already come when Kamira walked into the Jagged Swordsman, and the atmosphere inside gave her pause. The usual joviality was gone, and so were the bursts of laughter and lively conversation. Fewer patrons occupied the tables, and they seemed more serious. If she didn't see the familiar room, she'd go back outside to check if she'd walked into the wrong inn.

Yet when she scanned the surroundings, everything looked as it was supposed to. Some familiar faces among the patrons, and the same maids she'd seen so many times. Opyr wasn't at the bar, but that didn't alarm her. He often left the main room for the kitchen, overseeing the cooks or taking in deliveries from local merchants.

Veelk tensed as if he, too, had caught the difference in mood, but nothing in his posture suggested he was readying for an unknown threat, and she allowed herself to relax. They'd been away for three months, and the strain of the journey must be weighing on him. In hindsight, she shouldn't have rushed the departure from the cave. At the mere thought of the past few weeks, Kamira had to fight the urge to scratch the skin under her sleeves. The scabs were driving her insane, but her wounds hadn't healed yet, a sad realization that accompanied minor bleeding when she tried to remove the dried layer. With the constant itching of the healing skin, she could at least forget about the still-present numb echo of pain that lingered ever since the bone broken by Uganel had mended.

A maid noticed them and picked up a room key. Only then did Kamira realize she'd missed the warm greeting from the innkeeper's daughter.

"Lefna's not around?" Veelk asked.

Kamira hid her sneer. He missed Lefna more than he'd admit, but bringing it up meant he'd be quick to reciprocate with mention of Kamira's attachments to a certain adept, and she'd rather not hear such remarks with Koshmarnyk around. The prospect of being open about her feelings itched more than the scabs. At the same time, Koshmarnyk never pushed her for any promises for the future, which made her wonder whether it was courtesy or if he was trying to avoid making promises himself.

The maid's startled look washed away her playfulness and good mood. Kamira slowly took a breath, steeling herself for the maid's reply.

The woman pressed the key into Veelk's hand. "I'll get Opyr," she muttered, avoiding more eye contact, and ran to the kitchen.

Veelk stared at the maid's retreat. "There's bad news to come."

"Let's wait upstairs." Kamira touched his stiff arm. "Bad news is better dealt with in private." She also wanted to make sure that Koshmarnyk made it safely through Kaighal and into their room, as he'd insisted on splitting up before they reached the city. When Kamira insisted, he'd reminded her he was still a fugitive from Gildya's prison, and that memory only added weight to the burden of the situation. She cared little what other adepts thought of him, and should it come to that, both she and Veelk would stand by his side, but until she was done with her own task and free to pick her battles, secrecy was indeed a better choice.

They made it upstairs in silence. A gust of air brushed their faces upon their entrance into the room. Veelk immediately pushed Kamira to the side, but no sooner had his hand gripped his keshal, he relaxed, and she once more envied his ability to see in the dark.

"One day I'll kill you by accident," Veelk grunted while Koshmarnyk lit a candle.

The flame's light revealed the adept's arched eyebrow, but as soon as he inspected Veelk's face, concern replaced his good mood. Veelk threw their travel bags on the floor and paced the room in heavy steps.

"We're expecting bad news," Kamira explained as she moved past him.

Before Koshmarnyk could ask anything, a knock made them all turn their heads. The tension she'd noticed downstairs intensified into a sense of danger Kamira couldn't shake off.

"Come in!" Veelk's finger danced along his keshal's grip.

Opyr poked his head through the door, and upon Kamira's gesture, he entered. His face, tired but full of relief when he saw them, hardened when he noticed Koshmarnyk.

"He's a friend," Kamira said.

Koshmarnyk bent his head in greeting, but the innkeeper's attention had already turned to Veelk.

"A Devanshari man took Lefna." His voice trembled, but

his words brought information, not emotion. "He demands you come or he'll kill her."

Veelk's expression went blank as Kamira and Koshmarnyk exchanged glances. Neither of them needed a name or a description. Only one Devanshari had fled Veelk's assault, and only one could hate Veelk enough to go after Lefna. Guilt clenched Kamira's throat. The three of them could have defeated Phuran if only they'd bothered to track him down. Instead, they'd allowed themselves to forget about the threat, and Opyr and his daughter were paying the price.

"I paid a group of mercenaries to bring my child back." Opyr's mouth trembled, and so did his clenched hands. "Only one returned, mutilated... with another note."

Kamira poured wine and forced the mug into the innkeeper's hand. He guzzled it down with his eyes fixed on Veelk, and she dared not ask how long it had been.

"He wrote that if the next man who comes is not you, Lefna will lose her fingers." He shook his head. "I don't even know if she's still alive."

Veelk threw Kamira a glance, and she nodded. For years they had enjoyed Opyr's and Lefna's hospitality, and the time had come to repay them. If need be, Veranesh could wait a little longer.

"I'll go and bring her back," Veelk reassured the innkeeper, and his fingers closed around the keshal. She had no doubt he was already thinking about the fight to come.

Opyr's face brightened with relief. "Master Veelk..."

To Kamira's surprise, Koshmarnyk took a step forward, shaking his head. "If you go, the girl dies. She's not bait. She's his revenge. You took the most precious thing from him, and he'll do the same to you. You care for that girl, so if you go, it'll be to watch her die."

Opyr moaned, and Kamira placed her hand on his. His eyes, surrounded by dark circles, stared blankly.

"If I don't go, she'll die too." Veelk's face remained a stone. "He won't wait forever."

"Let me go first," Koshmarnyk said. "I'll let him believe I came for my own revenge, so if I fail, he won't hurt her, and you still have your chance."

Kamira bit her lip. Koshmarnyk had hardly been a match for Phuran back when they fought in the workshop, but both Veranesh and Veelk claimed the adept had gained a lot of prowess since. She was on the verge of offering to go with him, but she knew he'd refuse. The last thing he needed in a fight like this was to worry about her as well, and if she showed up, Phuran wouldn't believe Veelk didn't know. Yet there was something she could do.

"Take my bracelets with you," she said. "I won't need them for a while." Details could wait until after the innkeeper left the room, but she had no doubt Veranesh wouldn't mind. He seemed to like Koshmarnyk enough to be willing to help, and she couldn't take the nightflies to the Towers anyway.

Opyr glanced at her jewelry with curiosity, but then his gaze returned to Veelk.

Kamira had no trouble reading the mixed emotions on her friend's face. Veelk wanted to go, and he likely thought he *should* go, but at the same time, she knew him well enough to be sure he wouldn't blindly follow his feelings. No matter whether neither of them liked Koshmarnyk's argument, the adept was right: if Phuran wanted revenge, he wouldn't let Lefna go if Veelk yielded to the demand.

"My friend is right," Veelk said, his voice heavy and grim.

"That man wants me to see Lefna die. If I fail to get to him quick enough, if he sees me coming..." He shook his head. "I can't risk her life."

Koshmarnyk turned to Opyr. "I'll get your daughter back." He didn't say that he'd die trying if needed, but his expression made it clear.

Kamira bit her lip before protesting. One of them had to go, and Koshmarnyk had a better chance of bringing Lefna back alive.

Opyr remained silent but didn't hide his doubt as he searched his pockets and then pressed a crude map into Kamira's hand. "Let me know if you need anything." He rushed to the door, but before he left, he turned to Veelk once more, and the mage killer's face froze in pain.

Kamira threw an apologetic glance at Koshmarnyk. "I'm sorry. Fear and desperation must be weighing heavy on him," she said. A man who offered to risk his own life to save Opyr's daughter deserved better than being ignored.

With nothing else to say that would justify the innkeeper's hurried departure, she studied the map. From what she could gather, it led to the same place where Cahala had kept Koshmarnyk and the kidnapped girls.

"He thinks Veelk should be the one saving her, despite the risks involved." Koshmarnyk, unmoved by the treatment he'd received from Opyr, looked over her shoulder at the directions. "I'll set out in the morning."

"I'll wait five days," Veelk said grimly. "If you don't come back, I'm going after her."

"Fair enough."

In the silence that fell, Kamira said, "I meant what I said about Veranesh. If you take one of his imbued stones, you should be able to wake the nightflies."

Of course, he shook his head. "If I don't come back, and Veelk sets out, you'll need his help more than I do."

She snorted. "In five days, I'll already be in the High Towers, and Veranesh can't help me there. We can't risk that his presence will disturb what I need to do."

Veelk squinted, and his inquisitive stare brought her sudden discomfort. "What are you and that wretched demon planning, exactly?" he asked. "You're about to walk into the enemy's den completely defenseless."

"That's what I'm hoping the high mages will think." Kamira put all her effort into sounding confident. Sharing speculations she and Veranesh had about the outcome of their plan would do her no good. "I'll still have my magic at my disposal, so if needed, I can challenge even the archmages. But first, I need to talk to Pelina, and then get Ryell to do his part."

Veelk scoffed and shook his head, but he couldn't deceive her. His body was as tense as before. She sighed. They should have taken Phuran into consideration. So many other things could go wrong too, those very things they'd failed to consider beforehand. And with so many questions still unanswered, with Pelina and Ryell's roles vital but hardly predictable, her plan felt like a gamble.

Veelk paced around while Koshmarnyk repacked his bag, and they both seemed consumed by grim thoughts. With her own ones haunting her as well, she was convinced none of them would sleep through the night to come.

◦◦◦

THE JAGGED SWORDSMAN was nothing like Pelina had expected. Even if a poor student like her couldn't afford dining there, she had heard of their delicious meals and inviting atmosphere, but upon entering, she couldn't help feeling like she'd walked into a sandstorm of despair. Everything was in its place: patrons having loud conversations over their food, a musician playing a lively melody, and maids sharing jovial remarks as they served drinks. No shady men lingered in the corners, and no brawny brutes ruined the evening for others, and Pelina forced herself to focus on her task instead of searching for something that was likely only a reflection of her own anxious thoughts.

She scanned the room. No familiar faces emerged from the crowd, and she resisted the need to check the message once more. It had said "Jagged Swordsman," so either Kamira would be here or she would send someone to let Pelina know of any changes. And, in the end, if the arcanist insisted on meeting among other people, she must want to talk. If they had decided dealing with a high mage student was too much of a risk, they would have told Pelina to come to a less crowded place. Pelina shivered at the memory of the muscular warrior and his sharp blade. Her wound had since long healed, but the echo of pain and fear remained.

The table in the corner allowed her to take in the whole room, but the maids and patrons moving about made it hard to make sure she didn't miss anything. Kamira would likely find her, but Pelina didn't want to give up the advantage of knowing the arcanist—or her friend—was coming. If she was lucky, maybe the messenger would be the kind man who was kept prisoner by the Devanshari. Alluvendran, if she recalled the name correctly, seemed the friendliest of the three people she'd met there, but her arrangement was with Kamira. It would seem foolish to send someone else to talk.

She closed her fingers on the table's wood as the voices

around became annoying all of a sudden. Steadying her breath didn't help, and when her arms started to tingle, Pelina realized it wasn't her anxiety... her senses had picked up on someone using magic. *Friend or foe?* Energy teased her skin with no malicious intent. Like a string, it pulled and invited her to follow. As much as she enjoyed Irtan's teachings on the arcane arts, she'd never expected to put them to use so quickly. Back in the High Towers, she still relied on her taught and rehearsed high magic spells, not only out of habit, but to conceal her pact. A high mage who didn't use words to manipulate her magic would quickly raise questions among teachers and students.

The energy flowed from the stairs, and Pelina made out a dark figure standing in the shadows. *Kamira?*

She rose from her seat slowly, like any patron would, and made her way up, fighting the need to look around. Reason told her no one would follow her, since Irtan knew precisely where she'd gone and why, but she couldn't discard the possibility that other archmages wanted to spy on their rival's student. With the political tension in the Towers rising, despite those in power acting carefree, they must suspect Irtan was using her to his own ends. She almost laughed at the thought, but on the other hand, perhaps they weren't as wrong about it as she'd like to believe.

With her thoughts grimmer, she made it up the stars. Kamira waited at the top, shadows concealing her from the eyes of the patrons in the main room, and she indicated down the corridor, toward a cracked door.

"Go," she said. "I'll make sure no one follows."

The room looked like Pelina had expected, but when her eyes met the tribal warrior's stare, she twitched. His expression was grim, but at least he didn't act threatening, and his spear rested against the wall, far enough from his reach for her to not give in to her instincts and run.

"Come in. Kamira will join us in a moment." His voice had a morbid depth she didn't remember from their previous encounter, and it carried promises she wouldn't like to experience.

She stood in the middle of the room hesitating, until he pointed to a chair. Sinking into the seat was like a last-moment rescue before her own legs betrayed her.

"You seem nervous," he said.

He watched her with his eyes narrowed, and after giving it more consideration, Pelina decided his weapon was not as far from him as she'd previously thought. Pelina swallowed and nodded, feeling no reason to conceal the truth. "I've lots to tell her, and not much of it is good news."

"I'd be surprised if you brought good news from the high mages' den."

Kamira's entry saved Pelina for having to reply.

"I see you followed my instructions," Kamira said. She looked different too, and every now and then a grimace flashed on her face, as if moving about brought her pain. She took the free chair by the table.

"I did," Pelina replied. "Why didn't you tell me what the ritual was? Why didn't you warn me?"

Kamira arched an eyebrow. "Would you have performed it then?"

Pelina opened her mouth and snapped it closed, asking herself the same question. Now that she knew what the arcane arts could offer, the answer was obvious, but back then... "Maybe I would have. And maybe there would be fewer problems."

"Problems?" Veelk's voice made her fidget.

She bit her lip. All the way to the inn, she'd argued back

and forth whether she should reveal the truth to Kamira. Archmage Irtan had demanded she keep the arrangement with him secret, but Pelina had been around Tower games long enough to know which lies were worth the risk. No matter what she chose to say, it would be hard to conceal that she'd been the former first archmage's only apprentice. Besides, she was the one indebted to Kamira, and so far, Pelina hadn't proved her worth in any way.

"Archmage Irtan caught me performing the ritual," she said with a sigh of surrender. Even if such a confession was to seal her fate, she owed Kamira the truth. "He knew what it was and seemed... amused. But he caught me off guard, so he knows you're involved."

Veelk cussed, and his choice of words was a very creative mix of sailor's insults and some rough language Pelina didn't recognize.

Kamira narrowed her eyes. "What else does he know?"

"Not much. I... didn't tell him about Alluvendran." She turned to Veelk. "I made it sound like you came to rescue Kamira, and it was the Devanshari queen who committed all the crimes. He seemed to believe me, but... he knows that I came here, so if you still want my help, I'll have to tell him something. The more truthful it sounds, the better." At the thought of the possible consequences, she couldn't suppress a scowl. "If he senses I'm lying, he'll hand me over to Archmage Yoreus."

"Yoreus doesn't know?" Kamira leaned forward.

"No one else knows. Irtan keeps me close. I'm his student now. He gives me books to study demonolog— arcane magic. I'm sure he's playing a game against Yoreus." Pelina tried to condense weeks of events. "There's been a power struggle in the Towers. I just don't know what my role in his plan is. Or yours. He told me to keep helping you, but inform him of what you say or do."

Veelk sighed. "We need to rethink everything. She's not going to be of use if she can't do anything without the archmage watching her."

She couldn't blame him for his distrust. Even her honesty could have been carefully crafted to convince them both she was on their side.

Kamira shuffled through the parchments on the table. "No, I can still make it work."

"Make what work?" Pelina couldn't resist the question, even if she wouldn't be granted an answer.

To her surprise, Kamira handed her a piece of parchment.

Pelina inspected the precise drawing. "It's the initiation rite circle, isn't it?"

Kamira nodded, already drawing similar symbols on another page. Her speed and precision were envy-worthy. "It has additional symbols. I meant to give you a copy, but since Irtan will check on you, you need to memorize them instead. I'll give you another drawing to show to the archmage. You'll tell him the truth: that I asked you to alter the circle and said nothing else."

She stared at the parchment, but her basic arcane schooling offered her no clues. Besides, the initiation rite circle belonged to the high magic arts. "What do they do?"

"It's part of my plan," Kamira replied in a dry tone. "And that's all Irtan needs to know."

"You're right." Pelina blushed and focused on the unfamiliar symbols. They required her full attention. "What if someone notices the changes I make?"

"They won't." Veelk handed her a piece of crystal. "If you use this."

Pelina's eyes widened. "Hauhan's Graver!" The smooth blue jewel shaped into a chisel emanated delicate magic—any marking etched with it would be invisible until a ritual activated them.

"I'm surprised you recognize it," Kamira said. "Irtan really seems intent on teaching you arcane lore."

As subtle as it was, the compliment eased Pelina's mood. "He was amused by what I did. I don't think he'd would've even cared to punish me for making a pact if he hadn't discovered you were involved. But that might all be a part of his play against Yoreus. Some sort of revenge for being forced to step down."

"Irtan stepped down?" Kamira looked surprised. "That's the first good news I've heard in a while."

"How's that good news?" Pelina's forehead furrowed. "Yoreus is ruthless and won't hesitate to do anything if it'll help him prove he's better than Irtan."

Kamira's face brightened with a grin. "He's also more predictable. I need to finish this one." She pointed at the new drawing. "Which means we have time for a story. What exactly happened in the Towers?"

IRTAN SAT WITH A BOOK OPEN, but the old theories on demon origins were nothing more than a way to pass the time. His mind kept going back to the meeting Yoreus had held the previous night, and a chuckle rose in his chest whenever a memory of the new first archmage's face resurfaced.

Fyertash surely hadn't held back his words during that meeting. The demon played the situation well, constantly reminding Yoreus how little he was worth in comparison to any yalari. He came across as any other arrogant demon, and Irtan had had his share of amusement. He stretched in the chair. Being the first among the archmages was something more than a title, and even though Yoreus had all the traits of a future leader, his lack of confidence in the new role shone through his every word and reaction. He really wanted to force Fyertash to treat him as an equal, just like an adolescent boy demanding to be taken for an adult. Irtan didn't expect much more from Yoreus, since archmages rarely took time to study and understand demons, but at least dealing with Uganel should have taught him enough about their nature. Even Irtan himself, though on friendly terms with Fyertash, would never expect such respect from a demon. He shook his head in amusement. How the high mages' predecessors had managed to come to any agreement with those proud creatures centuries ago was a mystery in and of itself. They were either wiser back then, unspoiled by power and privileges, or the demons had gotten really desperate.

The door cracked open, and Pelina poked her head in as if checking the room, but once she saw Irtan waiting, she walked in with complete surrender on her face.

"You've been away for quite a while," Irtan said.

"She didn't come until late," Pelina murmured. "Then I got questioned about pretty much every moment since we last met. Just because she finds me useful doesn't mean she trusts me."

Irtan smiled. She hid her lies under frustration. Good— she was learning. "But you've convinced her."

"My guess is as good as yours." She shrugged. "She trusted me enough to give me another task." She handed a piece of parchment to Irtan. "I'm supposed to alter the initiation rite circle for her."

Irtan studied the new symbols and their placement.

He'd have to consult his books, but from first glimpse, he could tell the alteration wouldn't have any effect. By no means was Kamira a lousy arcanist, so either she intended to test Pelina's loyalty or there was something more to her plan. "Did she ask you to do anything else?"

"No. I tried to ask, but I didn't want to make her suspicious," she replied without batting an eye. "It's not like I'm her best friend."

"Maybe you should be?" Irtan arched an eyebrow. "You two have a lot in common now, except that you haven't gotten expelled yet."

Pelina's warm complexion paled, but she ignored his comment. "Will that be all, archmage? I'd like to retire." She sounded formal, like an obedient student who wanted to ensure she could be excused.

With that wit of hers and quick learning, in a few years, Pelina could become a quite successful high mage. Of that Irtan had no doubt. Pity she had first ended up with Kerl, and then gotten involved in plots and secrets. And as much as Irtan was fond of his young student, he'd use or sacrifice her without hesitation if it served his own goal. But then, he'd already paid so much for seeing his plan through. One more innocent life lost mattered little.

"I thought you had a task to do?" he asked. "Weren't you asked to alter the circle?" He gave the parchment back. "Since, I guess, it's supposed to be a secret, nighttime seems best for such a task."

"You'll allow me to do it?" Wide-eyed, Pelina took the drawing from him.

"I'll even help you." Irtan rose from his armchair with a smile. The more he thought about it, the more he believed Pelina was hiding something. He wouldn't put it past her to come up with a plot to conceal Kamira's real intent. "No one will question an archmage teaching his student of High Towers history, even if he chooses to do so in the dead of night." He walked over to the door while she still stood in the middle of the room. "I trust she gave you something to conceal the markings? Or was getting it a part of the task?"

Her hesitation revealed frantic considerations of lies, but then she nodded. "She gave me a Hauhan's Graver."

Such items were rare to come by. Making one required great skill and ample patience, but studying under Tijhran demanded both, so Kamira could have made one herself. Or, perhaps, her teacher had obliged. If not for his student's presence, Irtan would have sighed heavily. Recent events had driven a wedge between him and Tijhran, and he found himself wondering if he would end up shattering their friendship when he openly opposed Kamira. He had no doubt that Tijhran wouldn't take threatening or assaulting his brightest student lightly.

As Pelina walked to the door, he chased those thoughts away. He'd know soon enough.

On their way through the empty corridors, he asked Pelina random questions about the theory of high magic and delivered short lectures in a perfect scholarly tone. She stayed one step behind him and answered with a disheartened tone that sounded too genuine for her to simply be playing along with his little deception. Irtan hid a smile. She likely didn't want him to witness the alteration, which meant there had to be more to Kamira's task than his student had told him. But exposing the lie would bring him no benefit. Cornered, Pelina could give in and reveal the truth, but it was as likely that she had intentionally allowed him to see through her lies to conceal something else. Until he knew, he'd wait.

The initiation chamber, situated on top of one of the

towers, was crowned with a crystal dome ceiling crafted by high mages of the past. It refracted rays of moonlight, drowning the walls and floor in silver. In daytime, the magically aligned structure provided dispersed light, creating an illusion of gold mist—a perfect backdrop for the young and naïve students who were about to participate in their initiation rite, unaware the ceremony wasn't really about them. Their connection to the circle enforced Veranesh's prison.

Irtan nodded at Pelina, and she took several slow steps toward the circle on the floor before she pulled out the Graver. It didn't escape him how rarely she consulted the parchment. She must have memorized the symbols, but the closer she got to the end, the slower her etching became.

"You aren't adding anything else, are you?" He approached.

Pelina twitched then finished another symbol. It flashed with magic and disappeared, but it was enough for Irtan. The symbol wasn't on the drawing Pelina kept by her side.

"I can't help but wonder why you're allowing this." She wasn't subtle about changing the topic.

He couldn't blame her for such a crude attempt. Pushed on the defensive, she was more likely to slip, while a blunt remark like that fitted with the rebellious attitude she'd been hinting at in the past weeks. Maintaining a perfect balance between an obedient student and a woman disgruntled to be a tool, she could hide a lot of her reactions that otherwise could spark his suspicions, at the same time leaving an impression she wasn't a good player.

"I'm sure you are," he replied, pretending she'd distracted him from his previous question. Her need to change the topic told him enough already. "Are you done with your task?" He pointed at the circle.

She inspected the parchment with fake consideration. "There are two more on the parchment."

Irtan leaned forward with a sly smile. "And how many more not on the parchment? Because if she didn't tell you to add anything else, I'd be disappointed." It seemed safer to not mention Kamira's name. Many ears listened in on conversations in the Towers when the people speaking were convinced they were alone. Spying on an archmage in his private quarters would be difficult, but public spaces provided many opportunities, and he wasn't about to take chances.

"I'm just a pawn… for both of you," she responded with a shrug. "She might as well be using me to create a distraction."

He squatted down. His body rebelled against the strain and reminded him of his age. "A pawn, maybe, but a thinking one. And right now, you're trying to decide which is the bigger risk: letting me see the additional symbols you've been trying to keep from me, or not having a chance to come back to add them later."

Pelina's eyes settled into a frozen stare, and he couldn't read her. No reply came. Instead, she carved another symbol, one from the parchment. With only one left and with him watching, she couldn't add anything else or she'd admit to lying. She would have to try coming back later to finish the task.

There were other possibilities to ponder. He could find an excuse to move away and let her add the symbols, or arrange for her to slip off on her own some other evening, but that meant risking she'd get caught. Questions that would come could cast suspicions on himself. At the same time, he couldn't give up the desire to see at least one of the symbols Pelina wanted to hide from him, even if only for a moment. Kamira's goal could either become beneficial to his own plans, if she caused enough turmoil in the Towers, or foil them, and he had to learn more to act accordingly.

But all things considered, it was safer to give up a potential but fleeting advantage. His own plots would suffice, and he was too cautious to risk unknown consequences should Pelina get caught later or Kamira's efforts got in the way, and Irtan smiled as a solution presented itself.

"Let me make the choice easier for you," he said as Pelina finished the last symbol from the parchment. "Once you tell me you're done, I'll destroy the Graver."

19

K amira sat on the floor with old scraps of cloth on her crossed legs and a needle between her lips. She fastened the fabric together with little thought toward its end, perhaps a bag or a cloak, while rehashing all the points of the intricate lie she was about to weave. How much easier it would have been to simply tell Ryell the truth and ask for his help, but his ties to Yoreus made such thoughts a dangerous fantasy. Even if he didn't take part in the archmage's plots willingly, Atissa might be manipulating him. Besides, with Ryell's demon hate running deep, Kamira would have a difficult time convincing him anyway.

Veelk stopped sharpening his keshal. "Your conscience is going to kill you."

"I feel like I'm turning into a high mage." She didn't hide her displeasure. "When I became an arcanist, I thought I'd escaped their deception and intrigues, not that I'd take part in them." Of course, she also hadn't expected to come across a secret plot conceived by the high mages of the past.

He returned to his work—no reply was necessary. She'd

made her choice when she decided to stay loyal to Veranesh and keep her part of the agreement, so she couldn't complain. And if Ryell, even unwillingly, sided with the high mages, it made him an opponent, not an ally.

Knocking on the door, though she'd expected it, tensed her body, and Kamira took a deep breath. After Veelk nodded, she called out in a rehearsed, drained tone, "Come in."

Ryell entered, and she took in his appearance. His calm moves and face, aglow with a gentle smile, bore no signs of withdrawal. While she was away, he must have spent a lot of time with Atissa, and Kamira's doubts vanished like a dispersed lumisphere. As much as she wanted to allow herself doubt and believe that he had sought someone else to alleviate his withdrawal, she knew that was unlikely. If she was wrong, she'd offer an apology for her lack of trust after all deeds were done.

"I got your message." Ryell looked at her with a hint of uncertainty, as if he'd expected a warm greeting. "Though the high mage student who delivered it didn't tell me much."

"I didn't tell her much," Kamira replied. Using Pelina as a messenger was risky enough, but the high mage student had asked for an additional task to use it as a ploy should Archmage Irtan become too inquisitive. Kamira had obliged. Even though she considered it playing with fire, she had to leave the decision on how to deal with the former first archmage to Pelina.

Ryell sat down on the floor, and it didn't escape Kamira that he offered no greeting to Veelk. "How did your trip go?"

She couldn't shake the feeling he was hoping that whatever she was doing had failed. Especially after the quite desperate message she'd sent through Pelina.

"Worse than I expected, and a lot more painful." With the truths and lies woven together, she took her first step in the game.

She resumed sewing, and each move reminded her of the half-healed wounds on her arms, but the effort was worth it. The longer she persisted, the more likely Ryell would catch her subtle reactions to pain, those she couldn't readily fake.

He didn't disappoint, but his reaction exceeded her expectation. "By the Light, what did these barbarians do to you?"

"Watch your tongue!" Veelk said, and Kamira wasn't sure he was only pretending. "My people tried to help."

Ryell turned to him. "By making her suffer?! What kind of help is that?!" He let his words flow with disregard for the frown on Veelk's face. "Weren't you supposed to protect her? Or maybe you're doing as good of a job as you did with Lefna?"

As Veelk's hand tightened on his keshal, Ryell tensed, but his expression made it clear he didn't regret his words, nor would he back down when it came to blows. Kamira took the opening they gave her.

"Veelk," she said quietly. "Now is not the best time to pick a fight."

The glare she got could have been taken for hostile, and Veelk must have channeled some of his anger into it. Ryell glanced between them. Under the surprise on his face, she caught a glimpse of satisfaction. He must have wanted to drive a wedge between her and Veelk, and their little show had given him what he desired.

"Neither is it for listening to the insults of a high mage's toy." Veelk stood up and walked to the door. "But suit yourself. I'll be downstairs." He left, letting the door shut with more force than a casual departure would require.

Kamira kept her face neutral, despite the satisfaction she felt. With this perfectly played incident, she should be able to convince Ryell she was alone and out of options, and he wouldn't suspect any deception.

"He tried to help, and so did his people," she said. "And he suffers because of Lefna. But I apologize—this shouldn't be your concern." She put down her sewing. It had served its purpose, so continuing the painful endeavor would be nothing shy of torturing herself. "How have your days been? I heard news of Yoreus's advancement." She maintained a friendly face, but didn't intend to come across as naïve. Ryell could get suspicious if she didn't reveal a bit of what she knew.

"My days have been uneventful. I spend most of them helping my people. Gildya recovered the royal treasure, and Prince Allyv got crowned a king, but not much changed otherwise." He shifted, and she couldn't tell whether his uneasiness came from the memory of Cahala's death or trying to avoid mentioning Yoreus and Atissa. "I'd much rather hear what happened to you. Every time you set out, you come back wounded or scarred."

She held off a smirk. He had no idea how accurate it was, but at the same time, they'd only met after she had made a deal with Veranesh. Before that, her life was quite pleasant and uneventful in comparison. But it wasn't the time for such thoughts, and he wasn't the man to share them with, so instead she steered the conversation where she wanted it to go.

"I promised you answers, didn't I?"

His hesitant nod followed, as if he was torn between his desire to know and afraid of pushing her too far, but the spark in his eyes betrayed him. He wanted her to tell him everything. With such an invitation, she spun the story, a carefully concocted mixture of truth and lies prepared just for him. She told him of a malicious demon imprisoned in the old Towers and her own life being the key to his freedom, then of her supposed deception to convince the demon she was more useful alive. As Ryell's eyes grew wider, she followed with the account of her desperate search to break the spell the demon had on her under the excuse of finding a way to free him.

"Veelk's people tried to use their rituals to cut the demon off, but it failed," she said. "The demon will soon realize I'm not doing his bidding, and when he kills me, a good portion of this already scarred continent will die with me."

Ryell shifted uneasily. "There has to be some way," he whispered.

"I'm running out of ideas."

"What about the high mages? They defeated the demon once, right? They can do it again."

She inspected the needle in her hand, pretending to hesitate. "Or they might not believe me. If they kill me, they'll give the demon exactly what he wants. Why do you think I kept it away from them? Because of a silly grudge from years ago?"

"You don't have to face them alone," he replied. "I'll talk to Yoreus. He seems fond of you, and he's a man of reason."

"What makes you so sure?" Even with all her supposed desperation and loneliness, she had to stay true to her distrust to Yoreus, or Ryell could notice she was playing him. "He's the one who sent me to the old Towers in the first place, and has done nothing to gain my trust since."

When he fell silent, and his muscles tensed, her curiosity spiked.

"I think he knows the demon might have become dangerous," he said. "I've seen him talking to some adept from Gildya. They were sending a group of high mages and adepts to the ruins to have them sealed off."

A sudden cold washed over her. If the High Towers and Gildya Magna joined forces, they might be able to reinforce Veranesh's prison. "If the demon thinks it's my doing..." she muttered, letting her real fear add truthfulness to her words.

Ryell tensed. "You need to meet with Yoreus."

She was far from disagreeing. With this new information, getting into the High Towers became even more crucial. She needed to act before the archmages came up with another obstacle.

He reached out to touch her arm. Her hiss of pain was entirely genuine, and before she moved away, he grabbed her wrist and pulled her sleeve up.

"By the Light!" His eyes widened at the sight of Kamira's skin. "Is this what they did to you?!" He didn't let go when she tried to free herself from his grip, pulling the sleeve all the way up to her shoulder. "Is there more?"

She shook her head, withholding a remark that the scabs didn't look half as bad as they had right after the blending. "They stopped when they realized it wasn't working. It's just my arms and part of my back. It's not bad, and I don't remember the real pain."

Ryell exhaled and let her go. "So the journey was for naught. If you'd talked to the high mages back then, they'd have had more time to find a solution."

"I don't think arguing will change anything now." In the end, she'd agree to his offer, and even if he decided to leave, she could pretend she'd reconsidered, but she couldn't give up without a fight. The arcanist Ryell knew her to be wouldn't be convinced easily. "I picked what I thought gave me a chance."

"Will you let me help you?" he asked. "I'll convince Yoreus to talk to you. Maybe the mages have a solution."

Taking time to consider had to be a part of her play, but she'd already decided to cut the game short. She had to talk to Veelk and find a way to stop Yoreus's expedition from reaching the old Towers. In hindsight, she should have kept one of the nightflies to communicate with Veranesh, even if she couldn't take it to the Towers. But back then, she wanted to ensure Koshmarnyk had all help possible, and the demon seemed both eager to help him and trusting in Kamira to carry out their plan. Now she regretted he hadn't insisted on keeping an eye on her.

"All right," she said. "But if you don't come back by tomorrow evening, I'll head out to the desert." That should give Ryell a sense of urgency and leave the archmages with little time to plan. "And if the mages decide I'm better off dead..." She locked eyes with him. "This city's destruction will be on your conscience." Should it come to that, she doubted Ryell—or anyone else—would survive the magic surge, but it wouldn't hurt to put the blame on him if it helped her stay alive.

Ryell swallowed, and his eyes lost their focus. "I'll make sure he understands what's at stake," he said. Then he offered her a forced smile. "You aren't going to disappear while I'm gone, are you?"

"I'll wait for a day," she promised. She would wait longer if needed, but Ryell didn't have to know that. "I can't risk staying here, not with Yoreus's people heading toward the ruins." If things didn't go her way and Ryell failed or dawdled, she could still use Pelina to get into the Towers, so it was better if the high mages believed she was ready to set out for the desert, not sneak into their own domain.

"I'll come back with good news."

Ryell leaned over for a kiss, but she moved her head away. She might have already crossed the line that separated her from high mages or even her eagerly deceptive compatriots, but there were limits to her devotion to the game. There was hardly ever a time she considered Ryell a friend or a potential lover to begin with, and with her relationship with Koshmarnyk tightening, she would not betray him by seeking intimacy with another man.

Much to her relief, Ryell didn't insist. "I hope after you're free from the demon, I'll deserve one."

Swallowing a comment about Atissa, she let him read in her silence what he wanted to. At the same time, she had little doubt that after all was said and done, he would have no desire to kiss an arcanist who'd freed a powerful demon.

With no more words to come, Ryell shifted uneasily. He muttered a goodbye and a few more reassurances she didn't bother listening to. With her mind already focused on stopping the people Yoreus had sent to the old Towers, his departure was nothing but a relief.

When Yoreus finished sharing the news he'd heard from Ryell, silence fell in the room. He enjoyed the worried glances exchanged between the three other archmages, and only the neutral expression on Fyertash's face soured the taste of victory; the demon must be better at hiding his surprise.

"How do we know that arcanist isn't trying to deceive

us?" Loktra asked. "She lied to you before about the old Towers exploration."

He'd expected that question. At first, when Ryell brought the news, he'd suspected the same, but if she wanted to lure him out, she wouldn't be ready to meet on his terms, to come to the Towers. "It's possible, but from what I understand, her life is at stake. She seems lost and scared." He liked the image of a desperate, broken woman Ryell had painted for him, and even if it was only half true, he was looking forward to seeing Kamira's weakness for himself.

"Scared?" Kerl snorted. "That's something I'd like to see."

Irtan grimaced, and for a moment, an aura of authority surrounded him like when he used to be the first archmage. "I don't think the newly appointed third archmage should be the one speaking to her. Especially not the one who still wishes her ill." He turned to Yoreus. "If we are to be taken seriously, it has to be you. I understand you don't fully trust each other, but you've dealt with her before, and you're the one who represents the Towers' authority."

Suspicions surged, but Yoreus concealed his reaction. He'd expected the old man to put himself forward and argue he not only had the most experience, but could be seen as neutral. Instead, he'd taken a step back, and Yoreus couldn't shake the feeling he was missing another step in their game. Yet it wasn't the time to hesitate. Whatever the old archmage intended, Yoreus would find a way to counter it later. "The Devanshari man who brought the message said she'd agreed to speak with me. I'll allow her into the Towers for the meeting to be held here."

"Good. She'll be on our grounds and our terms," Loktra said. "But what if her story is true? What if her death frees the demon?"

Kerl's plump lips stretched into an ugly smile. "Isn't it a bit too convenient? The little gaharra would come up with anything to ensure her own safety."

Yoreus sent the third archmage a displeased look. Sobriety hadn't helped Kerl much, and he remained the uncouth boor he was before. The liquor must have brought out what was already there. But at least Kerl took the secret of high magic and the alliance with demons somewhat seriously.

"She's smart enough to know we won't buy into a tall tale like that," Yoreus replied. "If she still decided to come here, it means she's as desperate as I've been told."

"And what then?" Irtan asked. "Assuming it's true, we can't kill her, and we won't be able to lift the spell on her— that leaves us less than her lifetime to solve the problem. Provided the demon doesn't figure out that she betrayed him much sooner."

Yoreus allowed himself a triumphant smile. He'd spent the whole night and day coming up with a solution, so that he could ensure nothing spoiled his moment of glory. "We can isolate her from Veranesh."

Fyertash, who'd been listening in silence, grimaced, and all the archmages focused their attention on Yoreus. He let them stew for a couple of heartbeats, so that they could realize he was prepared for every possibility.

"I've been researching the spell performed by our ancestors, and I'm certain we can repeat it," he continued. "It worked on a demon, so it should work on a human too."

Loktra's eyes widened. "You want to—?"

"I'll do whatever it takes to ensure the High Towers' survival," Yoreus said. "Perhaps there's a way to sever that spell, but I prefer to be prepared. Moreover, a few days ago, I sent a group of mages and Gildya adepts to the old Towers.

They've been informed there is malicious magic seeping out from that place, and it caused the recent energy outburst. Therefore, they'll seal any entrances and bury the place deep under the sands." Yoreus allowed himself a sly smile. "To prevent any other dangerous events, of course."

Fyertash regarded him and nodded. "It should ensure no one else gets in and perhaps will limit the... prisoner's power. Wise move, first archmage. There might be some hope for you yet."

Yoreus cringed, fighting to keep his expression neutral. He'd had enough of the demon's presence. With no offer of any kind of help, the sooner he was gone, the better. "Will you be staying until all this concludes?" The thought that the demon would be lurking in Kaighal didn't put him in a good mood either. No matter how superb their demonic illusions were supposed to be, Fyertash's presence posed a risk. With the events that led to the fall of the Devanshari kingdom and the refugees present, people were more likely to cry "demon!" at anything suspicious than to discard it as a phantasm.

Fyertash's smirk told Yoreus his question was too obvious. "I'll inform other yalari of the situation and then come back." He headed toward the window. "We need to prepare in case you humans fail."

As soon as the demon departed, Loktra hurried to close the window. "So, the four of us will perform the spell? I trust you have it written down in some form?"

It didn't escape him that she hadn't mentioned exploring any other ways to actually help Kamira, and Yoreus smiled. Loktra might have many vices, but compassion was not one of them. Before he could reply, Irtan cleared his throat and shook his head.

"I won't be part of the spell if Yoreus thinks the three of

you can handle it. This is his plan, and if he's to become a true first archmage, he can't have an old man's shadow cast over him."

Yoreus narrowed his eyes. For the second time this evening, Irtan withdrew. Youreus wanted to claim the old archmage had to be part of the spell out of spite if nothing else, but there was truth in Irtan's words: Yoreus had to show that he didn't have to lean on the old archmage to succeed.

"The three of us should be enough," he replied with painful realization that, either way, he was losing. He would have admitted his own weakness or would have given Irtan what he wanted.

"As an additional precaution, you should use the initiation rite circle for the spell," Irtan suggested. "From what I understand, it might be the only place in all of Tyorane that is out of the demon's reach."

Kerl furrowed his brow. "But what about the initiation rite? What will we tell the students?"

Loktra snorted. "The students are the least of our concerns. It won't be the first time we've rewritten the truth, and in a way, this is better. If we're open about it, we'll make sure no one snoops around for the real secrets."

As much as the meeting proceeded according to Yoreus's expectations, it seemed that the archmages were bound to surprise him, save maybe for Kerl. Irtan undoubtedly was using it for his own game, no matter how helpful his remarks were, and Loktra offered insights Yoreus hadn't expected from her. "So, it's decided. I'll send for Kamira tomorrow evening, and I'll have the spell delivered to you by morning."

"That's less than a day to prepare," Kerl remarked.

"I'm sure you can handle it, *third* archmage," Irtan replied.

That brought an involuntary smile to Yoreus's face. He couldn't have said it better himself, and he allowed the old man a bit of satisfaction. The triumph was his and his alone, nevertheless. One more day, one more spell, and his troubles would be put to rest. Then, with order restored and Irtan having no reason to advise him anymore, leadership would be solely in Yoreus's hands, and with his success, no one would dare to question it.

20

The trees smelled of life, and Koshmarnyk inhaled their scent while he crossed the clearing. The building's dark shape stood out against the green, and its dark windows promised nightmares within, old and new ones alike. Pictures of the women imprisoned within and their deaths still haunted him. No secret was worth the lives of innocents, and he'd have rather faced Gildya's pursuit than seen people killed to keep his presence hidden. Possibilities ran through his head, but the voice of reason always reminded him that the decision belonged to someone else. Neither Veelk nor Kamira were killers by nature, and some nights the arcanist awoke gasping, her black eyes shining with magic as she reached out in desperation, half conscious, still enveloped in her nightmares. She rarely spoke about those nighttime torments, but he'd gathered enough from her meager responses to know those deaths affected her as well.

He sighed. It wasn't the first time innocents had paid for the struggles of the powerful, and to think he'd become part of the game himself stirred his conscience. Yet he had a choice, and he'd chosen to help Kamira and Veelk, and as he approached the building's main entrance, now broken into pieces, all the thoughts left his mind but two: *Find Phuran. Save Lefna.*

The stones in his body pulsated with energy, feeding his blood and muscles with power unreachable for common people, and he focused on the two stones he'd blended most recently. Veranesh's magic flowed through the back of Koshmarnyk's hands, and the nightflies came to life. They didn't move until the demon took control of them, but then their bodies uncoiled and lifted into the air.

"It's time," Koshmarnyk said.

The crystal creatures darted away without a single word from Veranesh, and he could only hope the demon would stick to the plan they had devised.

Pushing those concerns away, he stepped into the building. Its hallway was scarred with scorched furniture and disturbed soot. The deeper he went, the more obvious the signs of fighting became. Even without tracking skills, the adept recognized the battle had resulted in many dead. It must have been the mercenaries Opyr had sent, since even though Veelk had slain anyone in his way, Koshmarnyk remembered the building unscathed when they were making their escape. Dark blood marks on the floor suggested the bodies had been dragged out, and he studied the traces before deciding Phuran must have been upstairs when the attack started.

Cahala's chamber. Not the best place to hold one's ground, but Koshmarnyk doubted Phuran's reason to stay there was a tactical one. Everything he had in mind was meant to force Veelk in the same situation.

Koshmarnyk climbed the stairs, pausing to listen when they squeaked. No sounds and no attack came from the second floor, and Koshmarnyk had started to wonder whether Phuran was even inside when a quiet whimper and a rough whisper disturbed the silence.

"Don't cry. He'll come for you."

Koshmarnyk recognized his adversary's voice.

"He wouldn't leave you."

Approaching, the adept stretched his muscles, and the magic from the stones continued to aid him. His plan was simple enough—draw Phuran away from Lefna and kill him—but the details remained vague. He hated having to rely on circumstances and could only hope Veranesh wouldn't run into trouble.

The corridor ended with a tall window, and if he remembered correctly from his scarce visits upstairs, Cahala's room was halfway to it. He picked up a piece of broken furniture and tossed it. Glass shattered and rang as its pieces fell while Koshmarnyk hid in another room's entrance. Phuran would go to the window first, then check the stairs when he realized the glass hadn't been broken from the outside.

With his muscles tense, Koshmarnyk waited for Phuran to scout the length of the corridor, but the Devanshari warrior's steps were that of a ghost. When his shadow passed the entryway, Koshmarnyk had just moments to react.

With his knife ready, he lunged at his opponent, forcing him to defend himself, but Phuran's sabers met the challenge with one to parry and the other just grazing Koshmarnyk's neck and sending him back into the room.

"You!" Phuran's eyes widened.

"I'd have come sooner if I'd known you were still lurking here." A little deception never hurt in battle, and

Koshmarnyk could at least ensure Lefna wouldn't suffer consequences if he failed.

He lunged. He knew he had to press his assault to keep his opponent's twin blades defending, and press he did. Weeks of sparring with Veranesh had ensured he had enough speed. Phuran had to prioritize Koshmarnyk's blade, leaving him to suffer several aggravating knee strikes. But the saber-wielding warrior still had the upper hand, constantly driving his adversary back outside of his blades' reach.

"Leave now, and you might enjoy your life a while longer." Phuran moved to the side, opening an escape route from the room. "I'm not waiting here for you."

Koshmarnyk moved toward the door, until he was standing between it and Phuran. With a smirk, he lunged again, this time driving his opponent deeper into the room.

Phuran growled and burst forward with speed that came close to matching Koshmarnyk's. His blades split the air in search of the adept's flesh in a relentless series of swings, thrusts, and simultaneous strikes. Koshmarnyk had seen few that could wield long blades with such speed, but their swipes paled in comparison to the darting nightflies, so he kept his footing. Marks from his attacks gathered on Phuran's limbs, but all lethal blows were turned aside or failed to penetrate the stiff leather vest covering the Devanshari's torso.

A snide smile came on Phuran's face, and all too late Koshmarnyk realized his opponent had drawn him deeper into the room. In a mad dash, the warrior pushed past him and darted out of the door, making it clear he'd figured out the deception at work.

"Demon's blood!" Koshmarnyk rushed after Phuran, fear clenching his throat as the broad-shouldered man ducked into Cahala's chambers. *If he kills Lefna, I won't be able to look Veelk in the eye... nor Kamira.*

When he caught up to his opponent, relief overwhelmed him. The room was empty, and the opened window suggested that Veranesh had succeeded at his task. Lefna had to be safe already. But the moment of distraction cost him dearly, as Phuran spun and stretched a saber at him.

The blade missed Koshmarnyk's heart by a finger's width, and he recoiled in pain. He expected a deathblow to follow, but his opponent lost interest in him.

"Come out, you coward!" Phuran called out. "Come out before I slaughter your friend."

Koshmarnyk had to smile. As much as he'd rather survive the confrontation, at least with Lefna's escape, he didn't have to worry about its outcome. "Veelk didn't come."

He savored the moment as his words sank in, at the same time correcting the grip on his knife and taking a deep breath, readying for the last fight. The more he wounded his opponent, the further Lefna would get away.

Phuran spat as he turned his attention to Koshmarnyk. "So it's you and that demon's gaharra? Good enough. I'll get her after I'm done with you."

Koshmarnyk knew better than to reveal how much Kamira meant to him. Yet the anger boiling within didn't allow him for a dismissive response.

"No you won't." Veranesh's voice emanated with a new depth of coldness.

Phuran yelled in pain as he spun in place, whipping sabers around him. In his back, marking widening patches of crimson, two crystal nightflies protruded. As Phuran found no opponent, he turned back to Koshmarnyk, his motions slower and less fluid, and Koshmarnyk took his chance. The knife cut through the air and found the Devanshari's throat before the sabers rose high enough to deflect it. Phuran's face froze in disbelief, and he collapsed to the floor.

With no need to keep his battle stance anymore, Koshmarnyk fell to his knees. "Did you tell the girl to run?" The blood kept flowing between his fingers as he pressed his shirt and wound.

"I did," the demon replied. "But it would be wise if you pulled me out of this carcass so I can call her back."

"Why?" Koshmarnyk asked as he jerked the nightflies from Phuran's body.

The crystal creatures spun in the air, shaking off blood and pieces of flesh. "Because last time I wanted to leave for dead someone my pactee cared about, I wasted a lot of time on pointless discussions, and then even more on the actual lifesaving. If your wound is serious, I'll need that woman to keep you alive."

"I'm sure you could tell Kamira you did everything you could." Koshmarnyk couldn't resist a hint of sarcasm. He had never heard of demons being particularly caring. Even the protector of Veelk's tribe, Suzhaul, was benevolent only when it suited him.

One nightfly darted through the open window, while the other hovered above him, so he could hear the demon laughing. "We both know she's only going to believe it if I bring you back alive."

So much for gaining any insights in Veranesh's motives, but Koshmarnyk wasn't above taking the help offered. After all, being indebted to a demon was a minor problem in comparison to being dead. His strength abandoned him with his blood, and only the stones kept him conscious, so instead of prolonging the discussion with the demon, he used those moments to cut his shirt sleeve off and press it to the wound in his chest.

"Then let's hope the girl didn't run too far," he said as darkness took him.

~

AFTER THREE DAYS OF MARCHING, Veelk caught up with the expedition. The line of ten men and women moved at caravan pace, and hidden behind the dune's hump, he chewed on the rations, letting his body regain strength. If they kept their slow journey, weeks would pass before the expedition neared the old Towers, so a little rest couldn't hurt.

They tediously made their way through the sand, and their moves revealed they weren't used to strenuous travels. Yet they could still be formidable opponents when it came to a confrontation, especially in larger numbers. Telling mages apart from the adepts took Veelk only a moment, and he focused on the Gildya members, searching for the biggest threats. Some of the adepts carried weapons, but most were unarmed, so they likely had other tricks up their sleeves.

Veelk allowed himself a smile. This could be an interesting fight.

Any other time, he would be wary of the risks that came with the unknown, but with all that had happened recently, he yearned for the rush of adrenaline that would take his mind off everything but combat. He dug his fingers deep in the sand at the memory of what he'd left behind. Even if he could help neither Koshmarnyk nor Kamira with their tasks, he'd rather be around to see the outcome of their efforts. If his adept friend failed to save Lefna, Veelk had to take the risk and try rescuing her himself. At least there was some comfort in knowing that Phuran's desire for revenge would ensure the poor girl lived until Veelk showed up.

And Kamira... He couldn't help her once she got into the Towers. Even three days of rushing through the desert had not eased his anger at the plan she and the demon had concocted, which—upon insistence—she revealed before Veelk's departure. With so many things out of her control, she was setting herself up to fail, and whenever he thought of the risks involved, he thought of killing Veranesh with his bare hands. If that demon even regained his freedom, since it relied on Kamira's success.

Veelk could only hope that the archmages believed Kamira's death meant destruction of the city and would keep her alive. This way, should the demon's plan fail, Veelk would still had a chance of setting things straight. And if it meant slaughtering a bunch of mages, innocent or not, so be it.

That last thought brought him to the task at hand. The people traversing the sands might have not wronged him nor Kamira, but they were a threat to their plans. If Veranesh got buried under the desert or they had a way to strengthen his prison, they could thwart Kamira's efforts. Though he had to smirk at that thought—at the pace they were going, the demon could be freed already before they made it halfway to the ruins.

But he wouldn't let them get that far, because Kamira wasn't sure how much time she'd need. The expedition slowed down and scattered, and Veelk watched them with a smile. Each of them might be a seasoned traveler and perhaps even a fighter, but the way they set up camp told him they weren't used to working together. No wonder: Gildya and High Towers always vied for power in Kaighal, holding each other in contempt. Yoreus must have told some tall tales to get adepts to even set out with the high mages.

The sky above darkened, and Veelk slid down the sand, away from his quarry. He stretched his muscles, finished his food, and took the few sips of water he had left in his waterskin. He hadn't taken enough for his journey, as too much luggage would have slowed him down. He'd scavenge what he needed for the return trip from his opponents. Until the night drowned the desert in black, he had time to rest, but he didn't allow himself any sleep.

With the first stars coming up, he scaled the dune once again, and his feet sank into the sand with noise no greater than the wind whispering among its grains. The camp below was lit by imbued stone lanterns, and the elaborate tents explained why the group had been moving so slowly. Used to all the comforts Kaighal could offer to the wealthy, those mages and adepts had refused to give up their own convenience.

Most men and women were already out of sight, proving that even when sharing a mission, adepts and high mages didn't mingle. Only several guards stood posted, and none of them seemed overly concerned with their duty. City people, all of them, could not conjure all the dangers the wilderness could have in store for them, and dunes obscured threats almost as well as trees or rocks.

Veelk smiled and darted downhill, his weapon at the ready. Only when he reached the first of the guards did his keshal reflect the lamplight. Its blade, carefully crafted by Veelk's tribesmen, contained a part of Suzhaul's power, just like his scars did, and it cut through the enforced Gildya leathers, drawing sparks whenever it grazed an imbued stone.

The guard died before she could warn the others, and on his way to the next one, Veelk pinned two sleeping mages to the ground. The motion must have warned his next target, because he turned in time to meet his death. Veelk pierced his opponent's throat with a single thrust.

"Ambush!" someone called, and the camp came to life.

A mage threw a spell toward him, but the bolt of electricity just danced on the keshal's blade. Veelk destroyed the closest lamp, and shadows covered the battlefield. Magic still tingled his skin, reminding him of the many times Kamira had disregarded his presence between her and her target, but as he dodged under an attacking adept's blade, he focused back on the fight. His keshal pinned the assailant's leg to the ground, and Veelk's fist crushed her unprotected face, breaking her nose. The adept fell down, her body twitching, and Veelk was already turning to face other enemies.

A gust of magical wind disturbed the desert's calm face and brought grains of sand into the air. They whipped Veelk's bare skin, forcing his eyes to narrow. Two more men approached from the sides, and by their moves, he guessed they were now as blinded as he was. He waited until they closed in on him and spun his keshal high in the air, letting the wide blade take off two heads on its way.

The sand in the wind concealed his surroundings, and Veelk spotted the projectiles just a moment before they hit. His forearm caught the ice spikes bound for his face, and he brushed them off. *Time to kill some mages.* Even if most of their magic couldn't hurt him, their petty attempts were a nuisance and a distraction. The wounds stung, and the sand in the air promised more pain later, but they didn't affect his prowess. He darted through the whirlwinds, aiming at the silhouette by the lamp. Before the mage executed her next spell, likely a lengthy utterance unfit for quick skirmishes, Veelk's blade tore her stomach. Her incantation morphed into a scream, and Veelk sneered. A high mage would never be as good in combat as an arcanist was.

While the mage shrieked in pain on the ground, another man leapt from behind. Even in heavy Gildya armor his body weight wasn't sufficient to knock Veelk down, but the reinforced gloves closed around the mage killer's neck, forcing him to fight for every breath.

With the high mage's death, the wind perished too. As the sand fell, another silhouette emerged from the dark and swung an object with an imbued stone glowing in it. Veelk spun in place, turning his back—and the adept clutching it —toward the threat. A clay container shattered against metal, releasing thick substance and activating the stone.

Splashes of hot liquid reached Veelk's shoulders, burning into the skin and making it clear why the man in the armor screamed so much. The gloves' grip loosened, and Veelk freed himself from the burden. The man in the distance readied another sphere, and the imbued stone lit up on it. With no cover from liquid flames, Veelk didn't wait. He flung his lizard dagger. Its blade drove into the adept's forehead, and his body dropped along with the glowing sphere.

Only then did Veelk notice the bag by the man's leg: more spheres inside.

"Suzhaul's blood!"

He didn't wait for the sphere to reach the ground. He turned and dashed in a desperate attempt to outrun the fire. The burst of released flames roared behind him. Three heartbeats later, the explosion caught up with him, and Gildya-crafted flames ate through his skin, sending him flying and into the sand.

Veelk landed in the dune with eyes blurred from pain, but his ears caught the steady rhythm of wings beating the air. As a demon landed nearby, Veelk adjusted the grip on his keshal, even though he couldn't force his own body to stand up.

"I see someone did the work for me." The demon gave Veelk a calculating gaze. He was roughly Uganel's size, but his lean body made him look smaller even with the leathery wings, now curled behind his back. "Would you be, by any chance, the arcanist Kamira's friend?"

Veelk had expected the demons to have already learned Kamira's name through their contacts with the high mages, but seeing one in the desert reassured him they knew little of the plan. Good. Kamira would only have to deal with the mages.

"My name is Fyertash. I see you recognize the name." The demon grinned. "You made that coward Uganel speak before he died, didn't you?"

Veelk didn't reply. Even enhanced with Suzhaul's power, his body couldn't handle the vast burns, and weakness consumed Veelk's limbs, so if the demon kept talking, Veelk would die before he'd be forced to reveal anything of importance. He let his thoughts wander, reaching out to Kamira, who had to face her own challenge, and to Lefna, who—of this he was sure—would be saved by Koshmarnyk. If they'd had more time to spar, the scrawny adept would likely have taken him down in the end. He smiled. Even with himself gone, Kamira would still had someone to help her.

The demon came closer, and his silhouette concealed the starry sky. If the mage killer had any choice, he'd prefer the sky to be his last view, instead of an ugly face with a long nose that looked like a beak.

"I'll ask you one question, and if your answer satisfies me, you'll live." The demon looked down at him. "What is the name of the yalari Kamira has a pact with?"

If Veelk had any strength left, he'd use it up by laughing, but he didn't waste his breath on a reply.

"I see." The demon went down on one knee, leaning over Veelk. "I shouldn't have expected any other answer from Suzhaul's pawn."

KAMIRA DID her best to rein in her concerns as she climbed the stairs of the High Towers, seemingly serene and empty at night. Ryell's hand on her shoulder, though an attempt to comfort her, only enhanced her anxiety. She didn't want his touch to distract her, not when her thoughts already circled Veelk and Koshmarnyk, instead of focusing on the task ahead. She didn't worry about her friend as much as her lover. Veelk always came out of trouble victorious, while the possibility of Koshmarnyk dying in the woods made her skin crawl. She'd rather face a demon alone than suffer such uncertainty.

"Don't worry." Ryell's whisper brushed her neck.

How was she supposed to not worry? Even if Ryell couldn't know of all her other troubles, he shouldn't have forgotten she was walking straight into the enemy's den. On the other hand, the joy and hopefulness on his face suggested he'd never suspected the archmages could do something unsavory. A fool, that's what he was, but in the end, she needed a fool to get in.

Fighting the urge to push his hand off, Kamira forced herself to smile. Soon enough, she'd have to only deal with Yoreus.

It'd been years since she was a student here, but as they walked through the High Towers' corridors, it didn't take her long to realize he was leading her to the initiation rite chamber, not to the archmage's private quarters. Her smile shifted into a smirk. It seemed that Yoreus was preparing a deception, but one she could hope to use to her own advantage. Meeting in the chamber made her own plan easier, and perhaps she wouldn't have to risk too many lies... just like Veranesh predicted. She could see how he'd come to such a conclusion. If the high mages believed they couldn't kill her, they needed another way to stop Veranesh from breaking free.

She hid her thoughts as they arrived at their destination.

Ryell pushed the double door open, and they entered a brightly lit circular chamber Kamira had visited several times before. Had she more time, she'd admire the silvery glow coming from the crystal dome above the room and drowning everything in the moonlight, but the enchanting view was spoiled by the men and women waiting inside.

Yoreus stood in the middle, by the circle carved in the marble floor, while Loktra and Kerl were behind. He looked smug and confident, as if the first archmage's title made his pride swell tenfold, but she knew better than to disregard his skill. Deeper in the chamber, guards stood posted by the walls and tall windows, and Kamira couldn't hide her smirk. *So many people for one little arcanist.* At least Yoreus treated her as seriously as she did him.

Taking advantage of Ryell's confusion, she freed herself from his grip and stepped forward. The archmages behind Yoreus twitched, their expressions not as confident as his.

"This is not exactly what I'd consider a display of trust." Kamira stopped far enough from Yoreus to give herself a fighting chance, should it become necessary. "I came alone, as you asked." She offered no bow of courtesy.

Yoreus smiled. "I apologize." The tone of his voice told her otherwise. "We do want to help you, but we can't let you leave. There's too much at risk."

She snorted. In the end, they would win, but being too compliant would raise unnecessary suspicions. Yoreus had to be certain that he had the upper hand, and that she was simply being stubborn. "If I stay and you don't help me, you risk not only the Towers, but the whole city." Instinct urged her to bring up a barrier and defend herself, but she didn't give in. "I've deceived the demon for too long already. He'll catch up eventually." For once her heritage became useful, as no one questioned how a human could match a demon in a game of lies. If anyone could, it had to be a Tivarashan woman.

"Then I believe we don't have much time for petty squabbles, do we now?" Yoreus said.

"Enough for a bargain."

"I don't think you're in any position to ask for anything. You came to us pleading for help."

Kamira shook her head and joined the game archmages excelled at: cunning and manipulation. "I came to talk and didn't expect to be betrayed."

Ryell flinched, but she didn't pity him. Even if he wasn't aware of Yoreus's plan, he'd chosen to trust the archmage after everything she had tried to tell him about the High Towers and their leaders.

"You've made it clear you can't be trusted, and I'd be insane to," she continued. "If you refuse me the right to leave, I might as well fight you all. I'm sure the demon will show me some leniency if I bring this place down for him."

Kerl let out a short laugh. "What can such an insignificant arcanist like you do against us?"

"Insignificant?" Kamira sent him a vicious sneer. Kerl had given her a perfect opportunity to repay him for the way he treated her back when she was a student. "We have the same power at our disposal, you and I. But I don't have to steal it from the demon. He gives it to me."

She savored their pale faces when they understood. *The squabble just became less petty, didn't it?* Part of her wondered whether she'd survive such a confrontation, and if she didn't, how much damage the High Towers—and the archmages' pride—would suffer. The image in her head was satisfactory enough for her to yearn for a fight, but it wasn't only her life at stake. All of Kaighal needed her levelheaded.

Yoreus regained his composure first. "I'm sure none of us want to fight. You have to forgive the third archmage." He shot a warning glance at Kerl. "The recent weeks have been quite taxing for him."

He stepped forward, and Kamira put all her effort into not flinching.

"I think I know a way of severing the spell the demon put on you," he added. "But I can't guarantee it won't sever your pact as well. It's not something that was been done before."

Of course, there had to be a risk to his solution, and Yoreus had chosen one that shouldn't make her reconsider, but she still pretended to hesitate. "I'm willing to take the risk. I can make a new pact with another demon once this is done."

Her reply visibly pleased Yoreus. "I also think that it's been too long since the arcanists were excluded from the High Towers, chastised and loathed," he said. "Once all is done, I wish to offer you the ninth archmage's position in the Towers as recognition of your skills and bravery. You'd be the first arcanist in four hundred years to become an archmage."

Kamira let her surprise show. "That's unexpected." At the same time, she had to commend Yoreus. He'd played perfectly into the desires of the young student she once was, offering her everything she strove for... before she got expelled. Giving her a chance to rekindle all those ambitions, and without lengthy studying under some swine like Kerl, was calculated to blind her enough to ignore all doubts.

"You might feel betrayed, but we both want the same thing: to make sure the demon doesn't break free." Yoreus's words flowed like honey. "I'm willing to put aside the disagreements and send a clear message to all arcanists out there."

She laughed. "Finally understanding that keeping them away means no control over what they do?"

"She already thinks like an archmage," Loktra remarked. "So what will it be? Will you let us help?"

Kamira stared long into Yoreus's eyes. "What do you have in mind?" The tension in her voice was sincere. Everything depended on his reply, and if Veranesh's predictions weren't correct, she'd have to weave lies on the go to get what she needed.

He pointed to the middle of the room. "The circle is a part of the spell that keeps the demon trapped. And every student who goes through the initiation rite strengthens it. I've read some old high mage texts, and I think this might be the only place out of his reach. If you stand there, we can weave a powerful barrier around you to sever the connection between you and the demon and break any spells he has on you."

Once more, she pretended to take her time considering his words, but her thoughts kept coming back to Pelina. The message Kamira received the other day was brief but reassured her everything was ready. Yet she also had to consider Irtan. If the old archmage hadn't fallen for the false alterations, he might have found a way to add his own changes. She sighed. After a sleepless night spent on doubts and worrying about her friends, any outcome seemed better than none. If she wasn't willing to put all of Kaighal's fate on the line and stand her ground against the archmages, she had to take that risk.

"Very well." She walked over to the circle. "I trust you're prepared to start immediately?"

Triumph flashed in Yoreus's eyes when he nodded. "We can perform the spell whenever you're ready."

As she stepped in, the magic in the circle felt distorted and corrupted—something she hadn't noticed back when she was a student. It also bore the mark of Veranesh's energy, which confirmed both her guesses and Yoreus's words. The circle had to indeed be part of the spell that trapped the demon, and she sought comfort in that. "I'm ready."

"Clear out the room," Yoreus said.

The guards rushed outside, but Ryell hesitated at the door. Before leaving, he offered a small smile. "I'll see you when it's over."

Out of the corner of her eye, Kamira caught Kerl's sarcastic grimace, and it confirmed her suspicions. Yoreus's plan didn't include her walking out of the chamber. But then, neither did hers. Just like Veranesh had said, they only had one chance.

Without delay, the archmages began their chant. The complicated phrases, a mixture of the old arcane language and several dialects of the common language spoken across the world, flowed in a steady rhythm that amused Kamira, because the familiar melody of the first part of the demon-destroying spell, the binding, echoed within their words.

The magic around her condensed, and she could almost touch it, dip her hands into pure energy and change its stream, but instead she stood patiently. Too much was at stake to indulge in such inconsequential desires. Her mind, though, refused to be as idle as her body, and she found questions swarming her head. How had Veranesh felt four hundred years ago, in a similar situation? Anger and desperation for certain, since he destroyed three demons and channeled their energy to the human world in the attempt to free himself, but what else? Fear? Frustration? A sense of defeat? Or maybe apathy? The mere thought she could try asking Veranesh such questions once all was done lifted her mood. As willing to share knowledge as he was, he had never revealed anything a human would consider personal, and she doubted a proud creature like him would be willing to make such confessions.

Through the thickening barrier of energy, the archmages' faces became a blur. Kamira closed her eyes while she took in the sensation of the accumulated magic. Savoring the deep breaths she took as if they were her last, she let Veranesh's energy flow freely through her body. The scars instantly burned, but she remained motionless. Her own magic seeped through the circle, and she could only hope it returned to Veranesh's trap, as they anticipated it would.

Let's see how long it takes.

The archmages' spell solidified within the circle, trapping her in a crystal.

<<<<>>>>

Thank you for reading! If you enjoyed the book, please consider leaving a review.
Kamira's and Veelk's adventures continue in

Shadows over Kaighal

If you'd like to know how Kamira and Veelk met, sign up for the author's newsletter and receive your complimentary copy of Scourges, Spells, and Serenades – a collection that contains two stories featuring Kamira and Veelk as well as other short stories:
authorjm.com

ABOUT THE AUTHOR

Joanna might be a bit too cautious to do anything even remotely daring or dangerous herself, so she writes about daring adventures and dangerous magic instead. Yet, she found enough courage to abandon her life in Poland and move to Ireland, and then some years later, she abandoned her life in Ireland to move over to the US. She's determined to settle there, once she finally chooses which state to reside in.

When she's not writing or thinking about writing, she plays video games or makes amateur art. She lives the happy life of a recluse, surrounded by her husband, a stuffed red monkey, and a small collection of books she insisted on hauling across two continents.

You can find the full list of her publications and more about her at:

http://authorjm.com

and connect with her via social media:

facebook.com/AuthorJMac

instagram.com/authorjmac

indiepocalypse.social/@AuthorJMac

bsky.app/profile/authorjmac.bsky.social

threads.net/@authorjmac

x.com/AuthorJMac

goodreads.com/authorjmac

bookbub.com/authors/joanna-maciejewska

ACKNOWLEDGMENTS

They say writing the second book is harder than writing the first. I feel like I cheated, because when I first started, "By the Pact" and „Scars of Stone" were a single book, so my book two was, in a way, already written, waiting only for revisions and polishing.

It doesn't mean I would be able to get book 2 out without help.

As always, my husband Inq had been supporting me in every possible way, from writerly encouragement to mundane aspects of everyday life, and he's always generously lending me his "you can do it attitude" when I need it most.

Special thanks also go to Piotr Schmidtke, who multitasks as my alpha reader, beta reader, developmental consultant, and cheerleader, while managing his own busy life.

I always value the insights of my wonderful team of beta readers. Anna Suseł, Kamil Jach, Mikołaj Kamiński, Mariusz Kamiński, and others: thank you for your time and support!

The same goes for my writing buddies—J. Morgyn White, L.A. McGinnis, Chesley Cox, and Sara Marschand— your camaraderie makes writing a much less lonely endeavor.

Last but not least, a heartfelt thank you to Jake who once more designed a perfect cover for my book and to Arran who straightened up my second-language English.